MW00412669

Lincoln's Diary

a Novel

by

DL Fowler

This book is a work of fiction. Names, characters, places and incidents are either the product of the author's imagination or are used fictitiously. Any resemblance to actual events or locales or persons, living or dead, is entirely coincidental.

Copyright © 2011 by DL Fowler

ISBN-13:
978-0615445533

All rights reserved, including the right to reproduce this book or portions thereof in any form whatsoever.

For information email dlfowler@dlfowler.com

Harbor Hill Publishing

Dedication

To my family, especially Dad who passed on to me the
dream of becoming a novelist,
Judi, my wife who has loved me and supported me in all
of my dreams,
and Mom who laid the foundation for who I am.

In Memoriam

Joseph "Poppy" Emanuel
1915-2010

Lincoln's Diary

Prologue

"As God is my judge, I believe if I had been in the city, it would not have happened..." US Marshall - District of Columbia, Colonel Ward Hill Lamon.

Martinsburg, West Virginia, May 7, 1893

Colonel Lamon drew shallow, raspy breaths as he lay near death. He clutched President Lincoln's private diary to his chest. He had not opened it, even once, since the president delivered it to him just days before the assassination. Only Lincoln knew what it contained, and he never intended for its entries to live on after he was gone.

With the taste of death filling his nostrils, Lamon arched his back and wheezed, fighting to expel his final instruction – to keep the diary safe.

"You need to rest now, Father." Dolly tried to comfort him in his final moments.

Lamon reached for her arm. His eyes bulged as if his words would force their escape by any conceivable means.

President Lincoln's friend and bodyguard carried

two measures of guilt to the precipice of eternity. He had disobeyed Lincoln's order to destroy the diary, a failure he tried to excuse by complaining it was all he had left of his friend. On the other hand, he lamented obeying Lincoln's directive to travel to Richmond despite numerous threats against the president's life. By doing so he was absent from the Capitol on the fatal night of April 14. And Lamon berated himself for the remainder of his days. "As God is my judge, I believe if I had been in the city, it would not have happened."

When Colonel Ward Hill Lamon's last breath slipped away, his final instructions dissolved behind his lips.

After kissing her father on his forehead, Dolly pried the diary from his grip and whispered, "I love you."

Chapter One

Wicomico County, Maryland, October 13, 2010

Sarah closed her eyes and cupped the rickety glass doorknob. Her breath stalled and the knot in her stomach drew tighter. The truth about her father and grandfather had to be stashed somewhere in that old attic.

Grandma Cassie always sidestepped questions about the missing men in Sarah's life with "Both you and your mother were immaculate conceptions." And Grandma's myth got more mileage than the ones about the Tooth Fairy, Santa Claus and the Easter Bunny. Sarah clung to Grandma's story at least until she learned what 'immaculate conception' meant. Her enlightenment came about the time the blood on her underwear spun her into a panic.

Now, at thirty-something, it wasn't a question, anymore, whether they'd existed. Time had come for the truth about who they were. It didn't occur to her that the truth could hurt. Or that sometimes it killed.

The sound of a car door shutting on the driveway snagged her attention. Her eyes narrowed. Why hadn't the car made a sound coming up the magnolia lined asphalt? She cocked her head and brushed a handful of ebony curls away from her ear, focusing on the footsteps that creaked up onto the front porch. Had it slipped her mind that someone would be stopping by? That was unlikely. There was no extended family, and her handful of friends knew not to surprise her.

Sarah lingered for a moment at the attic door, but hopes the visitor would go away were driven back by persistent knocking. There was no recourse but to head downstairs and assess the hazy figure who was peering through the screen door. At the bottom of the staircase, she covered her cropped T with the practice hoodie she'd draped over the end post on the banister, and her hand laid hold of the lacrosse stick propped next to it.

Tiny beads of sweat dotted the man's forehead, uncommon for an October morning in Eastern Maryland. An edgy chill should have held over from the previous night. And by October, the leaves should resemble fire with various shades of red, yellow and orange fluttering against grayish-brown tree trunks. But an Indian summer held off the inevitability of autumn.

"Can I help you?" Sarah asked in an assertive tone, something she'd picked up working as a contract linguist assisting interrogators at State and NSA.

"Ms. Morgan?"

Was that a European accent, or was it just her imagination? After all, he'd only spoken two words.

"Yes, but –" Which Ms. Morgan did he mean?

"Sign here." The man lifted one knee as a makeshift prop for his briefcase. He laid a document on top of the closed lid and pointed to a line at the bottom of some printed text.

Sarah squinted at the document through the screen door and made out the name, Jennifer Morgan.

Still standing on one leg, the man wobbled a bit as he let out an impatient sigh. "Is there a problem?"

Sarah drew both hands to her hips and glared at him through the fine mesh screen. "Uh, well —" Looking back down at the document, she recalled the mental note her brain logged on catching the first glimpse of him. His tall athletic build suggested he played ball of some type in his college days. With his glory days behind him, he'd probably resorted to calling on lonely older folks, selling them stuff they didn't need, and Mom had likely been one of his recent victims. Not that there was any reason to be more suspicious of him than everyone else.

Sarah peeked up from the paper, her deep emerald eyes making a quick sweep of his face. "Actually, I'm her daughter. What's this about?"

"Is she home?"

"No." Sarah stared down at her mother's name printed on the page. Her voice softened. "Mom died a week ago."

"My condolences."

Sarah grimaced and gave him a silent nod. His accent was French, for sure.

The man lowered his briefcase and relaxed from his flamingo stance. "Do you know if anyone is managing the estate?"

Sarah looked away. "Yes, I'm all that's left of the family, so I get to be the Administrator." She didn't ask for that responsibility, but there'd been no one else to pass the job off to.

"A client of a law firm we do work for purchased some historical documents from your mother. I'm here to deliver a check." He opened his briefcase to retrieve an envelope.

Sarah propped her lacrosse stick against the doorjamb and pushed the screen door open. "Can I sign for her?"

"I'll have to see some identification." His look

was stern.

"Of course." Sarah excused herself for a moment to retrieve her wallet from the foot of the stairs, keeping an eye on the screen door all the while.

On her return, the courier examined her driver's license then studied her face. "Do you have a death certificate or something? To prove she's dead."

Sarah clenched her teeth. A lacrosse ref would have been fingering a penalty card, the only question – red or yellow. "You're kidding, right?"

He sighed again. "Okay, okay. I'll take your word for it."

She kept her eye on him and tucked her driver's license back into its designated slot in her wallet. "Exactly what documents are you talking about?"

"A letter signed by President Lincoln. Just a memorandum, actually." He glanced at his car, then back at Sarah.

She glowered at him, biting her lower lip.

He cocked his head and let out another sigh. "The memorandum instructed an aide to destroy some papers, a perfunctory sort of thing. But over the last couple of years, anything having to do with Lincoln seems to be fetching a premium."

Sarah planted one hand on her hip and held out the other hand, palm up, inviting him to produce the paper he wanted her to sign.

Once again, he lifted his briefcase onto one raised knee and laid the receipt on top for Sarah to sign. After scrawling her name, she glared at him and snatched the envelope out of his hand. The courier wasted no time retreating down the front porch steps to his car.

As the car disappeared down the drive, Sarah opened the envelope. Inside was a check from the Trust

Account of Easley & White, Attorneys at Law, drawn on Wells Fargo Bank, NA – Riverside, CA – Main Branch. The check stub identified the remitter as Thomas J. Moran, PhD. The courier was right. Ten thousand dollars was a lot of money for a simple instruction to destroy some documents.

´After taking a few steps toward the stairs, Sarah refocused on one particular word the courier used. He said 'documents,' not just one, but plural. Had he hurried out of there on purpose? Maybe he hadn't wanted to tell her everything.

Sarah stopped and stared up at the attic door, wondering if there was something valuable lurking behind it and whether Lincoln's memo was just the tip of the iceberg. Without taking the usual amount of time to study her next move from every angle, she launched herself back up the stairs.

Her hand slipped on the door knob, giving her pause. Not all the possibilities about her missing father were pleasant ones. Some came to her in nightmares suggesting things that were better off left alone. But wasn't the truth what she'd always wanted? And now, the truth might include some mysterious and valuable Lincoln papers.

She pursed her lips, remembering how Mom declared the attic off limits back when Grandma Cassie got too sick to make the rules for her own house. That was the first straw. When Grandma died and Mom inherited the house, Sarah had to escape. So she found a quiet little place near College Park across the Chesapeake Bay Bridge. The move didn't set well with Mom, but it helped Sarah salvage her sanity.

Now, Sarah shouldered the burden of cleaning up after two generations of Morgan women who never married. So whatever was behind that door begged to be unburied. If that included some precious Lincoln documents, it was a safe bet that Mom hadn't touched them. She never went upstairs, not even to clean the place out. "Digging through all those boxed up memories will just bring trouble" is what she always said.

Mom would only venture up to the attic when Sarah snuck up there as a young girl to hide from the household drama. On those occasions, Sarah would poke around for clues about her father and grandfather, keeping an ear out until Mom caught her and chased her back downstairs.

Grandma Cassie probably left that Lincoln memo lying around downstairs at some point, and that's how Mom got her hands on it. So yeah, there could be some valuable stuff behind that door. Like whatever President Lincoln wanted destroyed.

Sarah coaxed the door open just a crack, stiffening her resolve and squinting into the dimness, inhaling a whiff of stale, dusty air. She opened the door a bit wider and scanned for hiding places, shadows along the corners of stacked boxes or abandoned furniture. Her eyes studied silhouetted edges of support posts and any little nook or cranny where Mom could be lurking, ready to pounce and chastise her for stepping across the threshold. Scratchy recordings of Mom's scoldings echoed in her head. Sarah always cringed at Mom's voice telling her "No" for venturing up to the attic or for demanding the truth that was owed her. But of course, Mom wouldn't be up there this time. Mom was dead.

One step through the door and Sarah opened her eyes wide, taking in everything at once. A few boxes next to the wardrobe caught her attention. She edged toward them and lifted the lid from the box on top of the stack. It was full of Grandma Cassie's things. A dusty picture caught her attention and made her smile. The photograph showed her leaning playfully into Grandma's side. Mom stood like a pillar half an arm's length away from them.

Sarah couldn't remember who snapped the photo, but the occasion was clear in her memory. It would have been her fourteenth birthday, the only time that necklace ever dangled from her neck. Mom yanked it off the next morning, certain a boy had given it to her. Mom was right. His name was Nick.

Boys were taboo, especially if they were black, or heaven forbid, mulatto. Mom's racist paranoia was the catalyst for the rare conversations the two of them had that lasted more than two or three sentences. Those weren't actually conversations, though. Verbal combat was a better description for it.

Sometimes things got physical. And when they did it was one sided, giving Sarah practice at a valuable life skill. She didn't remember exactly when it happened for the first time, but at some point she discovered being alone in her imagination could be a good hiding place. So from that time on, whenever Mom went on her rampages, Sarah would roll up like one of those roly-poly bugs, shutting herself into an imaginary world where feelings could be invented.

Hiding in her fantasies, Sarah Sue Morgan held a firm grip on aloneness. And alone was her status quo. Grandma Cassie had been dead for some ten years, and Mom had always seemed dead. The two men who no one ever talked about – one should have been her father, the other her grandfather – never touched her life except through the veil of secrecy that shrouded their absence. In truth, they were probably dead as well.

Truth told, Sarah's reality sucked. So she camouflaged herself in layers of aloofness that even good intentions couldn't penetrate. People could compliment her complexion or exotic features, but their sentiments didn't register. Whatever people saw on the outside, inside she was just the freak her father didn't love. Who knows? Maybe there was too much of Mom in her. Or worse, maybe he had – no, don't go there. It can't be true.

Sarah shuddered from a chill that hit her out of nowhere. It was as if December's icy breath chased off the Indian summer afternoon. She shut her eyes and struggled to swallow, pushing back thoughts about her father – images from a recurring nightmare. Had he been some terrible monster? It was possible. After all, someone had to have done a real number on Mom to make her crawl into the deep hole she cowered in all the time that Sarah could remember.

Maybe no one ever talked about her father to protect her from the ugly truth. But that didn't stop Sarah's questions from having minds of their own. Was he the brute in her nightmare? Did he force himself on Mom? If that had been the case, why didn't Mom just get rid of her? Why did Mom keep a constant reminder of her worst horror? An abortion would have saved all three Morgan women a lot of grief.

Sarah's shoulders drooped. Her slender fingers caressed the picture frame once more before she laid it down on her lap and lifted the next item from the box, a leather bound portfolio. Thumbing through it, she found pages of notes in Grandma Cassie's handwriting. A long sigh flushed out of her. Grandma's half-empty journal reminded her of her own sporadic efforts to her counselor's mantra, "Journal every day." The third page caught her attention.

Uncle Joe is a jewel. He brought me and

Lake together. I'll never forget the summer of 1953. It has been the best ever. Lake teaches at the college, just like Uncle Joe. Of course, no one is thrilled about us – except me and Lake. That's because I'm 19 and he's ... well, he's older.

Lake can be awful moody. And when he is, his eyes turn dark and hollow like bottomless pits. Not that they look empty; it just seems that whatever's behind them is a galaxy away. You can't even see the shadows of his soul.

But he's so mature and intelligent. He hypnotizes me with ideas I've never imagined and can barely understand. He says his moods are a necessary burden. They help him see things that others can't. He said he got that idea from the diary he's always talking about.

Sarah flashed back to her freshman year in college. She had a flame and he was a professor, too. Back then, she fantasized that he seduced her for her mind, not her body. Of course those days, most girls treated their intelligence like a pimple you covered with makeup. Over the years, Sarah had come to view men as if they were acne.

She flipped over a few more pages.

Lake and I fought today. I told him his sad moods weren't necessary. He pulled a book off his bookshelf and waved it in my face. He said an old woman gave it to him. He met her on a train from out West during the war. He said it was a diary that belonged to President Lincoln. It talked about how he suffered from depression even when he was president. He called his depression melancholy.

Lake said there were details about the ugliness Mr. Lincoln touched in those moments of despair that he was afraid to talk about with others. He read me one of Lincoln's entries, "... great inspirations are forged in the cauldron of deep misery."

When he first showed the diary to me, I only pretended to believe it really was Mr. Lincoln's. I couldn't believe a teacher in Wicomico County would have a national treasure tucked away on his bookshelf. The more I fell in love with Lake, though, the more I wanted to believe in him, so I let myself believe in the diary, too.

Was it possible Grandma's old boyfriend gave her more Lincoln documents besides the memo Mom sold? Sarah dropped the journal on the floor next to her and dug through the box, setting aside things she'd otherwise take time to soak in – Mom's diploma and immunization record, old letters and random photos.

After emptying the box, she rifled through the drawers in an old dresser and dove into the antique wardrobe, flailing her hands across its bottom and into each corner like a blind little girl. When she came up empty, Sarah tucked the journal under her arm and headed downstairs to settle in for a long read. Maybe the journal would tell her if there was more Lincoln stuff to find. But first, a cup of tea sounded like a good idea – with two lumps of sugar, the way Grandma Cassie taught her to drink it. Luckily, she had filled the thermos with hot water at breakfast. There's nothing more frustrating than waiting for water to boil.

While stirring her steeped another entry grabbed Sarah's attention.

I hadn't seen Lake for weeks and didn't want to face him so soon after our fight, but I had to tell him Aunt Rennie died. I was still stinging from our argument. Just thinking about it sent a sharp pain up behind my eyes and made my throat dry and achy. The pain had a good side, though. It helped me remember what a jerk he could be.

That's all I could think about when I saw him, and I just blurted out, "Aunt Rennie's dead."

His eyes were dark and empty like the ocean when it's swallowed up by storm clouds and driving rain. He said that he'd heard she tried to have an abortion. I could tell what he was thinking by his tone of voice. He wanted to say, "I told you so." But he didn't dare.

I said I heard some back alley butcher botched it.

Sarah's throat burned as if a sheet of coarse sandpaper had scraped over her tonsils. Thirty-plus years earlier, abortions were different. Grandma Cassie's close encounter with that harsh reality must have been the reason Mom went ahead and let her be born, in spite of not wanting her. But it still didn't take away the sting of not being wanted. Tears welled up in her eyes as she tried to move on, looking for a new topic that would make her forget the rawness in her throat.

> *I still don't want to believe that Lake's dead. I cried for days when I heard. I still cry when I think about him, when I drive past the apartment. I couldn't even get out of bed to go to his memorial service. And later I was still too numb to get worked up about how he died. Someone said it was suspicious.*
>
> *A couple of days ago I saw a doctor. It's just what I was afraid of. I'm pregnant. Lake and I only went all the way that one time, just before we broke up.*

The sandpaper in Sarah's throat turned into a walnut-sized lump. She had a real grandpa. His name was Lake. But he was gone. Stolen from her. Leaving her without a single memory of cuddling in his lap or being spoiled the way every little girl ought to be. And since there was no father around, either, a grandpa would have come in real handy. She picked up the journal and cradled it in her hands to read more, hoping to reach across time and touch Grandpa Lake through Grandma Cassie's memories.

I haven't felt like writing for a while. I know I have to move on with my life. Lake's been gone for six months now. But I still hope it's him, even when I know I'm just imagining that I hear someone knocking at the front door. There really was someone there today, but it wasn't him, of course. It was a courier with a package from a lawyer's office. I was afraid to open it. What if it was something about Lake? But I opened it anyway. Inside the package was a dingy envelope that contained a coarse, yellowed piece of paper. And there was that damned diary that he seemed to love more than anything else, even me.

He'd insisted that the woman who gave it to him was the daughter of President Lincoln's bodyguard, and, according to her, Lake reminded her of her father's stories about Mr. Lincoln. It had something to do with them both having dark moods and deep, hollow eyes.

I didn't care whether the diary was real or not. I promised myself that I'd never open it. I didn't want to remember that part of Lake. Why couldn't he have just taken it to his grave with him?

Sarah stopped reading. Her achy throat turned

numb. The word "grave" made his death concrete and final. Her vague notion of a grandpa – what she'd not had, what she wished she'd had, what she'd hoped she might still salvage at least a bit of – it was all buried somewhere in the ground.   Indisputably gone, out of reach. Her treasure hunt had turned into a funeral without her having to move an inch.

Stroking the binding of Grandma Cassie's journal, Sarah fixated on the stains and ripples time had left on its leather cover. The loose paper peeking out from its pages escaped her notice until her mourning abated, seemingly of its own accord, and the journal was almost back into its box. The paper was crisp and neatly folded. A sheet of bright-white laserjet paper that had been tucked among coarse, yellowed pages. Sarah unfolded it.

The Executive Mansion

13 April 1865
Lamon: Please destroy.
A. Lincoln

1 May 1893
To Dolly: Please care for it the way I should have cared for you.
Your repentant father

April 18, 1942
To Lake: You can become a great man.
Your new friend, Mme. Teillard

Goose bumps tracked down Sarah's spine. Was she staring at a photocopy of some record of how

Lincoln's diary wound up in Grandpa Lake's hands? And was the original of that record what Mom sold to the professor in California? Maybe Mom had been up in the attic, after all, and found the journal. That photocopy was too crisp and the paper too bright. It had to have been made years after Grandma died. In that case, Mom probably knew about Lincoln's diary, too.

Her goose bumps turned to a heat rash as she seethed at what likely happened. Mom wasn't savvy enough to squeeze $10,000 out of a Lincoln scholar for some seemingly inconsequential memo. That meant someone probably scammed her out of the diary. Only the worst scum would fleece a mentally ill, dying woman.

Sarah jumped to her feet, and the blood rushed from her brain to her knees. Tiny bright dots swirled in front of her and her whole body went limp. Grandma Cassie's journal fell out of her hand, dropping to the floor. Usually, Sarah had more stamina, but she'd barely eaten for days and lacrosse practice hadn't been a piece of cake.

Kneeling down to steady herself, a dingy, coarse-edged parchment lying next to the journal caught her eye. It was thicker and more rustic than the pages in the journal, and in contrast with Grandma Cassie's impeccable penmanship, the parchment contained several lines of jerky handwriting in antiquated brown ink.

I will weep upon unhallowed ground
In rain or snow or dust,
Until the sacramental crown,
Has sealed its sacred trust.

Sarah studied the verse. Her imagination raced through myriad possibilities of where the poem might have come from. Could someone have torn it from

Lincoln's diary? Just touching it flushed a surge of adrenaline through her veins. It was as if her fingers had reached back through history and touched the hand of one of the greatest men who ever lived.

"Deep breaths," Sarah told herself. Her first order of business would be finding out whether Lincoln's diary was stashed away somewhere in the house. If not, her suspicions about Mom getting scammed would be confirmed beyond any reasonable doubt.

Chapter Two

No Lincoln diary, no treasures and no new leads on the two men whose absence left giant holes in Sarah's heart. Half way into the second day of searching the attic and packing, she taped the last box shut. The most interesting thing other than the journal and its contents was a draft of Grandma Cassie's last testament. The draft said Mom got the house, and Grandma's cash and securities went into a trust for Sarah to take care of. That's pretty much how things got handled back when Grandma Cassie died.

In any event, two generations of stuff stood ready to be loaded onto a moving van and sent to storage. Sarah gave the attic one last visual sweep to be sure she hadn't missed anything. Not a chance. Everything got moved and scrutinized at least once when she picked it up and put it into a box.

As far as Sarah was concerned, something wasn't right. What happened to Lincoln's diary? She dug through her bag for the envelope the courier had dropped off. The attorney's check had a phone number on it.

When the lawyer's receptionist answered, Sarah dove right in. "Hello, my name is Sarah Sue Morgan. I'm the administrator for the estate of Jennifer Morgan in Wicomico County, Maryland. We recently received a check from your office on behalf of a client, a Dr. Thomas Moran. Is there someone I could speak with regarding this matter?"

With the briefest acknowledgement, the receptionist put her on hold for several minutes. Sarah tapped her foot and glanced every ten seconds or so at the time display on her cell phone. Eventually, a man who said he was John Easley, a partner in the firm, interrupted the tinny sounding music mid-measure. His impatient tone made her want the music back. "I understand you have a question about the check we delivered to you on behalf of our client. What's the problem?"

Sarah explained that she needed to clear up some confusion about which documents her mother sold Dr. Moran and asked him to help her fill in the details. Easley replied that he couldn't disclose any information without his client's permission and told her to research the deceased's records.

Sarah inhaled a deep breath, almost audibly, holding herself back from blurting, "The 'deceased' has a name." Instead, she exhaled slowly and explained there were no records of the transaction. The lawyer offered his regrets but said he couldn't do anything. Even contacting Dr. Moran to get his permission to help her seemed to be a burden. He said his schedule wouldn't allow him to do so immediately, but he would make a note to follow up with the professor when he had an opportunity.

Sarah started to shout into the phone. "But —"

He didn't give her a chance. He said goodbye and hung up.

Staring at her cell phone, she ground her teeth. If only there was a way to reach through the receiver and grab Easley by his silk necktie to shake every drop of condescension out of him. Instead, her ringtone played harps and the display showed a familiar phone number, one she had deleted from her Contacts months ago.

Sarah pressed the phone against her ear and snapped, "I thought I told you to stop calling me."

The caller on the other end replied, "Honest, I'm not trying to get back into your life. I read your Mom's obituary and just wanted to offer my condolences, and see if you're okay."

"Look, Roger." Sarah rolled her eyes. "That's thoughtful of you, but you're not part of my life anymore. I'm handling things just fine. Besides if I weren't, I can't imagine how you could help."

"Say, I'm just trying to be nice here."

Sarah blew a loose curl away from the corner of her mouth. "I'm in the middle of something right now, so I'm a bit preoccupied."

"Well, if you're running into some issues settling the estate, I could recommend someone."

"It's not that. It appears that Mom owned a priceless Lincoln diary that she got conned out of for a song. I'm in the middle of tracing down some details."

"How in Hell would your Mom get her hands on something like that?"

Sarah gazed around the attic one more time. "That's what I'm trying to get to the bottom of. I might have to make a trip to L.A. to get everything figured out."

Roger snickered. "Look, it's not as if your Mom was playing with a full deck. You'd probably just wind up chasing windmills."

She shut her eyes tight. "That's exactly the kind of thing I'd expect out of you. Thanks for reminding me why we broke up. Have a good life." She tapped End Call and gripped her phone hard enough to strangle Roger. It wasn't as if she'd made up her mind to fly to L.A., at least not yet. But if it showed Roger a thing or two, it just might be worth it.

Sarah stomped out to her black FJ Cruiser and snatched up her computer bag. Her cell phone worked as a wireless modem for her laptop on previous visits to Mom's. But between the vagaries of wireless connectivity and the mysteries of computer operating systems, people just can't be sure about such things. And for Sarah, technology always pulled out all the stops to sabotage her plans when she needed its help the most.

This time, though, the technology gods knew they'd be beaten or at least worn down until they submitted. That damned diary had its hooks in her. So it didn't take long for her to own the search engine.

Her first attempt, a search for Dr. Thomas Moran fizzled – one hit, a psychiatrist. Next, Sarah skimmed back through the parts of Grandma Cassie's journal she'd read. There were names of the people who owned the diary before Grandpa Lake. One of them might lead her to the elusive Professor Moran. Mme. Teillard, the lady who gave Grandpa Lake the diary was her first target. Bingo! An entry reported that in 1912, Dolly Lamon Teillard sold Colonel Lamon's entire collection of Lincoln papers to George D. Smith as the agent for a collector, Henry E. Huntington. Later, Huntington deposited the collection with the Huntington Library, which he founded in San Marino, CA. Apparently, Mme. Teillard's sale wasn't as complete as that report indicated. She'd kept Lincoln's diary and gave it to Grandpa Lake years later.

A big library in California missed getting the diary. A professor in California possibly winds up with the diary. There could be a connection.

On the other hand, maybe Mom returned the diary to Dolly's family, instead of selling it. Though that wouldn't help her explain how Mom got such a good price for a simple memo, the angle was worth checking out. She went on searching, looking for names of Dolly Teillard's heirs But according to a family genealogy page, both Dolly's children died before her. One in infancy and the other at age nine. There were no heirs.

A call to the Huntington Library – their phone

number was on their website – didn't yield much information. However, one of the drones who got stuck with her call gave her the name and phone number of a rare books dealer who represented collectors of Lincoln memorabilia, Jackson Andrews.

Andrews took her call, almost too eagerly. Sarah hardly trusted the people she knew, let alone strangers. Her counselor once told her that paranoia and depression were related. She remembered arguing back, "I'm not paranoid. I'm just perceptive." That became her tagline.

Sarah resisted the temptation to bait Andrews with the poem that fell out of Grandma's journal. He only needed to know that Mom sold some Lincoln documents to a Professor Moran in California. She was just trying to make sure there were no loose ends to prevent her from closing her mother's estate.

Andrews told her he brokered some deals for Moran who taught history at the University of Redlands, about 60 miles east of L.A. He also thought Dr. Burgess, the curator at the Lincoln Shrine in Redlands, might have had some dealings with Moran.

Sarah asked Andrews if Professor Moran had mentioned anything about her mother. He hesitated. Finally, he said the professor made a passing remark about a woman back East who had some promising leads on documents that might advance his research, but he still hadn't found the smoking gun.

"What's that?" she asked.

Andrews muttered, "He has this bizarre notion that Lincoln planned his own assassination."

"Why does he think Lincoln would have done that?" Sarah squinted, wrinkling her nose.

"Moran's pretty much an opportunist who'll do anything for fifteen minutes of fame."

"Yeah, but Lincoln killing himself is pretty far out

there. Who'd bother to listen to him?"

"From what I gather, he's pushing some theory about Lincoln suffering from Post Traumatic Stress Disorder. Must be trying to tap into all those bleeding heart anti-war types who want us to believe defending your country turns you into a nut case."

Sarah wasn't in the mood for a political argument, especially with someone who gave the impression he was locked into an ideology. So she thanked him and checked out the University of Redlands website, scanning it for a phone number.

After dialing the main switchboard, the web of automated menus she got sucked into landed her in the Professor's voicemail. "Sorry, all my office appointment slots are booked for the next two weeks. Leave a message and I'll add you to the waiting list. If you're not one of my students, leave your name and number and I'll call when I come up for air."

After Sarah tapped End Call, her jaw tightened. Roger's condescending opinions still echoed in her head. But when was the last time they'd agreed on anything? Putting Roger aside, it made sense to confront this Professor Moran face-to-face. He could dodge her phone calls for months, which he would do if he had something to hide. On the other hand, sitting at his office door, she could catch him either coming or going. And in an eye-ball-to-eyeball confrontation, his face could betray a mother lode of lies. After all, her interrogation skills had gotten honed working with some of the world's the best.

Within minutes, Sarah booked a flight to Ontario International Airport for the next afternoon. Closing her computer, she promised Grandma Cassie, "I'll get to the bottom of this diary thing even if it kills me."

Chapter Three

As Sarah packed for the airport the next morning, her mind was still in a fog over the nightmare that kept her up half the night. She had woken with a start just past two o'clock, panicking over a vision of Mom rolled up like a fetus on the floor, moaning and sobbing – a large dark hazy figure hunched over her.

That dream almost convinced Sarah to cancel the trip. Maybe her subconscious was warning her that she was vaulting headlong into trouble out in California. It certainly scared her off from getting back to reading Grandma Cassie's journal. Was there some haunting secret lurking in its pages? Something to shatter the illusions she'd clung to for survival.

From her earliest memories, Sarah had created an image of what her father might have been like. And that was what she wanted the truth to be. Her heart went into a stall every time the idea of giving up on that truth snuck into her head. But the truth could prove her illusion was a lie. What if her heart was trying to protect her? Maybe the truth was more like that recurring nightmare that always left her wide-eyed and shivering, just like it did last night. Was her father the monster who hurt Mom? Was he the one who sent her over the edge?

On the airplane, Sarah sat squeezed between two oversized strangers in a narrow row of seats. As the plane taxied, the image that flashed through her mind was of rats trapped in a maze while some guy in a lab coat kept moving their cheese. She also thought she saw black smoke seeping into the passenger compartment. From the time the jet's wheels lifted off the ground, Sarah squirmed in her seat, not sure she'd survive long enough to reach cruising altitude to have access to something from her carry-on to absorb her attention.

By the time the pilot leveled off at 30,000 feet, Sarah had convinced herself to face whatever waited for her in Grandma Cassie's journal rather than go nuts like a trapped rodent. But something sucked her breath away as her hand touched the carry-on. This wasn't the time or place to learn some awful truth about her father. What if she came face to face with a devastating revelation just when the passenger in front of her dropped his seatback into her lap? And if Grandma's journal flopped out of her hand and into the guy's lap next to her, he'd see the whole ugly truth about her family. She'd probably make an idiot out of herself by getting up to go to the bathroom and retaliating against the passenger who had invaded her space with his seatback – she paid for that space by the way, thank you sir – by giving it a hard bump. But any pleasure that might give her would be undone when she had to fold herself up like a pretzel to slink down the aisle on her way to the world's tiniest lavatory.

Sarah wiped the clammy sweat from her forehead and decided to peruse some of the web pages she'd printed out from her research on Dr. Moran. On close examination they confirmed Andrews's sentiment about Moran. All the articles smacked of grandstanding and attention-grabbing controversies. The only supportive comments were on a blog that hyped Moran's case for Lincoln's complicity in his own assassination. The gist of the argument was that Lincoln might have sacrificed himself to spark public sympathy for his unpopular Reconstruction plan.

The blogger quoted Lincoln declaring he didn't have the right to put himself, not even his life, ahead of the work he was 'predestined' to finish. There was mention of Lincoln's mood swings just prior to the assassination. Associates said he was in the deepest depression they'd ever seen just days before his murder. Lincoln's brief euphoria the morning of his death was followed by an ominous dark mood as he left for the theater. And there was a citation referencing the "DSM-IV Criteria" that modern mental health professionals use for diagnosing Post Traumatic Stress Disorder. Lincoln allegedly manifested all of them. The source also pointed out that PTSD survivors can be prone to suicide, not as a result of overwhelming depression, but as a means of taking back control, especially when they are suffering a secondary wounding that reminds them of their original trauma.

Moran's most disturbing claim was that John Wilkes Booth wouldn't have found it necessary to rig the lock on the door to the President's box at the theater. Lincoln was purportedly a huge Booth fan. He loved the theater and saw Booth on stage a number of times. He even kept a scrapbook on Booth and memorized his favorite lines. Lincoln would have welcomed Booth into his box with open arms. So why do all the historical accounts have Booth going through such tedious machinations to get access to the president?

After the plane landed, Sarah's claustrophobia followed her down the concourse toward Baggage Claim. Her cell phone display alerted her to a waiting voicemail. It turned out to be Angela, a friend who hovered over Sarah the way Mom was never guilty of doing. Instead, Mom often dragged her into an abyss of despair. But Angela could suck the air out of a room and leave Sarah gasping for her last breath. Everything centered around Angela's latest drama or on fixing Sarah, even though Sarah couldn't count the number of times she had said, at least to herself, "I don't have a problem with me." And there was Angela's constantly pinging her about getting together or reminding her about lacrosse practice. As if Sarah would ever forget lacrosse, the one thing that always lifted her spirits.

Even before Sarah retrieved Angela's voice message, a text message popped onto her cell phone's display, "practice2nite – NEW FIELD@6:30." If Dr. Moran cooperated that would be all she'd have to give up. Missing a game would piss her off. There was nothing like being 'in the zone.' Just her with the ball, her stick, and the goal. The deafening silence as her willowy frame sliced through the air like the world was in slow-mo replay. Not even the bumping of bodies or the banging of sticks registered with her. It was like being one with creation, just like the ancient First Americans. That's where Sarah's mind was when she almost landed in a heap, just missing a collision with someone hurrying past her with luggage in both hands.

At the car rental desk, Sarah got upgraded to a midsized sedan, for the same rate as a compact. They were out of small cars. And by the time the congested eastbound Interstate toward Redlands greeted her, she was glad for the bigger car. It gave her at least an illusion of safety. Things were more intense than anything on the Beltway back home. Speeding happened on Maryland's Interstates, but at least some drivers back there took the posted limits seriously. Not so on this amateur NASCAR track with everyone pressing at full throttle, jockeying for inside positions and leaving only the slightest bit of daylight between cars.

Sarah leaned forward into the steering wheel and tightened her grip, habitually keeping an eye on her rearview mirror to track cars as they closed in on her. She cringed as people bobbed and weaved like wannabe slalom racers, using other cars to mark the course's gates.

Stealing peeks at the roadside while scanning for directional signs, her eyes caught glimpses of the fleshy billboards that dotted the landscape. The thought flashed through her mind, "Why do they degrade themselves that way?"

Soon after she checked in at the motel, Sarah's head hit the pillow, giving her an escape from the swarm of humanity. The change in time zones justified her need to sleep. But sleep was more of a convenient escape from confronting whatever lay in wait for her in Grandma Cassie's journal.

The journal stayed untouched the next morning when Sarah's internal clock, still stuck on east coast time, got her up early. There wasn't time for reading. It was more important to get to the university to catch Professor Moran before classes started.

Her thoughts were even farther away from Grandma Cassie's journal as she gazed at rows of palm trees that lined the freeway. The remnants of citrus orchards popped up here and there, too, but they must have been ornamental since hardly enough oranges dangled from the trees to squeeze out a quart of fresh juice.

The crisp sun-kissed morning contradicted stories she'd heard about Southern California's smoggy air. Smatterings of evergreen trees atop the distant mountain ridges stood out so clearly that Sarah could have inventoried them.   But on leaving the motel, the concierge had warned her that, eventually, the horizons would disappear behind a gritty, caustic-tasting haze that would blur the mountain peaks until they were mere silhouettes.

A few blocks after the freeway exit, Sarah found herself swallowed up in a suburbia of garden apartments and World War II vintage bungalows. She did a double take at the lawn bowling green on the edge of a large city park. And after turning right from University Avenue onto Colton, the pickets of palm trees in the median and parkways reminded her of a desert oasis.

The history department was located in an annex tucked between a large Grecian style amphitheater and an athletic field. Her adrenaline spiked at the sight of the women's lacrosse team scrimmaging. She smiled. In her last game, the ref carded her for trying to sneak in a hard check when no one was looking.

Gold block letters bolted to the annex's façade displayed the name Gannett Center. The word 'ironic' slipped out under her breath as she caught a vision of media moguls keeping historians under their thumbs. With no one around to greet visitors in the lobby, Sarah edged her way down a narrow hallway, passing a couple of closed doors. Nameplates at each doorjamb identified the faculty member who occupied the office. Halfway down the hall was an open door. The nameplate read "Dr. Thomas Moran." From behind a simple metal desk, which took up most of the sardine-can-sized office, a man peered up at her.

"Can I help you?"

"Dr. Moran?" Sarah asked, clutching her bag to her side.

He smiled broadly. "No, I'm Elliot, his research assistant. Is there something I can help you with?" Even under the fluorescent lights, his tanned face accentuated a pair of ocean blue eyes.

Sarah caught herself smiling back. Something about him seemed familiar. As he swiveled in his chair and stood up, his face left the impression it belonged in an old Morgan family photo. The problem was that there weren't any men in any Morgan family pictures she'd seen. "Oh, uh, I'm sorry. Uh, I just thought – I mean you just look like you could be a professor." For a moment, Sarah flashed back to her first semester at U of M when she almost lost her scholarship by investing too much energy into a TA. He was older, too. That was before the professor got into her head.

Elliot grinned and gestured across the desk at a small wooden armchair. "Thank you, I think."

Sarah shook her head and stayed standing. She let out a nervous cough and forced her mouth to form a sheepish grin. "I meant it as a compliment. I hope you weren't offended."

"No offense taken. In fact, if you drop by again, I'll make sure I'm wearing a tweed jacket with those leather patch things." He pointed to his left elbow. His bare forearms and half-sleeved biceps matched his bronze face.

Sarah held her hands out at her side. "Um, my mother sold some Lincoln documents to Dr. Moran just before she passed away. As Administrator of her estate, I thought I should make sure the documents arrived in satisfactory order." It was only partly a lie. "I was in the area anyway and learned the university wasn't far from where I'm staying. So I thought I might check in with him." Telling a bald-faced lie brought a chilly sweat to the back of her neck even while her face started to flush.

Elliot winced as he looked down at the desk. "Dr. Moran has taken the remainder of the week off to focus on some promising information he received relating to his pet research project."

Sarah grimaced. The walls in the tiny office felt like they were closing in on her, and beads of moisture collected along her hairline. Her hand waved off a hazy voice in her head as she reached into her bag and pulled out the poem that had fallen out of Grandma Cassie's journal.

"Wait, I have something my mother may have overlooked sending him." Sarah reached across the desk to hand him the poem.

Elliot's focus locked onto the four lines of verse.

"He had interesting taste – in poetry, I mean." Sarah wanted to make a good impression and hoped her observation sounded credible even if it was vague.

Elliot looked at her and grinned. His eyes were larger, even brighter than when they first caught her attention. "This is remarkable. It looks like Lincoln wrote it."

"Yes, that's my impression too." She was covering for not knowing enough about Lincoln's writings to venture more than a guess.

"Well, the handwriting is a dead give away for starters." He walked around the desk and stood next to her, pointing at the lines of verse.

Sarah drew a deep breath. "Of course." She covered her bluff with an approving grin, not being able to recall ever seeing a sample of President Lincoln's handwriting.

Elliot turned and looked out the office door. "This is about his mother's grave. We have stories about him sitting on her grave during storms as if he thought her body would float up out of the ground when the water table got too high. He did the same thing at Ann Hathaway's grave. He never talked or wrote about those graveside episodes, except for this." He held the page out by the edge of one corner.

Sarah smirked. "Really? I mean he actually did that?"

"Sure, he was just nine when his mother died, and he was pretty high-strung. But there was a reason for his worry. In the wilderness, water tables often lifted bodies out of their graves when it flooded."

Sarah held one hand up to her brow, shading her eyes from his. "Yes, I know he grieved a lot when she died, I'd just never heard about him sitting on her grave."

He smiled at her again, and this time the room grew less cramped. "Lincoln's family was very religious, and at nine, that would have affected his thinking. He became neurotic over the possibility that something might happen to her body before a circuit-riding minister got there to give her a proper Christian burial. On top of that, modern psychologists who've studied Lincoln's behavior think he may have manifested symptoms of Post Traumatic Stress Disorder stemming from an episode when he almost drowned in a creek at the age of seven. A playmate saved his life. Burying his mother and first love may have deepened the emotional wounds he suffered from nearly losing his life in that creek. Those memories could have inspired this poem. And it uses the same meter that he used in most of his poetry." Elliot kept staring at the poem.

Sarah studied his face, trying to read his mind.

"Where did you get this?" he asked.

Sarah lied again, "Oh it was just with my mother's things. It had probably been passed down through the family. I just thought possibly she might have neglected sending it to the professor with the other things." She shuffled her feet. "That's just one of the questions I wanted to clear up, but I'm only in town for a couple of days and was hoping I could meet with Dr. Moran personally."

Elliot smiled as he retreated behind the desk. "I'm sure that under the circumstances the professor will find the time to meet with you, even if it interrupts his research."

Sarah thanked him for his effort and asked, "What is he researching?"

Elliot picked up the phone's handset from its cradle. "He's spent more than forty years trying to prove that President Lincoln helped plan his own assassination."

"Why would he think that?" Sarah had already heard Andrews's point of view, but she thought Elliot might give her a glimpse into the professor's perspective.

"It all started with the recognition that Lincoln was a terribly depressed man."

"But didn't he manage to work through all that?"

"Not all the time. He actually talked about hanging himself several times while he was president. The thing that kept him going was 'finishing the work.' But he said his work was 'done' not long before he died."

"Did Professor Moran come up with this idea all by himself?"

"He got started on the theory in graduate school. I think it interested him because he heard some rumors about a Lincoln diary that supposedly eluded collectors. He almost gave up on finding it until he came across your mother, though I'm not sure why he thought she could help him locate it."

Sarah glanced away, not wanting him to see the skepticism in her eyes.

Elliot looked at her as he dialed the phone. "What other documents did your mother have?"

Sarah was spared from answering his question when Dr. Moran picked up on the first ring. And after a brief conversation with the professor, Elliot beamed as he reported Moran's willingness to meet with her at two o'clock that afternoon at his home in Grand Terrace. Still smiling, he wrote the professor's address and home phone number, as well as directions on a note pad. Almost as an afterthought, he wrote down his own cell phone number. "Call me if you have a problem finding the place."

Sarah wrote out her cell number and motel information for him, just in case Dr. Moran changed plans at the last minute. She hadn't made up her mind whether to go back to the motel, but with several hours to kill, it was an option.

Before Elliot could raise the question again about other documents, she distracted him by asking for directions to the Lincoln Shrine. He drew a rough map and described how to find the Shrine tucked behind the Smiley Library and across the street from the Redlands Bowl, a large outdoor theater and the centerpiece of the city's downtown park.

On her way out into the hall Sarah turned. "Say, is there a Starbucks close by? I'm dying for a latté."

"Yes, it's on your way to the Shrine. After you turn left on Orange Street, you'll go under the freeway. It'll be just a block or two past there on your right."

After thanking him for his help, Sarah started down the hall toward the lobby.

Elliot called after her, "Oh, wait. I'll walk you out."

Sarah looked back as he pulled the office door shut behind him. She must have worn some hint of surprise on her face.

"I'm headed to class. I'm covering lectures for Dr. Moran this week."

"Well, I did get a little lost wandering down here from my parking spot. Maybe you can point me in the right direction."

"I'll do better. I'll walk you to your car just to be

sure you don't get lost again."

Sarah started to object.

As Elliot held the door for her on their way out of the building, he explained with a smile and a glint in his eyes, "Don't worry about me being late for class. They can't start without me."

Chapter Four

When Sarah showed up at the Lincoln Shrine a bit before noon, the sign next to the locked entry door said the place opened at one o'clock. Part of her wanted to go back to the motel, just to be alone and away from the masses of people who by her estimation outnumbered the combined count of pollutant particulates and gritty granules that had started to collect in the late morning air. But the motel room would be more oppressive than the unfamiliar frenzy of people darting in every direction. Grandma Cassie's journal would be sitting on the nightstand leering at her.

It didn't take long for an alternative plan to pop into her head. Making a dry run to the professor's home to be sure she didn't get lost later. According to her cell phone's GPS, he lived only 15 minutes away. But, as can be typical for modern technology, the GPS got her lost somewhere near her destination. And its persistent announcement, "Destination on your left," had her twisting every direction in her seat. There was only a vacant lot and a stand of scruffy, low hanging trees where her destination was supposed to be.

Sarah made several passes through a nearby neighborhood, studying house numbers without any success. An older couple out for a walk tried to help, but their directions got her more lost. She sputtered at herself, knowing she'd missed a turn somewhere. And ending up at the top of a steep hill that overlooked an uninhabited canyon triggered the onset of a headache. No houses, just withered grasses and dead-looking shrubs in variegated shades of amber ranging from parched-earth-wheat and brown-mustard to dustings of bleached-cocoa.

From the top of the hill, she stared out across the

basin at rows of lanky palm trees that resembled mop-topped pencils. They formed a picket along the foot of a stark steel-gray mountain range. It was a different landscape from anything in Maryland. Everything looked browner, drier and less tame. Home was better. The growing lump in her throat agreed.

After composing herself, Sarah wiped a mist from her eyes, wheeled her rental car around, and started back down the hill to take another stab at finding the professor's house. Within a few hundred feet, her GPS had guided her back to the vacant lot, but this time a narrow driveway caught her eye, something that escaped her before. It veered off the street, angling between two rows of oleanders into an untended landscape. Several droopy pepper trees canopied the entry to the driveway, obscuring a sprawling, rambler-style house from every angle. The pepper trees reminded her, in a way, of the willows that grew along Maryland's rivers. Earlier she had missed the sign that hung on the fencepost, and almost overlooked it a second time. It displayed the professor's address, barely visible.

Sarah stopped her car, threw it into reverse, and backed up just past the driveway to get a better view of the house. As she peered through the gauntlet of vegetation that made the house difficult to see, a light-colored, late-model sedan catapulted out onto the street. It appeared so suddenly and went by so fast it wasn't possible for her to get a clear view of the driver. But it had to be the professor. After all, he gave the impression he did everything in a hurry – answering the telephone on the first ring and blundering out into traffic. Hopefully, he was a little more deliberate about his research.

When her adrenaline surge subsided, she eased her car forward a few feet before an inspiration brought her foot to the brake and a smile to her face. It wouldn't hurt to do just a little snooping around the professor's house. If he'd been working on the documents he got from Mom, they might be lying out in plain sight. So after parking her car down the street from the driveway, she reached for her cell phone. A quick call to Moran's house phone, which no one picked up, was her cue that it was safe to take a look around.

Sarah hurried some fifty yards toward the front door, passing neglected remnants of landscaping from an earlier era when the house likely belonged to someone who cared about such things. On her left, between the house and her parked car, several granite boulders, some as much as six feet high, jutted out of the ground. Knowing they'd give her cover if the professor returned before she was done with her snooping gave her cause to smile. And the boulders would check Moran's progress if he pursued her back to the car. It would be like weaving through a maze of defenders on the lacrosse field.

The front door was locked, as was the one at the back of the house. All of the windows were batted down, too. It looked like there was no getting in. But on the far side of the house, the side closest to the street where she parked her car, a set of French doors provided a clear view into Dr. Moran's study. The top of his desk was only about ten feet away.

Sarah squinted, straining to read anything visible from the top layer of papers that littered his workspace. It was hopeless. So she started scanning the room for something that resembled a century-and-a-half old leather portfolio. Presumably, that's what Lincoln's diary would look like. But nothing popped out.

It was no wonder. The place was a mess. Books and papers covered the floor, some in piles as if they'd been tossed out of sight whenever they didn't help advance the professor's research. One-half of a bookend set, Lincoln's bust, lay on its side at the corner of his desk next to an errant shoe. The shoe was lying on its side with only the toe visible, as if Moran had slipped it off while he was deep in thought. She grinned. Obviously, the guy was a bachelor and didn't have anyone to pick up after him.

Running her fingers through her dark curls, Sarah stood back and studied a panel of three narrow windows aligned vertically next to the French doors. The middle window was open just a crack. Her mouth felt like it was filled with cotton as she pressed her thumbs against the edges of the window screen. She hoped to find a way to dislodge it without leaving any signs of forced entry. And when the screen gave just a bit at the bottom, her breath hung up in her chest. The tabs were on the outside. Someone put the screen in backwards.

A smile unfolded across her face. It wouldn't be long before her cell phone camera could capture shots of the Lincoln documents that Moran practically stole from Mom.   Those documents had to be the lead the professor's research assistant said he was working on.

Once the screen was out, Sarah slid the window open as far as it would go. It would be a tight fit, but there was a chance of getting in. She started by stretching her left leg into the study with only her toe touching the floor. Next, she grabbed the edges of the window like a gymnast gripping a set of still rings and swung her right leg in, but her butt got hung up as she tried to pull herself all the way through. Twisting her body to align the widest part of it along the diagonal of the window frame, got her in a good bit farther.

But her ribcage was pressed against the window frame and her breast got hung up in the top corner.

Pulling her arm down by her side and pinching her shoulders together only gained her a couple of inches. There was not way to wedge her shoulders through the window. Even willowy bodies have their limits. Sarah grunted her lungs empty and gave her torso one last shove, leaving a painful dent in her arm without making any progress.

Not yet accepting defeat, she bit down on her lower lip and extracted herself from the window. It was time to try a different approach. But the headfirst entry didn't work either. Her shoulders were just too wide.

Frowning, Sarah pulled her head out of the window and replaced the screen. In no time, the boulders were behind her that would have provided cover if her unlawful entry attempt had been interrupted. At the street, she peeked through a buffer of oleanders to check for passing traffic or nosy neighbors before dashing to her car.

Her pulse didn't drop to normal until she was well on her way down the hill toward Loma Linda, a medical and university community at the southwest edge of Redlands. With her blood sugars hovering near the danger zone, eating moved to the top of her priorities. If something didn't make it into her stomach soon, someone's life might be in danger. Fortunately, a fast food joint caught her attention. And even though ground mystery meat wasn't her typical fare, a burger and a Coke averted an emergency.

At about two o'clock, when Sarah returned to Dr. Moran's home, the last thing she expected to find was a fleet of police cars and the place crawling with uniformed officers. Yellow crime scene tape cordoned off the entrance to the professor's house.

Detective Glen Hetherington, Homicide Detail, approached her. "Can I help you?"

Sarah glanced away from his laser stare. Was he about to bust her for her aborted attempt at breaking and entering? "Uh, I'm here for an appointment with Dr. Moran."

Detective Hetherington's eyes accused her of something. "I'm afraid he isn't able to keep your appointment, Ms – "

"I'm Sarah Sue Morgan. I have some business with the professor regarding, uh, some historical documents." She paused. "So, what's going on here?"

"Well, he's indisposed at the moment." Detective Hetherington smiled, though his vagueness put her on edge. Was he waiting for her to volunteer some telltale knowledge about the crime scene?

"Is he in some kind of trouble?" she asked.

"Not any more. I'm afraid he's dead."

"Dead? How? When?"

"Can't say just yet. We're still processing the scene."

"I can't believe it." She covered her mouth with her hand. "I was at his university office just a few hours ago. I heard his research assistant talking with him on the phone."

"What kind of business did you have with the professor?"

Sarah froze as images of her attempted break-in flashed through her mind. The shoe. Could Dr. Moran have been dead already when she tried to climb through the window? Was he lying there behind the desk with only his shoe visible? That was just too surreal. Murders happened on cop shows and in the news. How had she stumbled into the middle of a murder scene?

Looking up at the detective, she collected herself and explained about the courier who showed up at her mother's front door. The check he delivered from Dr. Moran was too small for the kind of documents Mom owned. It seemed best to confront the professor in person.

Detective Hetherington smiled and shook his head as he repeated the word "confront." He countered that she could have saved herself a lot of trouble and expense by handling the matter by phone or email, "… unless of course, you had some other motive for seeing him in person."

Sarah cringed at the word 'motive.' All she wanted was to find out whether the professor had taken advantage of her dead mother. "That seems like the kind of thing that needs to be handled in person."

The detective's smile dissolved. "Yes, there are some things that can only be handled in person. I'm all too aware of that."

She stared up at him, wrinkling her nose and squinting hard as if trying to read his mind. "What are you insinuating?"

"How did you plan to handle this thing?"

"Not the way you're thinking."

"How do you know what I'm thinking?" His laser eyes made her wonder if he could read her thoughts.

"Isn't it obvious? You're investigating a murder."

"No one said anything about murder. I only said that the professor is dead."

"Then?"

"Then what?"

"Then he was murdered, right?" Sarah pressed.

"It's possible. Is there something you want to tell me about that?"

"No!"

"Is that because you don't want to?"

Sarah stumbled over her words. "It's because I'm just guessing. A man is dead and his house is swarming with cops. There's crime scene tape across his door. You don't have to be a genius to connect the dots."

"No, and you don't have to be a genius to commit murder, either. You just need a motive and opportunity. The means usually present themselves. By the way, can you account for your whereabouts today, until, say about an hour ago?"

"Why, I was –" Sarah stopped cold. The truth wouldn't sound good.

"Yes?" He continued to glare.

Was this what it felt like to be smeared between two thin pieces of glass and peered at through a microscope? "I drove around the neighborhood, just to make sure I could find Dr. Moran's house. I saw him drive off. I guess he hurried out for a short errand."

Hetherington raised one eyebrow. "Is that all you did?"

"No, after I found his place I went and got a bite to eat." Sarah knew she couldn't hesitate or stumble. But telling him everything was out of the question.

"Will anyone at the restaurant recognize you?"

"Doubtful." She almost whispered her answer. "I went to a drive-thru. And I paid cash. I tossed out the receipt with the bag." Sarah closed her eyes, waiting for him to unload on her.

"Right. Why don't you hang around for a bit until we're finished processing the scene. Officer Wiley will keep you company while I check on some things."

Sarah's knees wobbled as Detective Hetherington turned and motioned to a young female officer. The temperature dropped the second she was out from under the detective's glare. Now that's how it feels to be on the other end of an interrogation.

Except for the few moments it took Officer Wiley

to write down Sarah's contact information, along with her rental car and hotel particulars, the two women stood for most of an hour without a word.

Their silence continued until Detective Hetherington returned with more questions. "Exactly what kind of documents did your mother sell the professor?"

"I'm not sure. That's why I wanted to see him. But they involved Abraham Lincoln."

"I was afraid you'd say that." He shook his head. "My uncle was a homicide cop in Pasadena. He's retired now. But for some reason, one particular case dogged him. Over 50 years ago, a young guy from back east turned up dead in an alley off Colorado Boulevard. My uncle never did solve that case. He still talks about it today."

"I'm sorry. But I don't get the connection."

"The only lead my uncle got in that case was a note they found in the dead guy's wallet. It was apparently instructions for his lawyer to pass on Lincoln's diary to a girl from his hometown in Maryland." Detective Hetherington scratched his head.

Sarah fought off the reflex to swallow hard and hoped he didn't notice the obvious. Maryland. Lincoln's diary. Dead man's girlfriend. Could he see the chill creeping over her body? "I hope you have better success with this case." If Detective Hetherington had already connected her to Lincoln's diary, he probably would have handcuffed her on the spot and stuffed her into the backseat of a squad car.

"By the way, it's kind of interesting how you decided the professor's check was too small for what your mother sold him, even though you didn't know what she actually sold him."

Sarah froze.

"You better stick around for a few days. I'm sure I'll have more questions for you very soon." His eyes looked as hard as steel.

"Should I get an attorney?"

"I don't know. Do you think you need one?"

Sarah didn't answer. She turned and made a b-line back to her rental car, pretending to ignore his insinuation. Hiring an attorney would only make it look like she had something to hide. Innocent people don't need lawyers.

A few steps before reaching her car, she looked over her shoulder at the detective. "So I imagine I should deal with the professor's attorney about my mother's documents."

Hetherington shrugged his shoulders. "Not my department. But there is something I'll be glad to help you with."

Sarah turned around and stared at him, holding out her hands and inviting him to finish his thought.

He pinched his left earlobe and grinned. "We'll keep an eye out for that missing earring while we're poking around here. If we find it, I'll be sure to let you know."

Sarah's left hand shot up to ear. Her face telegraphed panic. Instant replays of the morning flashed through her mind. When could it have come off?

Chapter Five

Murderer. Sarah's stomach churned and horror took charge of her emotions. Her eyes darted back and forth from one passerby to another. What kind of person kills? How could people think of her as one of those mug shots on *America's Most Wanted*? Five foot eight inches, one hundred sixty-five pounds. A snake tattoo on his right forearm. Pockmarked complexion. She wasn't that kind. But that's how Detective Hetherington saw her.

A couple nearby caught her eye. They were flirting with each other. Their smiles, the glints in their eyes, the way they moved in their chairs, and their subtle fidgeting with their hands. Sarah noticed it all. When the lovers got up to leave, each of them nonchalantly hooked a thumb into the other's belt loop.

She kept watching them as they walked away from the umbrella-shaded table where they'd been sitting. Their fingers played with the idea of sliding into the other's back pocket. They hadn't noticed her – consumed by each other's attention. Sarah glanced at the printing on the side of her paper cup, trying to evade memories of the disasters she routinely invited into her aloneness. But the losers she'd dated were nothing compared to what Hetherington thought she was capable of. How can you tell if somebody's a murderer?

The harp ringtone on her phone begged her to answer it. The number wasn't familiar. The area code in particular didn't register with her..

"Hi, this is Sarah."

"Sarah Morgan?" The caller sounded vaguely familiar.

"Yes."

"This is Jackson Andrews. I'm the rare books

dealer. We spoke on the phone recently."

"Oh, yes. I called you the other day."

"I hope you don't mind. I captured your number from the caller ID."

"No, I mean sure. It's fine." She did mind, but he caught her off guard. Unprepared to give an honest response. Why would he be reaching out to her?

"It's awfully sad. I mean it's terrible what happened to Dr. Moran. I hope you two were able to connect before the tragedy."

"I'm afraid I got into town too late." Sarah ran her free hand through her hair. Why was he calling?

"You came out to see him?"

"Yes, I had an appointment to see him earlier this afternoon about some items he purchased from my mother."

"I don't want to seem crass, but is there anything I can do to help, uh, any unfinished business you might have regarding the Lincoln materials you mentioned when we spoke?"

She opened her mouth, but held her words in check. People like him must be why the condor is mistaken for California's state bird.

Andrews pressed her. "Precisely what documents did your mother leave behind?"

"Excuse me?" Sarah shouted into her phone.

"I'm sorry. I don't mean to come across insensitive or rude. I just imagined since you're in the area it would be a good idea for us to meet in person. And I imagine you're under some time constraints. You'll be heading home soon – right?."

"I'm not going anywhere right now, thanks to Detective Hetherington."

"Oh my. Does he think you killed Dr. Moran?"

"I happened to drive up to the crime scene in the middle of their investigation, so that made me a convenient suspect."

"But, you're not. You didn't –"

"No, I didn't kill anyone."

"Is there anything I can do to help? I mean, do you need an attorney or something?"

"Do you know any good criminal attorneys?"

"It's not something I'm familiar with personally, but I have contacts who might help."

Sarah shook her head. "I'm joking."

"Of course, but it's certainly not a laughing matter." His show of sympathy won him a few points.

"Well, maybe it would be good for us to meet.."

"Great! I can meet you at your hotel for lunch. Where are you staying?"

"At the San Bernardino Hilton on Interstate 10."

"Tomorrow about noon?" he suggested.

"That's fine. Just ask for me at the front desk – Room 415."

When the call ended, Sarah looked at the time display on her phone. She closed her eyes and rubbed her temples. Her throat was dry and achy. How had she gotten herself into this mess? Why had the whole paranoid notion of Mom getting scammed sent her all the way across country chasing windmills – just like Roger said? It wasn't as if Mom could cause any more trouble from six feet under ground. When Sarah was all argued out, she decided to go back to the motel. For the moment at least, it was the next best thing to escaping back to Maryland.

After closing her motel room door behind her, Sarah flipped the deadbolt and set the chain before making a direct path to the nightstand by her bed to check the time on the digital alarm clock. Her tired grin acknowledged the habit. Or was it a compulsion? Upon walking into a motel room, she'd always secure the door first, then check the display on the digital clock.

Grandma Cassie's journal glared up at her from the nightstand. Her vacant eyes stared back, her mind refusing whatever the journal wanted to tell her. What if her father had –? No, don't go there. If that's what they hid from her all her life, fine. Who needed to know something like that? Her breath hung in her chest just as it did on the airplane when her hand stalled on the zipper of her carry-on bag, refusing to retrieve the journal. That time she had avoided facing its hidden truth by idling away her in-flight time playing Sudoku on her phone until its battery died, leaving her to peruse the in-flight catalog.

Afraid or not, the journal was getting under her skin like an itch that refused to go away until it got scratched. Her eyes focused on the journal's rippled spine. Her slender fingers traced the edges of its worn leather cover. It slid into her hand almost like it had a mind of its own. She picked it up and flopped down on the bed, expelling her breath with what felt the last of her energy.

I was furious when Jenny told me she was pregnant.

Sarah swallowed hard. Her heart fluttered. Was she the baby?

I wasn't angry that she had been careless. It was me who failed her; I hadn't been a very good example for her. She had no idea what being in love meant because I hadn't shown her what it was like to love another man after Lake was gone.

I really didn't think she had been careless, anyway. I was sure she'd done it just to spite me and to spite God. It was her way to say she hated me for depriving her of a father. I was sure she picked him because she thought it would hurt me all the more. He had a reputation for being angry, rebellious and disrespectful and for never being content with his place in life. Everyone said he was just a troublemaker.

No wonder it never felt as though Mom loved her. She was just a protest – an angry, in your face 'screw you.'

She kept trying to convince me that the war had changed him for the better. And that he had changed her, too. I was supposed to believe Vietnam had made him into a man, and not an angry, temperamental or depressed one like so many of his kind. I thought she was just trying to con me.

I knew for sure she was going to tell me she was going to get an abortion. The horror of Aunt Rennie's death hit me again. I was petrified just like Lake always got paralyzed by feeling things so deeply.

Sarah winced at a sharp pain behind her eyes. But

if Mom didn't want her, why did she keep her?

*I couldn't believe it when my Jenny asked
me to teach her how to be a good mother.
I melted. The tears just poured out of me.*

Sarah's head felt like it would explode.   Her
throat seized up and tears rushed down her cheeks.   So
where did Mom's love go? Why didn't she ever feel any
of it? She paged ahead, looking for more about Mom and
her father.

*I had been floating on air since she told
me they were going to get married. But
that's all gone now. What they did to him
was unspeakable. Jenny might as well
have died with him. She's been a ghost
ever since. When little Sarah was born,
she didn't show any emotion. She's never
been able to hold that precious little girl.
Even now, her arms are limp, her
shoulders sag and her eyes are hollow.
The only times she shows any feeling at all
is when she gets angry.*

Her father was a good guy. Sarah wasn't Mom's
daily reminder of some horrible rape. Mom loved him
and the two of them were going to love her, together.
Sarah tore through the pages, searching frantically
for her father's name. Who was he? What was his name?
What happened to him?
A rude hammering jolted her motel room door.
Sarah sat straight up in bed, muttering to herself, "Who in
Hell could that be?" She dropped the journal on the

nightstand and hurried toward the door.

A voice boomed from the hallway, "Police! Open up!"

"Just a second." Sarah fumbled with the deadbolt. Instinct told her to leave the door chain in place.

"Police, let us in."

Sarah thought she recognized the voice. Someone pushed a badge into the narrow opening along the doorjamb. It was Detective Hetherington's ID.

"Search warrant," he announced as Sarah struggled with the door chain.

Once she released the chain, the detective and his entourage pushed their way through the half-opened doorway. Sarah fell back, giving way as they strode into the room. They walked right past her, except for Hetherington who slapped the search warrant into her chest. As they started rifling through dresser drawers and unloading her luggage onto the bed, Grandma Cassie's journal caught her eye. A chill settled over the room, giving her a shiver. She rocked back and forth, hugging herself, trying to wipe the goose bumps off her arms.

It took the police over an hour to search the tiny room. They even dismantled the bed and took down the cheap artwork. At one point, an officer handed Grandma Cassie's journal to Detective Hetherington. He skimmed a couple of pages and looked knowingly at Sarah. "Bedtime reading, I suppose?"

Her face went blank. He could have painted any response on it he wanted to imagine. And he probably did.

"Bag it," he said.

Her heart – it had been pounding like a rock band drum soloist run amok – skipped more than a beat. What was her father's name? Losing Grandma Cassie's journal right at that moment was like having a winning lottery ticket snatched right out of her hands.

As Detective Hetherington left, he turned to Sarah and reminded her, "Don't leave town.   We'll be in touch."

Alone again, Sarah sank back onto the bed and covered her eyes with one hand. She'd gotten herself in deep. Who knew what Grandma Cassie's journal said? For sure it proved she knew about Lincoln's diary – probably the same one that was involved in the decades old murder Hetherington's uncle couldn't solve. Maybe the journal even mentioned Dr. Moran. That would be just her kind of luck. Then, there was that bonehead attempt of hers to sneak into the professor's house. Maybe Hetherington had already found her earring. Probably on the floor inside the study, next to the window that was too small to crawl through. Even if he hadn't found the earring, there would be fingerprints and a stray hair or two. She pulled a pillow over her face. The stupidity of her predicament only fed her frustration – a screw-up as bad as any of Mom's. Now, it was her own fault the secret about her father was under lock and key again. And Hetherington would lock her away soon, as well.

What was his name? What awful thing did they do to him? Sarah tossed the pillow aside and stared at the ceiling, taking long, deep breaths. She covered her face with the pillow again and tried not to imagine what it had been like for her father to face some unspeakable horror. After nearly two hours of repeating the cycle, covering her face and throwing the pillow aside, exhaustion had its way with her and sleep took its turn.

Chapter Six

Brrring – brrring. A light blinked in sync with the raspy ringtone on the motel phone. Sarah stared through the sleepy residue in her eyes at the alarm clock display – eight o'clock. Who could that be?

The cheery voice on the other end belonged to the front desk clerk. He asked something about accepting an outside call. She rubbed her eyes and mumbled her consent, bracing herself for an inquisition by the laser-eyed Detective Hetherington. Both feet were planted firmly under her, and her defense arguments were in formation on the tip of her tongue, ready to counter any accusations he might level against her. But her knees became wobbly when the caller greeted her in a swirly European accent.

"Madame Morgan, I represent parties who are keen on acquiring Mr. Lincoln's diary, along with any collateral documents you might have."

Sarah struggled to speak, finally stuttering, "I'm sorry. I didn't get your name."

"That's because I didn't give it. I have no interest in cordialities. I am simply posing a straightforward business transaction. Now, are you interested or not?"

"I'm sorry. I don't have anything that's for sale."

"Madame Morgan, you might want to reconsider. Your refusal could cost you more than any artifacts would be worth."

"Pardon me," she shouted into the phone.

"There's no need to shout, Madame."

"I'm giving you a simple, straightforward 'No.'"

"I would hate to be put in the position of having to be clearer about the consequences."

"I'm sorry, this conversation is over." Sarah

slammed down the receiver and sat on the edge of the bed, staring at the motel phone. A few seconds later, she glanced at the alarm clock and stared again at the phone. "What the –. He threatened me."

Sarah bounced off the bed and scurried to her bag. Detective Hetherington's business card eluded her for a moment, but when she pulled it out it captured her focus for a long minute. Would he think she was a freak of some sort? But, how else would he know someone else wanted that damned diary?

On the fourth ring, his voicemail greeting answered. At the beep she unloaded. "Detective Hetherington, this is Sarah Morgan. I need to report a threatening phone call I just got from someone who is looking for – uh –" Sarah caught herself, not wanting to admit her main aim was finding Lincoln's diary, "– my grandmother's journal. Call me when you get this. I think it's about time you started protecting the innocent, rather than persecuting them."

Sarah collapsed on the bed. Her big mouth always got her in trouble. She closed her eyes tight and covered her head with a pillow, hoping to shut out the world. Tears welled up behind her eyelids and started to trickle down her temples. Her body knew how far her emotions could be stretched, so sleep rescued her from the eye of depression's storm.

At half past eleven, Sarah bolted straight up. The display on the digital clock broke through her mental fog and registered on her brain. Jackson Andrews would be there in half an hour.

She vaulted out of bed and made a b-line to the shower which took forever to warm up, and when it did, it fizzled into nothing more than an annoying trickle. In fact, it drizzled out even slower than the blood that trailed down her calf after she nicked herself shaving. On top of that, a fingernail broke as she rummaged through her makeup case.

The final straw was discovering no clean underwear in her bag. How could anyone rinse two-day old panties in the sink and get them dry in two minutes? Not even a hair dryer could do the job on an elastic band. But why did that matter, anyway. Andrews would never get a chance to see her in her underwear, not even if he was her father. Geez. Why did she think every man who's at least twenty years older than her could be her father?

When Sarah's cell phone played the harps, the digital clock caught her eye. It read 12:00 – it was already noon.

"Hello," she answered.

"Sarah Morgan?"

"Yes, who's this?" The voice sounded vaguely familiar, but it wasn't Andrews.

"It's Detective Hetherington. I'd like for you to come down to headquarters."

"I have a lunch appointment. Can it wait?"

"Who's your date?" he teased.

"Does it matter?"

His tone became stern. "Everything matters."

"His name is Jackson Andrews. He represents collectors of rare books and documents." Sarah didn't want to ruffle him by continuing to play coy.

"Sure, come in after you're finished with Jackson." He paused. "And give him my regards."

Almost as soon as she tapped End Call, the harps played again. This time it was Jackson Andrews. She told him she'd be down in a minute.

It actually took her five minutes. The elevator wasn't cooperating. It was impervious to the tap-tap of her fingers drumming on her thigh as it stopped at every floor. Why shouldn't it be slow? It just wanted to make her even later.

About a step-and-a-half out of the elevator, Sarah realized her key was still back in the room – and the door was locked. One more delay wouldn't matter. A stop at the front desk just meant Mr. Andrews would have to wait a bit longer.

She glanced several times at the display on her phone while waiting her turn in line. An older couple, probably in their eighties, wanted the front desk clerk to explain every minute detail of their bill, not just once or twice. How many times did he have to tell them that their AARP discount did not apply to the room taxes?

Once Sarah got to the counter and explained about the key, the clerk asked to see her driver's license and asked for her room number. It took a couple seconds for him to code a new key. Her thank-you was forced as he offered her the new key. But the he pulled it back from her, remembering the twenty-five dollar charge for lost keys.

"You've got to be kidding," she said.

"I'm sorry." The clerk pouted, exaggerating his sympathy. "But that's our policy."

"Just charge it to room 415," Sarah sputtered.

"Yes, of course it's room 415." The clerk rolled his eyes.

As she turned away from the clerk, Sarah noticed a man watching her from within earshot of the front desk.

"Ms. Morgan?"

"Yes?" Sarah replied.

"I'm Jackson Andrews."

Sarah sized him up in an instant. A man of about sixty who shaved twice a day, once in the morning and once after his midday tanning session. Someone who stepped out of a 1960s college yearbook, the preppy fraternity boy section. On such a warm October afternoon in Southern California, there must be a reservoir of sweat under his wool tweed sports jacket and starched button-down light blue oxford dress shirt. His idea of casual appeared to be 'sans necktie.' And his passion for English Leather almost choked her.

Sarah apologized for being late. He excused her with a condescending sigh.

She relayed Detective Hetherington's greeting, and Andrews nodded in polite acknowledgement. Reading his reaction was like gleaning feedback from a professional poker player.

When asked how he knew the detective, Andrews told her their paths crossed during an embarrassing misadventure at the Rose Parade many years ago. Actually, the incident involved the detective's uncle. But back then, every law enforcement agency in Southern California got involved in crowd control for the Rose Parade. It just happened that her Detective Hetherington had partnered with his uncle for the overnight shift.

"Enough with the ancient history," he said. "Tell me more about what brings you all the way across the continent."

"Well, apparently," Sarah traced the edges of her napkin with her slender fingers, "my mother sold an old Lincoln paper or maybe papers to Dr. Moran. I just wanted to be sure he didn't take advantage of her."

"In that case, I can understand why the detective suspects you. Anyone in your position could have flown off the handle and clubbed the bastard in the head."

"That doesn't sound very helpful." Sarah knotted her brow.

"I'm sorry, but I am trying to be helpful. I just think you should get into your opponent's head before you do battle. That way you can know how he's likely to react, rather than mistakenly believing he'll always think like you do. Besides, you're not the only one who had an axe to grind with the professor. He liked scrumming around in the muck, throwing garbage around just to see what he could make stick. The truth never mattered to him. He wouldn't hesitate to dirty someone else's good name just to have his own fifteen minutes of fame."

"Whose name do you mean?"

"Just about anyone's. But in this case, President Lincoln's, of course. He wanted to make Old Honest Abe look like a lunatic. He claimed Lincoln tried to commit suicide by arranging his own assassination." Andrews pursed his lips. "And don't worry about the detective. If he becomes a problem for you, I can help handle things." He smiled as he inspected his manicured nails. "I have plenty of influential friends."

"Thanks, I may need to take you up on that." Sarah took a sip of water. Her mouth had been dry since her plane touched down in Southern California.

"If you don't mind, I could use just a bit of your help, though." Andrews studied her face for clues she might take his bait.

"How could I possibly help you?" she asked.

"Do you know any particulars about the documents your mother may have owned and which of them she might have been willing to part with?"

"Since she's dead now, I guess she parted with everything." Sarah coughed into her water glass while starting to take another drink.

"Well, if this makes you uncomfortable –"

"No, I'm sorry. I didn't mean to be rude."

"No harm, no foul."

"All I know is what I read in my grandmother's

journal. It said my grandfather gave her the diary. He died under suspicious circumstances when they were young. She mentioned the diary several times in her journal. My grandfather had insisted it belonged to President Lincoln."

"Well, that's hardly likely," Andrews scoffed. "Lincoln wrote reams of notes and journals, and he didn't hide anything. He seemed to presume that posterity would want his every thought to be on record. It doesn't make sense that he would have kept any kind of private diary."

"I understand what you're saying. My grandmother didn't think it made sense that a small town professor would own anything that important. But in her journal, she said my grandfather told her that Lincoln kept a diary of things that embarrassed him so much he couldn't share them with anyone. And tucked inside her journal, I found a hand written poem that looked like it could date back to Lincoln's time. In fact, Dr. Moran's research assistant is positive that Lincoln wrote it."

Andrews sneered. "Not a very trustworthy source, those academics."

"Well someone is taking the diary seriously. I got a threatening phone call this morning from a man who demanded that I sell him the diary and anything else I had related to Lincoln. He said he didn't want to have to explain the consequences if I didn't."

"Did he identify himself?"

"No, but he had a thick accent, probably French."

"How did he know that you might have something to sell?"

"I don't know. As far as I know, only you and Dr. Moran's assistant knew why I came out here. Of course, Dr. Moran probably knew, too. But he died shortly after we were in touch."

"Well, he still may have had time to mention it to someone. Or his assistant could have said something." Andrews unfolded his napkin and stared off into the distance. "So, is there anything else?" He draped the napkin over his lap, waiting for her response. As he waited, he alternately rubbed his finger tips and tapped them together.

Sarah toyed with her napkin as the server set her plate in front of her. Her answer gestated in her head while she chewed her first bite.

Andrews took several bites as he waited her out.

Sarah swallowed then sighed. "There was a document that came with the diary. President Lincoln addressed the first entry to a Colonel, ordering him to destroy something. His name was Lamon, I think. A French lady who gave the diary to my grandfather signed the last entry. I'm certain she was the Colonel's daughter, and I think the document was a record of everyone who had possession of Lincoln's diary."

"That's all very interesting." Andrews sniffed in a quick breath. "How much of this did you tell the detective?"

Sarah checked herself. Did Andrews really need to know the cops had taken Grandma's journal? She decided not. "I didn't tell him any of this. And I don't think he's connected me to Lincoln's diary, at least not yet."

"That's good." Andrews leaned back in his chair and rubbed his chin.

"Why is that good?"

"Because if he knew you traveled all this way looking for the diary, that would damage your case. It would mean you had a motive for killing the professor."

Sarah wanted to blurt out 'I wouldn't kill anyone.'

But instead, she leaned over the table and whispered, "What motive could I have?"

"As I said, if you knew about the diary and didn't find it with your grandmother's effects, you naturally assumed that the professor duped your mother out of it. What did he pay, a measly forty or fifty thousand?" Andrews grabbed the edges of the table and pulled himself toward her. She could feel his glare. "Well, he cheated her and you out of a small fortune. He should have been clubbed in the head."

Sarah leaned back in her chair and folded her arms across her chest. "How did he die?"

"How would I know? I – I wasn't there." Andrews sat back and tightened his jaw, folding his arms across his chest as well.

"But you said it twice, 'clubbed in the head.' Is that how he died?"

"It's an expression." Andrews chortled. "Some people say 'drawn and quartered.' I say 'clubbed in the head.'"

"Well Mr. Andrews, thanks for lunch. But Detective Hetherington is expecting me at the Sheriff's Office. I'd better be going." Sarah stood and reached to shake his hand, not that she wanted to touch him, not now, after he came so close to admitting that he was an actual murderer. She extended her arm straight out and flexed her fingers, determined to grip his hand with all her strength and give it a firm pump.

"Is there anything I can do to help?" He stayed seated and studied his manicured nails once again, ignoring her handshake offer.

"If I get in over my head I'll be sure to call," Sarah promised. "But, I've managed this much of my life without a man's help. I can probably get out of this thing on my own, as well."

Andrews snickered. "I see. So what are you going to do?"

"I have a plan."

"It's always good to have a plan."

Sarah detected a hint of anxiety in his tone. It was a slight quaver. She'd watched interrogators pounce on faint clues just like that during interviews at NSA. She grinned. "When I find the diary, I'll have found the killer."

Chapter Seven

Sarah took long, poised strides on her way through the motel lobby, headed out to the parking lot. But when it appeared Andrews hadn't followed her, her pace slowed almost to an amble, and her shoulders slumped. Putting distance between herself and Andrews, a possible killer, only took her closer to someone who believed she was capable of murder, Detective Hetherington.

Back in her grade school days, police public relations officers wanted her to believe the police were her friends. But these days, too many media stories covered accounts of convicted murderers getting vindicated after years behind bars. Of course, that kind of thing didn't happen on TV cop shows where investigators followed the evidence and always nailed the right 'perp.' TV cops never jumped to conclusions or rushed to judgment like real ones sometimes did.

And most certainly, Detective Hetherington wasn't the objective type. Her counselor would probably say she was being paranoid, but she hardly had to be perceptive to notice that Hetherington and Andrews knew each other. And how believable was Andrews's account of how they met? Maybe that was their cover story. They could be working together on a cover-up using her as their scapegoat. If that was the case, Hetherington would find convenient excuses to dismiss any evidence that didn't point at her.

The Grand Terrace Homicide Detail worked out of the San Bernardino County Sheriff Department's Central Station, almost a straight shot north from the motel, just off Waterman Avenue. The drive had none of Redlands' charm. It showcased a collage of newer commercial zones sandwiched between empty hardpan lots. Some of the grimy parcels weren't actually vacant. Their brownish-gray 1950s concrete industrial buildings simply blended into the dusty landscape. Not even the air conditioning in her rental car could filter out the area's grungy taste.

After about ten minutes of aggravating stoplights, Sarah made a right turn off Waterman onto Third Street. A couple of blocks later she spotted the Sheriff's logo, a seven pointed gold star embedded on a desert-mauve masonry sign marking a parking lot on her right.

A beveled stub – part of a perimeter wall that partially enclosed an entry patio – greeted her like an overbearing usher guiding her into someplace she'd rather not be. The building's reflective glass exterior created an illusion that she'd been shrunk to the size of a mouse and led into an imposing outdoor interrogation arena.

Inside the lobby, inmates wearing orange jumpsuits filled up several rows of benches. The sight of them sparked the flight instinct in her. Had Hetherington already reserved one of those in her size? Sarah almost turned and sprinted to her rental car. The airport ticket counter and a boarding pass for a plane home were about half-an-hour away. But running from problems didn't come easy to her. That's why her lacrosse team always let her play 'first home' position.

After a few moments of deciphering the confusing lobby layout, Sarah followed a uniformed officer to a small, sparsely furnished, air-conditioned – too well air-conditioned – and dimly lit conference room where she was left to wait. Tiny hairs on the back of her neck tingled as she wondered whether someone was watching her on closed-circuit television.

When Detective Hetherington entered the room, a grin accessorized his smug tone. "How was lunch?" he asked.

"Do you mean the food or the company?" She scanned his face for any signs of a hidden agenda.

"I'm acquainted with the food. How was Mr. Andrews?"

"He tells me that you two are old friends. So you must know what he's like."

"Since he's still at large, I apparently don't know him well enough." The detective's smile dissolved.

"Should I take it that you're not friends, then?" She smirked at him.

"I don't get along with bad guys, Ms. Morgan."

"Okay, tell me Detective, have you ever met any good guys?"

"It's my turn to ask the questions."

She pursed her lips.

"Did you two discuss Dr. Moran?"

"Yes."

"And?"

"He was shocked that you consider me to be a suspect." She stressed the word 'shocked.'

"Is that so?"

"Yes."

"At this point you're what we call a 'person of interest.' Anything else?"

"You mean about Dr. Moran?"

"Anything."

"Yes, I told him about the phone call I got this morning."

"You mean the 'threatening' Frenchman."

"Yes."

"And?"

"He blew it off. Said the guy must have thought I

had more stuff that I was planning to sell to the professor."

"Will he get a chance?"

"Not from me."

"Why not?"

"I don't know what he thinks I have. I only have my grandmother's journal. And it's too personal to sell."

"Did you two talk about anything else?"

"Well, he said that Dr. Moran deserved to be 'clubbed in the head.'"

"That's an interesting choice of words. Quite specific." Detective Hetherington folded his hands on top of the table.

"He said that it's just a figure of speech. You know – like 'drawn and quartered.'"

"Drawn and quartered?" Hetherington cocked his head. "Haven't heard that one in a while."

Sarah waited for his next question.

"Why does Mr. Andrews think the professor deserved to die?"

"I don't think he said that exactly. I just got that impression since he questioned Dr. Moran's intentions."

"Like slandering the name of a great American just to buy a few minutes of fame?"

"Exactly!"

When Detective Hetherington's face didn't show the slightest tic in response, Sarah's body tensed. Maybe he shared Andrews's sentiments and wanted Moran dead, too. Maybe he was trying to throw her off with the 'bad guy' charade. They could be in on it together. After all, he almost repeated Andrews's words exactly.

"Now, Sarah, tell me about the journal we took from your motel room."

"When can I have it back?"

"Not right away. For the time being we're treating it as evidence in a homicide investigation."

She couldn't camouflage the stress in her voice. "I thought you said I wasn't a suspect."

"What reason would you have had for killing him?"

"None."

"What documents did your mother sell him?"

"That's what I wanted to find out."

"Did she sell him Lincoln's diary?"

Sarah's face flushed and she squirmed in her chair. My God, he knows. He must have read the journal.

"Were you trying to get him to return Lincoln's diary because you thought he cheated your mother out of it?"

Sarah's voice quavered. "I didn't know what she sold him. That's why I wanted to meet with him."

"You could have asked him that over the phone. But if you were set on getting a particular kind of revenge, you'd have to fly out here."

"You think I came all the way out here planning to kill someone for stealing something I didn't even know for sure existed?"

"Oh, I think you knew it existed."

"I know it existed. I just don't know if it still exists, and if it does, where it is."

"You didn't find it at Dr. Moran's?"

"I never went inside Dr. Moran's house."

"You talked to a couple on your way up to his place, and nearly a half an hour later another witness saw you speeding past an elementary school on your way down the hill. You had plenty of time to go inside, have an argument, kill the professor and search the place."

"It took me that much time just to find his place. And, I saw him pull out of his drive just as I got there."

The detective grinned. "Of course you did." His smile dissolved as quickly as it had appeared on his face. "We'll figure out soon enough that you were in the house. DNA has a funny way of helping us get to the truth. And if we get real lucky, that missing earring of yours will show up, too."

Sarah decided to take control of things. "Did you find the diary?"

Hetherington ignored her question. "Let's talk about your grandmother. What's her name?"

"Cassie Morgan." Sarah paused. "She's been dead for over ten years."

Hetherington looked away. Sarah had sensed more sympathy from her neglected houseplants.

"Your grandfather's name?"

"All I know is that his first name was Lake."

"I see." Detective Hetherington hesitated. "And your father's name?"

Sarah hung her head. She answered in a near whisper. "I'm afraid I don't know his name."

Neither of them spoke right away.

After a bit, Sarah raised her head and volunteered, "And my mother was Jennifer Morgan. She died a couple of weeks ago."

"I'm sorry."

Sarah stared down at the table again.

Detective Hetherington stood up and slid his chair back under the table like someone trying to be inconspicuous when they ducked out early from a meeting. As if putting their chair in its proper place somehow erased the fact that they had been present.

"How did you find Jackson Andrews?"

"Someone at the Huntington Library referred me to him."

"Why?"

"As I told you, I wanted to find out what my mother sold Dr. Moran."

"Why did that matter?"

"Because, if she sold him the diary, he cheated her out of it."

"And that made you angry."

"I couldn't be angry because I didn't know whether or not she had sold it to him."

"But if he refused to return the diary, you probably snapped? He told you he didn't have it and you refused to believe him."

"Well, there you have it. I guess I'll just have to find whoever stole Lincoln's diary from his house. Whoever killed Dr. Moran must have taken it."

"All I have to prove is that you were in his house. I already know you were in the neighborhood when he died."

"How are you going to prove something that never happened?"

"How are you going to prove it didn't?" Detective Hetherington grinned.

Sarah stared back with a blank expression.

"That's enough for now, Ms. Morgan. I'll be in touch." As Hetherington opened the door, he looked over his shoulder. "Oh, there is one more thing. Does the name Tyrone Wallace mean anything?"

Something about the way he looked at her was different.

"No. Should it?" she asked.

"Not necessarily. Just thought I'd check. You know, for someone who's supposed to be bright, you don't appear to know very much. You aren't making it easy for me to believe you."

Sarah hung her head and stared down at the table

again.

Hetherington didn't wait for her to get up. He disappeared into the hallway, leaving the door open behind him.

Sarah had no recollection of walking out of the Sheriff's headquarters after her interview with Detective Hetherington. When a blaring siren snapped her back to reality, her eyes blinked several times as she got her bearings.

Her world had become like an interminable 'Gravitron' at the county fair, but there was no lever for the operator to grab so he could stop it if things spun out of control. Was this kind of pressure what made people confess to heinous crimes they didn't commit? Did they just get sucked into some alternate reality where they believed their accusers, having lost track of the truth? Was she going to tumble into that kind of insanity?

How long had she been sitting there in that parking lot, frozen like a statue behind the steering wheel? That didn't matter. What was important right then was taking charge of the situation, proving her own innocence. And the starting point would be finding out everything possible about Professor Moran and anyone who wanted Lincoln's diary badly enough to kill for it.

Chapter Eight

Sarah found Elliot working away in the professor's cramped office at the University.

When he looked up at her, her cheeks warmed and her greeting came out like a question. "Hi, I'm Sarah Morgan. I stopped by the other day to see Dr. Moran."

"How could I forget someone like you?"

He moved some files from the chair he was using as a makeshift table and offered her a seat. She wedged her way between the corner of the desk and a stack of storage boxes and slid onto the chair.

"I'm that memorable?" Her face flushed more as their knees almost touched.

"Believe me. You're very memorable."

At such close quarters, getting a whiff of his scent was hard to avoid. It was a familiar one that carried her away to a fuzzy, nostalgic memory. Leaning closer to him – it wasn't a conscious choice – an alarm sounded in her head. The layers of aloofness she hid under, like a stack of Grandma Cassie's handmade quilts, had begun to peel away. There had to be some way to escape Elliot's force field before things went any further, but it couldn't be something that made her sound stupid. Sarah sat up straight and surveyed the stacks of boxes around them. "Wow, I'm surprised Detective Hetherington let you keep anything to work on."

"I had enough warning to set aside a few things and make copies of most everything else. I put it all in the custodian's closet before they showed up with their search warrant." He winked.

"Is that legal?"

"I can't see how making copies would be illegal. And the rest of it is just stuff that doesn't matter."

"I see." She didn't see, exactly, but winning an argument wasn't as important as his cooperation. She leaned forward in her chair. "So what do you think happened?"

"Well, I don't think some attractive young woman –" he impressed her with the 'attractive' and the 'young' parts "– came all the way from Maryland to kill someone who paid too much for an innocuous piece of paper."

Sarah sat back. "So you know the detective thinks I did it?"

"Yes, and I'm sorry if I'm responsible for you being in trouble. Honestly, I wasn't trying to throw you under the bus."

"You had to tell him the truth."

"I only said you came here and made arrangements to talk with Dr. Moran about a document your mother sold him."

She folded her arms across her chest. "Do you think there was just the one document?"

"I saw your mother on that TV show – you know, *Antiques Road Show* – showing the appraiser a note in Lincoln's handwriting. When he asked if it was all there was, she just shook her head and frowned. I got the impression there might have been more at some point." His quizzical expression suggested he expected Sarah to know exactly what he was talking about.

Sarah glanced at the boxes, hoping to hide her cluelessness. Mom on a TV show?

"Anyway, she owned a document that Lincoln signed and wanted to know how much it was worth. I didn't take it seriously. I only mentioned it for laughs, but Dr. Moran got all wound up and told me to track her down. The professor shocked her when he offered $10,000 for the document in spite of the fact that the guy on TV appraised it at half that value."

Sarah pinched the bridge of her nose. "Did she give any details about the rest of the stuff that was gone?"

"No, but the professor was convinced the secret Lincoln diary he'd been looking for was part of it. Of course, I thought he was just grasping at straws."

Sarah leaned forward again, trying to read any secrets his face might betray, not quite ready to trust him with her family's secret. "Why did he think she had Lincoln's diary?"

"Because the memo suggested that whatever accompanied it, Lincoln didn't want it to survive him. And as I said, he was grasping at straws. After his prostate cancer scare a couple of years ago he was determined to find any evidence he could to prove his thesis."

"I see, but didn't Lincoln pretty much wear his feelings on his sleeve? I mean he left reams of papers behind that told how he felt about almost everything." Her piercing stare was calculated to give the impression she could hold her own on his turf. He didn't have to know her information came from Andrews.

Elliot shifted his weight slightly to one side, tilting his head a little closer to hers. "Just the opposite. It's true he left volumes of writings and he expressed himself freely on most things, but he didn't confide his deepest thoughts to anyone. Not even his confidant and bodyguard, Colonel Lamon. Psychologists are beginning to understand that Lincoln was an extreme introvert and he trusted no one with his most intimate thoughts. In fact, he worked hard at camouflaging his introversion by acting like an extrovert. Apparently, many introverts do that."

"What was so special about this Colonel Lamon?" Hopefully, he didn't expect her to know that.

"He was Lincoln's bodyguard and had been a close personal friend back in Illinois before the White House. Lamon obsessed over Lincoln's safety. He even slept in the hall outside Lincoln's bedroom to keep assassins from getting to him. He kept a file of death threats. There were more than 80 of them when Lincoln died."

"So how did Moran plan to get the diary if my mother said she didn't have it?"

"He tried to get her to tell him what she'd done with it. But as far as I know, he came up empty."

"So you weren't involved with any of those conversations?"

"No. Dr. Moran handled it all himself."

Sarah held back a satisfied grin. "Well, my grandmother was different from Mom. She didn't hold things back. And her journal was full of references to a Lincoln diary my grandfather had given her. I presume she left the diary to Mom."

Elliot lurched back in his chair. "My God! You mean the diary is real. And that poem you showed me – someone might have torn it out of Lincoln's diary?"

Sarah sat up straight and grinned. "I'm pretty sure the diary is real. But I don't know what happened to it. I couldn't find it in Mom's things."

"So maybe Moran talked her out of it after all. That would explain some things."

"Explain what?"

He leaned forward again. "I couldn't help but get suspicious. Something didn't feel right the last few weeks. Moran got very secretive after he got his hands on your mother's document – started collecting his own mail and packages. He even told me not to answer the phone anymore when he was out."

Sarah edged forward in her chair, leaving barely enough space between their knees for a wisp of air to pass through. "So, Dr. Moran might have swindled her out of the diary. But who else wanted it badly enough they'd kill him for it?"

"Do you remember me mentioning Moran's theory about Lincoln planning his own assassination?"

"Yes. You said Moran had a couple of theories."

"Well if Lincoln hand-picked his own assassination team like Moran suspected, the diary might name names. And many of his collaborators' heirs might not want to suffer the embarrassment of being targeted by every talking head and late night comic on television."

"After all these years? What would they be afraid of?"

"Losing their families' legacy and their wealth. Or maybe they'd just be paranoid. Face it. Rich people can get paranoid over pretty small stuff."

"Still, that doesn't sound like a motive for murder."

"True, but Moran's murder may have been unplanned. The whole thing could have started as a simple burglary and just escalated. And there are a lot of people who'd want to keep a private Lincoln diary under wraps."

"Like –"

"In addition to the families of those who might have helped him plan his assassination? You can start with people who are afraid it could say something to hurt Lincoln's reputation, or others who might want to alter it to be sure it would be incriminating enough to destroy the myths surrounding Lincoln's god-like persona. Oh yes, don't forget about the Todd clan, his wife's people. Some of them think Mrs. Lincoln has been maligned enough, and a private Lincoln diary might include revelations that would give her fragile reputation a final and fatal blow."

"Why? What could he have said about her that would make her reputation any worse?"

"One rumor is that she planned to elope from the White House with some European playboy. But Lincoln confronted the man and booted him out before they could go through with it."

"She did what?" Sarah gulped.

"Mary Lincoln was a bit loony. What can I say? But some of her heirs might prefer we remember her as a nut case, instead of us thinking she was the White House slut"

"Are you saying Mrs. Lincoln might have planned the assassination to get even with him for spoiling her elopement ?"

Elliot's eyes widened. "After all, Robert, their oldest son, tried to cover up something. He fought, successfully for a while, at least, to get her declared insane so he could take over her affairs. During that time he burned all of her correspondence that he could find. But forget about Mary Lincoln for a moment, any number of people might have wanted to suppress a private Lincoln diary."

Sarah combed her fingers through her curls. "Other than Mrs. Lincoln's family, who would be afraid of the diary?"

"To start with, some people believe our national identity and our international reputation are closely tied to the ideals Lincoln championed. They worry our national security would be compromised if his reputation was tarnished in any way. I know that sounds extreme – but after all, it's extremists I'm talking about."

"But isn't the theory that Lincoln plotted his own assassination a bit far fetched? He was almost like a super hero." Sarah shook her head.

Elliot nodded. "Maybe, but Dr. Moran had a couple of angles that made at least a little sense."

"How so?"

"Well, first off, if Lincoln planned his own murder during an episode of severe depression, the assassination angle might have been a smokescreen to protect his children or to soften the blow on the nation. And whoever helped him probably would have been taking advantage of his depression to further their own private agenda. For instance, instead of planning the assassination herself, Mary Lincoln might have used his depression to manipulate him into hatching his own plot."

"Yes, I've heard that Lincoln was severely depressed."

"It's well known that Lincoln suffered from acute chronic depression. His friends put him on suicide watch at least twice by the time he was in his early thirties. So he was emotionally fragile even before two of his four children died and before he became responsible for a bloody war that tore families apart, including his own. He was depressed before he found himself trapped in a terrible marriage. A lot of people have taken their own lives over lesser tragedies."

Sarah cocked her head to one side. "I see what you mean."

"The truth is that his emotions were more fragile than most peoples'. And recently, psychologists who've studied Lincoln's life believe during the winter of 1864-65 he faced the three things that triggered his two previous suicidal episodes. It's just that on the third time around, the triggers were stronger and he was arguably weaker."

"What were they?"

"Extremely bad weather – especially winter

storms. Death of a loved one or recalling the death of someone he loved deeply. And finishing a period of intense work. As long as he immersed himself in some grand cause, he could usually stay on top of what he referred to as his 'melancholy' episodes."

Sarah's eyes turned dark and empty. That's why she'd started playing recreational lacrosse, to keep her evenings occupied so depression didn't overtake her in her aloneness. And so far, the pace of activity over the past couple of days had kept her from plunging off into an emotional abyss.

Elliot nudged her. "Sarah, are you okay?"

"Oh, sorry Elliot. It's a bit overwhelming."

"Say, do you feel like getting some air? I have to run some things up to the Dean's office."

Sarah hesitated, studying his face, not wanting to change anything about the moment. In fact, listening to his baritone voice transported her back to Grandma Cassie's kitchen and the oldies music she adored so much growing up. Sometimes her imagination let her believe her father and grandfather had rich, mesmerizing voices like those old singers.

When Elliot smiled at her, she lowered her head and pivoted in her seat toward the door. "Sure, I don't mind taking a walk." Then she looked up at him. "But first, do you mind if I get a little personal?"

He grinned. "How personal?"

Sarah glanced over at a bookshelf in the corner behind the desk. "Just wondering – I expected a research assistant to be a bit younger."

"Oh, I'm not a professional student, if that's what you're thinking. I had a good career – made lots of money on Wall Street. But that wasn't me. When the market took a dive, I decided it was time to face the truth." He chuckled. "I'm in love with history, so I decided to go back to school."

She nodded her approval.

Elliot stood up and grabbed some things off the desk. He gestured toward the door, still smiling.

Sarah's eyes narrowed. "So why would Lincoln have just cashed in his chips right at that point in his life? I mean he'd just started his second term."

"You mean he'd just delivered his Second Inaugural address that included the words, '...but woe to that man by whom the offense cometh ...' which some people think was a confession of his own deep sense of remorse over his role in bringing on the war."

Sarah nodded. "You have a point."

Elliot guided her up the steps along an amphitheater that was carved into a hillside. From its roost on top of the hill, the Administration Building looked down on every corner of the campus. "January 1865 was exceptionally stormy. Mrs. Lincoln, never having gotten over young Willie's death, began talking about him incessantly. She even dragged Lincoln to a séance right after New Years to prove that she'd talked to the boy's spirit. On top of that, Lincoln knew the war would end soon and so would the insidious institution of slavery. His hatred of what he called 'this scourge on the human race' propelled him for much of his adult life. The very obsession that had kept him sane would no longer require his attention."

Sarah sighed. "Yeah, I understand the average time a man lives after he retires is about two years. A feeling of uselessness sets in."

Elliot opened the door to the Administration Building as Sarah angled past him, smiling. "Yes, but there are other indications that Lincoln had slipped into a deep depression. During the winter of 64-65, he got so sick that he held cabinet meetings from his bed. And that winter he told Harriet Beecher Stowe he wouldn't live to see peace. At the end of January 1865, when the Thirteenth Amendment was certain to become law, Lincoln said something like 'the job is finished,' paraphrasing Jesus' last words on the cross."

"Okay, but why wouldn't he have just hanged himself, instead of going through all the trouble of arranging an assassination?"

"Well, I suppose for the same reason some people offer to explain why Jesus let the Romans crucify him. He knew he'd have more influence dead than he did when he was alive. His death made him one of the most influential people in world history."

Sarah stopped at the foot of the stairs that led up to the Dean's office and scowled. "But Lincoln was different. He never claimed to be God."

"No, but he was quite a control freak. After he re-entered politics in 1854, he refused to give in to anyone – not Congress, not even the Supreme Court. By the time he died, he'd gotten his way on everything he'd set out to do, except Reconstruction. And he knew he was going to lose that battle. It could be that he figured his assassination would galvanize the public behind his Reconstruction plan, snatching victory out of the jaws of defeat."

"Actually, that lines up with something I was reading about Post Traumatic Stress Disorder and how some victims commit suicide in order to take control of a situation, rather than out of despair or hopelessness."

"True, and Lincoln may very well have suffered from PTSD. In fact, he experienced a long series of traumatic events – most of them threatening either his life or someone's he cared about deeply – any one of those traumas could have resulted in severe PTSD symptoms. But Lincoln wouldn't likely have pulled the trigger on himself." Elliot put his hands on his hips. "He couldn't even stand violence against animals. When he was about ten, he shot a turkey and was so traumatized that he never went hunting again. And he went ballistic when he saw other boys terrorizing the neighborhood cats."

As they started up the staircase Sarah asked, "You're not making this stuff up, are you?"

"No, I'm serious. Now, a few nights before Lincoln died he told his wife and several others about a dream. He said he dreamed that he wandered downstairs in the White House and found a crowd of people sobbing and wailing around a flag-draped coffin. A soldier told him they were mourning the President's death. He'd been shot."

Sarah's eyes widened. "Talk about premonitions."

Elliot nodded. "On the night Lincoln was killed, he sent the last of his bodyguards home early. Two days before, he had already dispatched Colonel Lamon, his most trusted bodyguard, to Richmond. By the way, according to the note Moran bought from your mother, Lamon was the person who Lincoln ordered to destroy some mysterious document – possibly his private diary."

He palmed the back of his neck as he made his next point. "Now here's another interesting idea. On Lamon's way to Richmond, it would have been easy for him to make a detour to Mary Surratt's boarding house where the Booth conspirators frequently met. If he made that side trip, he could have given Booth a message from Lincoln having to do with the assassination. But then again, maybe Lincoln just wanted to get Lamon out of the way so he wouldn't interfere with a different plot he had hatched without Booth's help."

Elliot opened the door to the Deans offices and

held it for her to go in ahead of him. The receptionist acknowledged Elliot with a scowl as he dropped a file on her desk and flashed an impish grin. Without a word, Elliot wheeled around and ushered Sarah back out to the hallway.

As they headed down the staircase, Sarah tapped him on the wrist and asked, "Why was she so rude?"

"I'm just a lowly TA to her."

"She must not know you very well." Sarah smiled.

A reluctant grin unfolded on Elliot's face.

Sarah looked away from him and squinted as she asked, "Why didn't they teach us any of this stuff in school? I mean the stuff about Lincoln's depression."

"Like I told you – there are people who believe the myths we've been taught are necessary, as if the truth could threaten our national security. But to be entirely fair, back at the time of that horrific national tragedy, the average guy on the street needed those myths to cope with what had happened. And it almost became unpatriotic to believe anything else. So historians have cherry picked facts and made up excuses to marginalize any evidence that didn't line up with the Lincoln that people needed to remember."

Sarah turned back and studied Elliot's eyes. "Did Dr. Moran have run-ins with any of the people you think might have wanted to suppress the diary?"

Elliot pushed the door open, motioning her back outside the Administration Building. Once they were outside, he lowered his voice, almost to a whisper. Sarah leaned close to him so she wouldn't miss a word. "Moran got his share of hate mail from members of the Sons of Freedom, an ultra right-wing group. They're obsessed with the notion that the country's image and our sense of national pride could suffer if anyone tainted Lincoln's reputation. They're vigilant about hushing up anything that might make Lincoln appear human."

Sarah touched his arm. "But I've heard people claim Lincoln was anything but right-wing. In fact, I had a libertarian prof who thought he trashed the Constitution, and a Fox-News-junkie neighbor of mine thinks he was the worst president ever."

Elliot stuffed both hands in his pockets. "You're right, but these Sons of Freedom guys are pretty extreme, and like most extremists, they spin the facts to fit their ideology. Lincoln supported workers' rights. He created a government run centralized banking system, not a central bank owned by the big banks. He wasn't afraid of massive government borrowing to fund infrastructure projects. He insisted he had the power to seize private property. And he believed that 'popular sovereignty' – today we call it 'states rights' – was an 'invention of the devil' that only existed for the purpose of perpetuating slavery. In his mind, the Tenth Amendment only provided states the power to make laws that carried out the principles of the Declaration of Independence. None of his ideals lined up with what conservatives or libertarians believe today."

Sarah pressed him. "What about other groups?"

Elliot prompted her to start walking back to Dr. Moran's office as he answered. "Well, there were a lot of other people Lincoln could have named in a diary as co-conspirators, people who were supposed to be his friends, but who would have benefited from having him out of the picture. For instance, many abolitionists didn't believe in racial equality, especially if it meant giving former slaves the right to vote. Lincoln made a host of new enemies across the political spectrum when he endorsed universal suffrage just before his assassination."

Sarah rubbed her forehead. "Wasn't that the logical result of emancipation?"

"Hardly." Elliot's eyes grew darker. "Even in the North there was a strong sentiment that the Constitution only guaranteed protection to white males. Many abolitionists expected that the slaves would be shipped back to Africa. Even Lincoln thought that way for a while."

Sarah laughed. "What's changed?"

Elliot grinned. "But, let's not overlook the infamous robber barons who made a killing by defrauding their investors and bilking the government. Lincoln was on to them, and he even forced one of the biggest railroad tycoons in the country to resign – and that guy had been his biggest client before he was elected President."

"The President can fire a CEO?"

Elliot nodded. "Lincoln believed he could do anything that helped the Union win the war. And as far as he was concerned the railroad was an essential weapon in the war effort."

Sarah held up both hands. "But the Constitution doesn't give the President that kind of power, not even in times of war."

Elliot gestured down the hill toward Gannett Center. "Well, not everyone agrees with you on that. But anyway, Lincoln believed that the Declaration of Independence took precedence over the Constitution. Any time someone, even the Supreme Court, disagreed with him, he argued that the Constitution couldn't be applied in any way that undermined the principle that all men are created equal."

Sarah winced. "I bet that was a bitter pill for strict constructionists."

Elliot added, "Then there were the Radical Republicans who wanted to punish the South after the war. They were irate over Lincoln's Reconstruction plan. And Vice President Johnson opposed it, too. So with Lincoln gone, they expected no resistance in getting their revenge on the South."

"Are you suggesting there might have been members of Congress, or even his own Cabinet, who helped him pull off the assassination?" Sarah shook her head.

"Or the bankers – mostly the ones tied to the big European banks. They complained that Lincoln betrayed them when he hijacked their plan for reinstating the central bank. Instead of making it a privately owned bank that could essentially operate as a shadow government, Lincoln insisted that it would belong to the people. Lincoln had a habit of stealing the capitalist agenda and finding ways to make it work for the common man."

Sarah broke in. "I've heard people speculate that bankers killed Kennedy because he planned a government takeover of the Federal Reserve."

Elliot shrugged his shoulders. "Well in Lincoln's case they'd have been glad to help him carry out his own assassination. He didn't make any friends among the rich and powerful when he said, 'Labor is the superior of capital and deserves much the higher consideration.' Bankers were particularly unhappy. They simply wanted power. In fact, it was Mayer Rothschild – he was kind of the godfather of the powerful European banking cartel – who said, 'Give me control of a nation's money and I care not who makes her laws.'"

Sarah tapped his arm. "You're making Lincoln sound like a socialist."

Elliot ignored her complaint. "With the war

straining the country's resources, big European banks had the clout to take over our economy. They tried using New York banks as proxies to promote a scheme to reinstate a central bank. Their plan was to become hard-money lenders to the Union by way of the central bank and to strap the federal government with a pile of debt at exorbitant interest rates. The European bankers had already sunk their fangs deep into the Confederacy's jugular. The South was borrowing directly from the European banks without using a central bank to launder their money. If those bankers had succeeded in taking control of both economies, it wouldn't have mattered to them who won the war."

Sarah stopped again and folded her arms across her chest. "And they called themselves our friends."

"They still do." Elliot shook his head and motioned for her to continue walking. "But, Lincoln turned the tables on them. After setting up the government run centralized banking system, he issued his own currency. So he didn't need private financing anymore." Elliot grinned. "Nobody could out-think the guy. That's why his enemies hated him and his political backers didn't exactly love him either."

Sarah rubbed her forehead with the tips of her fingers. "Okay, so there were a lot of bad guys running around, but I still don't get why would any of their descendents care today about what the diary said? It's not like anyone can take their loot away from them now, or put them in jail."

Elliot sighed. "Probably none of this stuff would matter to the general public, but as I said, that's not the point. If someone's descendants feared potential fallout from their family's involvement in a 150 year old act of treason, they'd likely do whatever it took to keep the whole thing secret. Especially if they worried it was going to hit them in the pocketbook or cut the legs out from under their social status. Remember, after Lincoln died he became a martyr, a cult hero. It became fashionable to love 'Old Honest Abe,' and it still is. People exploited claims of friendship with Lincoln to build their fortunes and family legacies. If that was all a lie on somebody's part, the story might get legs and not go away. And if cable news could boost their ratings by skewering some big name, well –."

Sarah grinned. "And for some people, it wouldn't matter whether the public cared. All it would take was for them to be afraid someone might care."

"Especially if they depended on that someone to feed their ego – the press, business associates, social circles, constituents if they're in politics. Once again, people who are obsessed with power and money often get paranoid enough to take extreme actions just based on the fear, rational or irrational, that part of their world could slip away. Think Watergate. Nixon had his re-election locked up, but he was so paranoid of losing even a single vote that he committed a criminal act and ended up in disgrace."

Sarah caught his elbow and turned him around so he could see her eyes. "This little history lesson would be a lot more helpful if you could give me some names of people who might have killed Professor Moran."

Elliot smiled. "I'll get some details put together for you, but two names you should focus on are Huntington and Stanford. They were close political allies of Lincoln's, but they had reasons to worry he'd turn on them. He'd already taken down one railroad tycoon, and they were pulling the same types of scams."

Down at the parking lot, Sarah pressed him again. "So you think someone connected to The Huntington or

Stanford legacies stole the diary and killed the professor to stop him from proving his theory about Lincoln's death?"

Elliot waved her off. "There's another possibility. Some people believe Lincoln did more than anyone in history to expand the power of the federal government. By tearing down his reputation, they might be able to turn popular opinion against the institutions he established. It could spark a fervent revival of the Jeffersonian ideals that Lincoln hated. Libertarianism would rule. Those people might have worried that Dr. Moran wouldn't go far enough in using the diary to discredit Lincoln. If they had the original document, they could doctor it to prove anything that fit their needs."

"Like what?" she asked.

"Like the rumor that he was gay, for instance." Elliot laughed.

"Wow. Was he?" Sarah's jaw hung open.

"Doubtful," Elliot snickered. "Here, let's go back into the office and I'll get some contact information for you."

Back at Dr. Moran's office, Elliot grabbed a pen and wrote something on a sticky pad that he pushed in front of her. "Here's a place to start."

She read the note. "Jackson Andrews 909-555-6679."

"What's this for?" she asked.

"He's an old codger, probably in his nineties by now, a retired antiquities dealer who co-founded the Sons of Freedom. You should talk with him. But be careful. Just tell him that you have some Lincoln memorabilia you want to donate to the Lincoln Shrine. He's been a big supporter of the Shrine. If he agrees to meet, that will give you a chance to size him up and ask a few questions about his organization."

She stared at the note, reluctant to tell him about her earlier meeting with the younger Jackson Andrews.

Elliot pointed to the stack of boxes. "And by the way, if you want to look through any of these, just give me a call."

"Thanks, Elliot," she replied. "I just might take you up on that. But there's just one more thing."

"Sure."

"Wouldn't the kind of conspiracy you've talked about been awfully risky. I mean, could it have been pulled off and kept under wraps?"

"Yes it could – especially if the trigger-man who ended up dead, unable to talk, was a Southern sympathizer who was already hell-bent on killing Lincoln. And then suppose the other conspirators, the people who got away with it, were powerful enough to control the investigation and write the history we all studied in school."

On her way back out to the parking lot, Sarah dialed the elder Andrews's number. He told her he'd be happy to meet with her the next morning, but he liked to get an early start on the day, so it would have to be around seven o'clock. He also warned her that he didn't think he would be much help. Sarah figured seven o'clock would be the same as ten for her, so she agreed. Besides, starting early meant she'd have more time afterwards to do other detective work.

Chapter Nine

Dinner alone. Of her many aloneness rituals, Sarah almost enjoyed eating by herself. She especially disliked being interrupted by telephone calls or uninvited guests – not that either occurred often. Worse of course, would be getting collared by strangers in a public dining room. She stared up at the pair in front of her thinking, 'This isn't a social visit.'

"Ms. Morgan?" The woman wore a navy blazer, tan pants and plain white blouse. Her companion brimmed out of his undersized sports jacket – his necktie cinched loosely and yanked to one side, exposing his unfastened top button.

"I'm sorry. Do I know you?" Sarah asked.

The woman flashed a badge. "I'm Agent Salazar. This is my partner, Agent Conrad. We're with the Treasury Department."

"I see. Did Detective Hetherington send you?" Sarah crossed her arms tight against her chest and stared at Agent Salazar, clamping her molars with all the pressure they could take.

"I understand you have a valuable piece of history in your possession." Agent Salazar braced her hands on her hips.

"You're dead wrong about that."

"Interesting choice of words for a woman accused of murder." Salazar cocked her head.

"I didn't kill anyone." Sarah uncrossed her arms and snatched the linen napkin off her lap. She pinched one of the napkin's pleats and drew her fingers down the entire length of its fold.

"That's not really our concern," Salazar pressed.

"We've been informed that you recovered a historical document that's the rightful property of the United States Government."

"You've been misinformed."

Salazar grinned. "And I'm supposed to take your word for that?"

"Exactly what document are you referring to?" Sarah sat back in her chair and crossed her arms again.

Salazar leaned forward and planted her palms flat on the table. "I understand you have President Lincoln's private diary."

Sarah laughed. "I wish."

Salazar straightened up.

Sarah's grin faded. "Look, my guess is that whoever killed Professor Moran has the diary. But, why do you think it belongs to the government?"

"Our job is to impound the diary. If you think you have an ownership claim, you should get a lawyer. In your case, maybe two lawyers."

"You can't just walk up to someone and demand they turn over anything you think might belong to the government."

"You're right," Salazar smiled as she reached into her blazer's inside pocket. "Here's a federal court order. We're impounding it on National Security grounds."

"Well, I don't have it. Detective Hetherington already served me with a search warrant. He would have taken it if it had been anywhere around me." Sarah looked down at her napkin. "I'm sorry to disappoint you, but finding the diary is why I flew all the way out here."

"So you want us to believe that Professor Moran didn't have it?" Salazar asked.

"I don't know if he had it. I never had the chance to meet him. But if he did have it, whoever killed him probably knows what happened to it."

"So you aren't clever enough to stash it somewhere and fly out here pretending to be hunting for it, just to throw us off its trail?" Salazar's stare made Sarah cringe.

"Why don't you tell that one to Detective Hetherington? It'll blow a hole in his motive theory." Sarah looked over at Agent Conrad, hoping to escape Salazar's grilling.

Salazar countered, "Why don't I suggest to him that you might have staged the murder to make it look like someone else has the diary?"

"If you think I'm hiding Lincoln's diary, go search my mother's house. Be my guest." Sarah glared at Salazar.

"We've already been there. That's the first thing we did when the tip was called in."

Sarah swallowed hard. "What tip?"

"That's confidential," Conrad broke in.

"You searched her place without a warrant?" Sarah gritted her teeth.

"We had a warrant. Wasn't our fault no one was there to serve it on," Salazar snarled.

Sarah continued to glare at Agent Salazar as she strained for a response.

"So, you're still looking for the diary?" Conrad asked.

"Yes, as if my life depends on it." Sarah caught a hint of empathy in his tone.

"Look, we intend to get our hands on that diary." Salazar interrupted, but her stare had softened a bit.

"So do I," Sarah said.

"We'll be in touch." Salazar nodded toward the restaurant lobby, signaling to Conrad that she was ready to leave.

Agent Conrad backed away from Sarah's table to make room for Salazar to lead the way out.

After the agents left, Sarah picked at her plate. When a tentative bite of Alfredo sauce curdled on her tongue, she pushed her dish aside and asked for the check.

Back in her room, Sarah practiced her usual ritual – lock dead bolt, set chain and check time. The display read five past nine o'clock, and the house-phone sitting next to the digital clock blinked in harmony with its ringing. Crap. That better not be Mr. Andrews cancelling.

The voice on the other end of the line sounded like someone trying to talk under water. "You have something I want – your grandmother's journal. Give Professor Moran's murder a rest and wait for my instructions. If you do as you are told, you won't get hurt."

Sarah lofted the receiver onto the bed and covered her mouth. Someone was stalking her. Her eyes locked onto the phone. Moran's killer could be on the other end of the line.

A muffled noise kept gurgling from the phone. Sarah reached over and picked it up, staring into the earpiece. The garbled noise was still there. Closing her eyes, she put the receiver up to her ear and stuttered something unintelligible into its mouthpiece.

The voice that interrupted her stuttering made her quiver, "Sarah, that was rude. I need you to promise you're going to behave from now on."

"I'm sorry," she stammered. "I promise."

"Now that's more like it." The line went dead.

Sarah threw herself onto the bed, burying her face in a pillow. Something told her to call Detective Hetherington. No, he'd just think she was a flake, or worse, he'd accuse her of making another desperate attempt to throw his investigation off track. The irony of it all, an innocent person accused of obstructing justice for wanting to be treated justly. Both hands pummeled the bed until her wrists ached, and tears spilled down her cheeks leaving her whole body limp.

After a while, having lost track of time, she sat up and wiped her eyes with one hand while brushing her hair back with the other. She picked up her cell phone and dialed Elliot's number. The sound of the first ring paralyzed her. No, he'd think she was a drama queen. She tapped End Call and covered her eyes with one hand while clutching the phone to her ear with the other.

The familiar tone of harps reverberated in her ear, only much louder than usual. "Oh great! He called back." Then Sarah looked at her phone's display and scowled.

"Hi Angela."

"Just checking in. I haven't heard from you in a couple days."

"I didn't realize I was supposed to report in on a daily basis. We must be getting serious."

Angela laughed.

Sarah sighed. "So what's up? Is the Steven thing under control?"

"You mean Sean?"

"Sure." Sarah rolled her eyes.

"He's history. I'm just calling to see if everything's going okay out there."

"Thanks, things are fine." Sarah didn't dare tell her the truth, even though having a cheerleader could fill a sinkhole inside her.

"You don't sound fine."

Sarah flopped her head back onto a pillow. "Just stressed is all. How are things with you?"

"How stressed?"

"Don't pretend you're my mother."

"I'm not. Your mother wouldn't have noticed you're stressed."

"That's not fair."

"It's true."

Sarah grimaced. "But it's still not fair. She did her best."

"Whatever."

"Look I have to get some rest. I have an early booty call tomorrow."

"What kind of booty are we talking about, sister?"

Sarah rolled her eyes again. "Just business – goodnight." She tapped End Call before Angela could say anything else. In a few short minutes, sleep saved her from a dizzying night of instant replays and second-guessing every misstep that had landed her in her current misery.

Chapter Ten

The elder Andrews's tedious directions saved Sarah from getting lost in the maze of old neighborhoods that meandered around the Redlands Country Club. If she'd relied on her GPS, it would have gotten her lost again. Andrews's 1950ish Usonian inspired home crowned a steep hillside that was guarded by avocado trees. The orchard – deployed helter-skelter like a detail of snipers defending the resident against potential sneak attacks – spread from the base of the hill all the way up to the arc-shaped lawn in back of the house. As she drove up the hill, past the grove to the entry gate, Sarah girded her mind for battle.

But when she stepped out of her rental car, the tenseness in her body dissipated. The sweet October morning caressed her senses, chasing last night's anxieties deep into her memory banks. As Southern California slept, an offshore breeze had pushed a fresh supply of pristine air off the nearby mountain slopes, evacuating the previous day's gritty smog. And as the sun broke, its rays mingled with the air's coolness, yielding a dewy vapor laced with the scents of rose petals, citrus blossoms and freshly cut grass. The air tasted like a summer salad.

Pushing 90 years old – from which direction it wasn't obvious – a tall, wiry Jackson Andrews, Sr., greeted her with the energy of a man half his age. Nevertheless, his pale, age-spotted complexion suggested he'd gained enough wisdom by now to avoid prolonged exposure to the sun. Sparse wisps of silver hair capped his narrow, oval head, and his bluish-gray, ochre-edged eyes accented his grayish-yellow teeth. As he ushered

Sarah into a large open living room, its territorial view took her breath away. The striking panorama flooded into the room through floor-to-ceiling bay windows that dominated the house's north face.

"Thank you for seeing me," she said, smiling.

An impish twinkle danced in the old man's eyes. "Believe me, the pleasure's all mine. Please have a seat." Andrews gestured toward an embroidered teal sofa.

Sarah sat on the sofa. Andrews sat in one of two matching club chairs arranged opposite her. A dated Danish style coffee table separated the sofa from the two chairs. "I bet you say that to all the girls."

"Yes. But I suppose you don't have much to worry about from an old buzzard like me."

"Now don't undersell yourself, Mr. Andrews."

He took her teasing in good humor.

Sarah's smile dissolved. "But I am afraid this is a business call."

The gleam went out of Andrews's eyes. "You know, it used to be that attractive young women like you didn't involve themselves in business matters."

"Yes, but times have changed, haven't they?"

"Well, not all change is good, is it? Now what kind of business brings you all the way out here from the enchantment of Chesapeake Bay?"

"As I explained on the phone, my mother inherited some Lincoln artifacts from my grandmother. Without consulting me – I'm all that's left of the family now – she sold part of the collection to Dr. Moran at the University of Redlands."

Andrews sputtered. "Good for nothing maligner, despicable fraud!"

"Well, it certainly has me concerned. I've heard some pretty bad things about him, and now he's dead."

"Got what he deserved, I'm sure."

Sarah recoiled. "I'm not sure anybody –"

He cut her short. "Believe me. He's devoted his career to bringing down the greatest man who ever lived. And he didn't care one wit if he tore down our great country in the process. He's a traitor, and traitors should be dealt with severely. Otherwise, democracy's future is on shaky ground. If you ask me, there are too many liberal-minded socialists trying to destroy this country from the inside. They're as dangerous as terrorists. Hell, they are terrorists!"

Sarah held her tongue, though it took all of her resolve. To salvage the conversation, she tried to change the subject. "I'm concerned that he might have taken advantage of my mother."

"Well, I don't doubt it. Men like Moran don't have any scruples. He probably planned to doctor whatever documents he acquired so he could use them as so-called evidence to slander Mr. Lincoln. I'm sure that taking advantage of a poor, naïve widow would have been a piece of cake for him."

Sarah didn't bother to correct him on her mother's marital status. "Well, what should I do? I don't know exactly what he got from her or whether he gave her a fair price. And there are other things still in my possession that I'm prepared to part with to the right party." She lied, hoping the old man would fall for her bait.

"Describe the documents your mother sold him." Andrews squinted and turned his head so his good ear was trained on her response.

"That's part of my problem. I'm not exactly sure. She sold Dr. Moran at least one item. But it referred to another document that I haven't found in her effects. I presume the professor bought it as well."

"Go on."

"Okay, according to my grandmother's journal, my grandfather left her a note that President Lincoln signed."

Andrews's eyes grew wider as he leaned closer. "What kind of note?"

"It instructed a Colonel to destroy the accompanying document. The Colonel added a comment underneath Lincoln's signature, telling his daughter to take care of the document he was supposed to have destroyed."

"Meaning that he wanted her to destroy it for him?" Sarah had no way of knowing that behind his eyes, Andrews was guessing she was talking about Colonel Ward Hill Lamon, Lincoln's close friend and bodyguard. He had even met the Colonel's daughter, Dolly Lamon Teillard, when he started his antiquities business. She introduced him to General George S. Patton who helped him get connected with the Huntington Library. General Patton's father was one of the original trustees of the Huntington Trust.

"I don't think so," Sarah replied. "He said he wanted her to take better care of it than he had taken of her."

"That's all very interesting. But it hardly seems like something that would interest the professor. It sounds more like the kind of curiosity that would get donated to the Lincoln Shrine."

"There's a little bit more that might explain his interest."

Andrews raised both eyebrows. "Go on."

"I understand that the professor had some bizarre notion that Lincoln planned his own assassination. And my grandmother received a diary along with the note my mother sold Dr. Moran. I'm thinking the diary is what

Lincoln wanted the Colonel to destroy." Sarah studied Andrews's reaction.

Andrews coughed and sputtered. If there was such a thing as a condescending, skeptical cough, he did it. "Diary? You said a diary?"

"Yes."

"My dear child, Lincoln didn't write a diary." Andrews pulled his shoulders back. "He never kept his feelings a secret on any subject. Everything he ever felt he wrote down in letters and papers, or talked about in speeches that have been published dozens of times over. I'll bet the bastard planned to use your mother's little memo to prove some fictitious diary got missed by an army of Lincoln scholars, and that it contained some kind of suicide note."

"But my grandmother's journal says my grandfather read the diary to her."

Andrews waved off her suggestion with a flick of his wrist while he tightened his jaw to stifle the alarm her claim had set off inside him.

Sarah pressed him anyway. "The Colonel's daughter also made an entry on Lincoln's note when –" Sarah knew she was taking a big risk "– she gave the diary to my grandfather."

Andrews's face couldn't hide the rush of adrenaline that coursed through him. Sarah wondered if his rosy cheeks and sweaty brow betrayed the same rush that addicted him to chasing down rare artifacts before he retired from the antiquities business. Or was he just a man at the end of a lie?

Andrews's face softened. "What do you need from me?"

"Elliot, Dr. Moran's research assistant –"

His jaw drew taut and his eyes flamed when she

mentioned Elliot. "Yes, I know who he is."

"He said you might help me find a place for the rest of my mother's collection."

Andrews practically spat out his reply. "Well that may be the first noble thing the little bastard has ever done!"

Sarah blinked. She tried to form the words to defend Elliot, but she couldn't get them out.

Andrews warned, "Be very careful around him. He's cut out of the same cloth as that despicable professor. He must be up to something clever, and he's trying to hide it by sending you to me like some Trojan horse."

Sarah collected her thoughts. "He seems harmless enough. In fact, he suggested you might help me arrange a donation to the Lincoln Shrine."

"No, not the Shrine." Andrews paused. "I have another idea."

"What do you mean?"

"I'll put you in touch with my son. His name is Jackson as well. He took over the rare books business when I retired. I'll bet he can get you a very tidy sum, that is if you can lay your hands on this alleged Lincoln diary."

Sarah looked away, still watching his face out of the corner of her eye. "I've already met your son. He helped me locate Dr. Moran."

Andrews cocked his head. "Funny, he never said anything about that."

"I traced him down through the Huntington Library. It was the best lead I could find on Google."

"What's a Google?" he asked.

"It's an internet search engine."

Andrews waved his hands in front of his face as if he were wiping away an infestation of cobwebs. "Don't bother to explain. You young folks can have your internets and computers and whatever."

"Well, I'd like to consider selling him the diary when I find it. And since I never found it in my mother's effects, I assume she sold it to Dr. Moran along with Lincoln's note."

Andrews shook his head. "No, I'm thinking your mother didn't have any diary. But Moran probably planned to fabricate one and use the note as evidence to prove its authenticity. It wouldn't be the first time someone tried to put words in Lincoln's mouth after he died."

"What makes you think that?"

"If the police recovered something of that significance from Moran's home, I would have heard by now."

"Isn't it possible that Moran bought it from my mother, but his killer stole it from him?"

"Well if that's what happened, I'd lay you odds his research assistant did it."

Sarah pursed her lips and shook her head. "I'm not sure he's the type."

"If Moran cheated your mother, the little bastard probably tried to blackmail him and clubbed him in the head when he refused to pay."

Sarah froze. He used the same expression his son had used. Sarah muttered under her breath, "Clubbed in the head."

"What was that? I'm sorry, you'll have to speak up. My ear drums are getting a bit thick."

"I asked, do you think Elliot will continue with Dr. Moran's work?"

"If not him, someone else will try to. The world is full of liberal pinheads and revisionist historians who are hell-bent on undermining what's left of our national pride." His voice was so pitched it almost hurt Sarah's ears. "It's their disrespect for everything good about America that inspires terrorists all over the world."

"What are the chances that the Sons of Freedom, or some group like them, broke into Dr. Moran's house to steal the diary? And when he caught them in the act, they killed him." She knew it was a risky question, but her patience was running out.

"That's a preposterous idea! We're not a bunch of thugs." He glared at her as if she'd crossed a boundary that he never let anyone transgress.

"Or maybe someone got jealous because Dr. Moran landed the 'holy grail' of Lincoln artifacts." Backpedaling might get her out of deep water.

"That's utter nonsense."

He stood and gestured toward the front door. "I think it's time for you to leave."

Sarah stood up, too. She could tell he was straining to be civil. "I'll see myself out."

Chapter Eleven

Old man Andrews gave Sarah a solid reason to suspect his son killed Dr. Moran. He used the exact phrase the younger Andrews had used, 'clubbed him in the head.' Either those two knew more about Moran's murder than they were letting on, or they were telepathic.

On her way back to the motel through Redlands's grid of quiet streets and frequent four-way stops, Sarah's heart fluttered a bit, thinking about Elliot. But it was okay to be thinking about him, after all he promised to get her more information on the Huntington legacy. And considering the fact that her call to the Huntington Library led her to the Andrewses, any possibility of a deeper connection deserved exploring.

Okay, so she and Elliot just met. Was it too soon for any kind of attraction? If it was, why did her breath leave her whenever his image popped into her mind? But an inner voice warned her not to let her guard down. Men are like porcupines. They might be shiny on the outside, but they can stab you with those same quills when you cuddle up next to them.

In spite of those cautions, though, Sarah melted when she found Elliot in an empty classroom at Gannett Center, sitting under a portrait of Abraham, Martin and John that hung next to a photo of Bobby Kennedy. He'd surrounded himself with stacks of boxes and was pouring through photocopies of articles he'd collected for her.

He looked up and smiled. "I didn't expect to see you this morning. Did you strike out on getting a meeting with old man Andrews?"

Sarah shuffled her feet and glanced away as she confessed, "Oh, I met him this morning up at his place.

But I think I wore out my welcome when I asked him if someone from the Sons of Freedom might be capable of killing Moran."

"Direct, aren't you?"

Sarah looked at him. "I tried being coy, but I guess I got impatient."

"So you came back here for sympathy?"

Sarah allowed a timid smile. "Yes. I guess so, since you're the only person who's been the least bit sympathetic since I got here."

He smiled back. "So I win the race by default? Impressive."

Blushing, Sarah answered, "Would it sound better if I said I didn't need other alternatives?"

He grinned. "How can I not be flattered by that?"

Sarah pounced on his graciousness. "By the way, is there some way I can connect with the Sons of Freedom without going through Andrews?"

"Well, like most organizations, not everybody gets along. In this case, one particular guy would be just as happy if old man Andrews croaked."

Sarah moved closer. "Who's that?"

"Reverend Davis. He's a retired minister – lives in the Crafton Hills area on the east end of town."

"What's his beef with Andrews?"

"Conservatives and Libertarians only co-exist to defend themselves against a common enemy."

Sarah shook her head. "Like whoever's in their way."

Elliot looked down at the papers he'd spread out in front of him. "I'm not sure I'm the one to call him. He thinks the University is an abomination. His church used to provide most of our funding, but that ended decades ago. He says we're a bunch of degenerates."

Sarah frowned. "So I'm better off calling him

myself."

Elliot shrugged. "Yeah, but I can give you his contact information. Just be warned, though. He doesn't have much tolerance for people who don't see the world through his lenses."

"So I should hold my tongue this time."

"Not just that. You'd better buy an old fashioned dress that covers down to your ankles."

Sarah teased, "We're getting a little possessive, aren't we?"

Elliot laughed as he shifted in his chair. "And do you think you can dredge up anything that resembles a sweet southern accent, something that sounds like old fashioned revival-speak?"

"It is such a blessin' to meet you, Brother Elliot." Sarah snickered.

Elliot laughed aloud. "That works."

"I come from rural Maryland, Brother Elliot. Good gracious dear, we're just a rock's throw away from ol' Virginie where our Lord first manifested revival-speak. I think it was in the vicinity of Lynchburg that his blessing poured out on some fine fundamentalist brethren. Now 'course if you ask an Oklahoman, he'd argue mighty fierce on that one. He'd say it happened somewhere near Tulsa."

Elliot teased, "And don't bother putting on any makeup, especially no lipstick. It's an invention of the devil."

"No worries. I don't use the stuff unless I have to."

"I'd noticed. You're a natural beauty." Elliot winked.

His compliment jolted her like someone shooting off a flare gun inside a dark gymnasium. She scrambled to escape its glare. "Say, can I still take you up on your invitation to check out those boxes?" She nodded at the stacks of Dr. Moran's copied archives.

"Sorry if I embarrassed you, but beauty like yours is hard to overlook."

His smile had dissolved. Maybe he wasn't kidding her about the beauty thing. Her face flushed hotter. She nodded again at the stacks of boxes.

"Sure. Where do you want to start?"

"I'm not sure. Just give me any one of them."

Elliot stood to get a better view of the labels on the boxes before moving several of them off one of the stacks so he could get to a box near the bottom. "See what you can find in here." He set the box on the corner of the table.

As Elliot pulled back a chair for her to sit in, she caught a glimpse of his ocean blue eyes and smiled. "You're such a gentleman, but I think it'll be a little easier if I stand while I'm digging through stuff."

Elliot returned her smile. "Can I get you something to drink?" He reached in front of her and lifted the lid off the box he'd set on the table.

Her breath halted for a second. "Water would be fine."

"I'll be right back." Elliot held her gaze as he turned and walked toward the hallway.

After a moment, Sarah turned and looked down at the box, but only for a second. She snuck a peek over her shoulder and watched him disappear down the hall. A smile lingered on her face even as the box began to absorb her attention. Each item deserved to be handled with reverence. Her face turned somber as she realized the artifacts in her hands were remnants of a life that no longer had a voice. Those boxes contained the only means by which Dr. Moran would be able to tell her how and why he died.

When Elliot returned with a bottle of water, he found Sarah still standing, fixated on a pair of old newspaper articles from the *Pasadena Star-News* – one dated December 27, 1955 and the other, six months later. The first article told about an unidentified body that turned up on Giddings Alley near Pasadena City College. The second article identified the deceased as Lake Matthews, formerly a college professor from Wicomico Teachers College in Maryland. It said his killer remained at large.

A chill clung to Sarah's spine. Was it possible Grandpa Lake died almost three thousand miles from home? According to Grandma Cassie's journal, Grandpa Lake taught at the college in Wicomico. She stood motionless and mute. Her complexion had turned gray.

"Are you okay?" Elliot asked.

Sarah continued standing. Her eyes remained glued to the newspaper clippings.

"Sarah?"

She kept staring at the picture of Lake Matthews.

"You look like you've seen a ghost."

Turning toward him, her deep emerald eyes were locked in place, focused elsewhere, as if nothing within her reach had any meaning.

He repeated, "Are you okay?"

She blinked as if she'd just woken from a trance. "What are these about?"

Elliot skimmed the first article. "Gee, I don't remember ever seeing them."

Sarah focused on his face.

He strained for an explanation. "They must have fallen out of one of his personal files."

Sarah pressed him. "Doesn't it seem odd that he

would have old clippings like these that don't appear to have any connection to Lincoln?"

"No." Elliot laughed. "He kept everything. He was a pack rat, a disorganized one at that. I wouldn't be surprised by anything you'd find in these boxes."

Sarah set the articles down at one corner of the table. "Do you mind if I hang on to these for a bit?"

"I don't see a problem. Feel free to borrow anything you think might help."

She emptied the remaining contents of the box onto the table and sat down. In front of her was a random array of items that bore no obvious connection to the professor's primary research. She found copies of more newspaper clippings, which she set aside with the others. One, cut out of the *Pasadena-Star-News,* covered a USC professor's suicide on the day after Christmas, 1969. His name was Martin Deery. The other clipping, this one from the January 22, 1953 edition of the *New York Times,* reported Dorothy Teillard's passing at the age of 93.

Sarah looked up from the table. "Elliot, does the name Tyrone Wallace mean anything to you?"

"Can't say it does, why?"

"Oh, a thought just popped into my head. Hetherington mentioned the name, but he didn't give me any details about why it might be important."

"No, I've never heard it before."

Sarah sifted through more of the box's contents. There were some old theater ticket stubs, airline-boarding passes, a hodgepodge of restaurant and motel receipts, tickets to the Tournament of Roses Parade and something that set off alarms all through her brain, copies of donation receipts that were addressed to J. Andrews. The amounts were the same, twenty five thousand dollars each. The dates were consistent, December 26 of each year going back at least a couple of decades. The charity's name that appeared at the top of each receipt was 'USC Society of Lincoln Scholars, c/o University of Southern California Alumni Association, 635 Childs Way, Los Angeles, California 90089.'

Sarah got up from her seat and shoved a handful of the donation receipts under Elliot's nose. "What are these about?"

Elliot scrutinized the documents and grinned. "Poetic justice."

"What do you mean?"

"Andrews, Sr. donated to Moran's research every year without knowing it."

"But how did Dr. Moran get his hands on these receipts?"

"That is a bit of a puzzle. Whenever I asked him about it, he just stared at me and told me to get back to work."

"And what was Moran's connection to USC?"

"That's where he got his BA and Masters."

Sarah sat back in her seat. "I think I need to make a trip to L.A."

"When?"

"Now."

"I'd go along, but I have classes to cover."

"I understand. Hey, but it's awesome of you to offer." Sarah smiled at him then turned her attention to calculating her next move. "Say, do you want to meet me at the motel tomorrow morning for breakfast? I can give you a report on my research, and after that we can come back here and go through the rest of this stuff."

"Sure, where are you staying?"

"The San Bernardino Hilton. What about nine?"

"It's a date," he agreed.

She liked his choice of word 'date.' "Oh, I'm in

room 415. I mean, just in case you want to call up to the room when you get there."

"Of course." He smiled as he watched her tuck the trove of evidence he'd given her into her bag.

"Oh, don't forget these articles." Elliot gathered the photocopies he'd made for her.

Sarah beamed as he nestled the articles in her hands, coming within a whisker of touching her.

He walked her out into the hallway.

"Thanks" was the only word that managed to slip off her tongue.

Chapter Twelve

Sarah slid behind the wheel of her rental car, telling herself she was nearly two decades too old for high school crushes. At the ramp to westbound Interstate 10, explanations for the donation receipts started parading through her head like faces in a police line-up. She was concentrating so hard on the array of possibilities that her phone's ringtone almost played out unnoticed.

The caller ID displayed Jackson Andrews's name. She'd stored his name and phone number in her contacts list when he called earlier, before he all but admitted to being a cold-blooded killer. But with the business of his father's donation receipts, who knew what secrets the two of them might be keeping. Curiosity won out over revulsion.

"Hello, Mr. Andrews."

"Hi, Sarah. I just thought I'd check in to see if I could help in any way."

Sarah felt nauseous just hearing his voice, but remained focused on the traffic and the possibility of prying loose an important clue. "Actually, you can. I'm on my way into L.A. to do some research. Do you have time to meet me around dinner time?" Her stomach turned again.

"Yes, I'd be happy to buy dinner. Why don't you buzz over to my office in San Marino when you're done? I'll take care of making reservations."

"That's fine." She didn't plan on being hungry, anyway. "How do I find you?"

"I'll text you my address. You have GPS, right?"

"Sure," she replied. "Can we be flexible on the time?"

"Certainly, I'm sure the restaurant will accommodate us whenever you're ready. By the way, what brings you out to L.A.?"

"I'm just following up on some leads. My first stop is USC. I'm not sure what comes after that."

"What kind of leads?" he pressed.

"We can talk about that at dinner." He didn't need to know what she was up to, even if he was in a position to make introductions for her at his alma mater. "Right now I'd better concentrate on driving. This is a real jungle."

"I can understand. I'll wait for your call. Drive careful, now."

"Thanks." The End Call button saved her from hurling, though her stomach continued to roil for a good fifteen minutes.

The stories about L.A. traffic were true, especially the parts about traffic jams that turned miles of eight-lane thoroughfares into parking lots. About half way into the city – her car idling in standstill traffic making its own contribution to Southern California's polluted skies – the familiar sound of harps reached her ears again. This time the display showed Angela's name and number.

"Hi Angela, look I can't talk right now, I'm trying to drive this insane interstate into Los Angeles. I need to focus on the road. Call you back later, okay?"

Angela didn't pick up on the tension in Sarah's voice. "Say girlfriend, we need to talk. Somebody has to knock some sense into me. I can't get Sean out of my head."

"Look Angela, I said I can't talk right now. This traffic is insane."

"Sarah –"

"I said I'll call you when things aren't so hectic. Goodbye."

Sarah tapped End Call and turned off her cell phone. Traffic crawled at a snail's pace all the way to the University Park Campus in the depths of the L.A. jungle. Her GPS led her to a parking structure close to the alumni headquarters. She didn't expect to get any luckier than that. Her good fortune continued when a couple of carpooling commuter students gave her directions to Alumni House. They described it perfectly and with a measure of pride, a late 1870s two-story Georgian style wood frame house that happened to be the first building constructed on the University Park Campus site. It stood out partly because the surrounding buildings went up during a late 20th Century construction spree.

A petite woman named Vicki greeted Sarah at the Alumni Office. Her greeter appeared to be clinging to midlife like an overboard passenger gripping onto a life ring. But more than likely, her midpoint had already passed her by. Vicki's wardrobe looked like it could have been ordered out of an early 1980s Spiegel catalog, and while she applied her makeup precisely, her choices of blush, lipstick and eyeliner were of the same vintage as her clothes. Most out of step with her age, however, were a girlish voice and matching sorority sister effervescence.

Vicki explained that the alumni headquarters' current location – a new facility was already under construction – wasn't the only thing that was temporary. She had agreed to fill the role of Administrative Assistant to the Senior Director of Alumni Relations only until a permanent staff person came on board. The previous person left six months before.

Sarah asked Vicki about the USC Society of Lincoln Scholars, and learned it served as a vehicle for one of the university's alumni to raise funds for research projects.

"Would that be Dr. Thomas Moran?" Sarah asked.

"Yes, it would."

"Well, who could I talk with about his donors?"

Vicki's perkiness faded, and she drew her shoulders back. "I'm afraid that information's confidential. As I told the detective earlier, we can't release that information without a subpoena."

"Do you mean Detective Hetherington by chance?"

"Why, yes." Vicki's eyes widened. "I think that was his name."

"So, you know he's looking into Professor Moran's death?"

"He told me something happened to him." Vicki's smile returned, joined by a gleam in her eyes. "I'm going to miss the old buzzard."

"Did you know him well?"

"Somewhat, but not well enough." Vicki winked.

"What sort of person was he?"

"A bit of a loner. Even as a student, he was that way." Vicki buffed her nails on the cuff of her blouse.

"So you knew him back then?"

Vicki's smile faded again. "Yes, he was a TA in one of my history classes. I didn't get to know him well until the prof – his name was Deery – committed suicide. At first, the police thought Thomas killed him. But eventually, they called it a suicide. The whole thing shook Thomas up pretty bad, and I tried to take advantage of his grieving. I wanted to get something going between us, but, it never worked out."

"Why did the police think Dr. Deery killed himself?" Sarah watched Vicki's face.

Vicki stared back, planting her hands on her hips. "Well, there were no signs of a struggle, and there were rumors floating around at the time."

"What rumors?"

"According to the campus scuttlebutt, Deery slept with an alumn's son. That kind of relationship could have cost him his job. But he got off easy. They only made him break off the affair. In any event, the incident sent Deery into depression."

"Did he leave any kind of suicide note?"

"No." Vicki fidgeted with the cuff of her blouse.

"Why did they suspect Moran? Was he gay too?"

Vicki sighed. "Well, he didn't date, and he kept to himself a lot, in spite of the fact that he was a real hunk. Believe me, I tried to get into his pants any way I could. Deery was Thomas's thesis advisor, and they were always arguing just like an old married couple."

Because Vicki was a student when Deery died, Sarah figured her to be around sixty. It was likely she was a real hottie back then, since even at her current stage of life she might be rather attractive with some updating.

Sarah asked, "What do you think really happened?"

"My best guess is that Deery got tangled up in some kind of lovers' quarrel that went bad. His lover's father cleaned up the scene so nothing could point back to his son, and the authorities looked the other way." Vicki peeked around the office. "Rich alumni can be very influential when they want to be."

"One last question, if you don't mind."

"Sure."

"Does this alumn have a name?"

"As I said, the whole thing got covered up pretty well. But I do recall the father was supposed to be a classmate of Deery's back when they were undergrads here. That would have been in the 40s, I think."

"Does the name Tyrone Wallace ring a bell?"

Vicki hesitated and rubbed her forehead. "Sorry, nothing sticks out. And I think I'd remember a name like Tyrone. After all, we're practically next door to Hollywood."

Sarah gave her a vacant look. "Sorry, I don't get it."

"Tyrone, as in Tyrone Power. He was a movie legend in the 40s and 50s."

"If you say so." Sarah grinned. "By the way, do you have copies of annuals that go back that far?"

"Not here, but there's a complete archive at Doheny Library."

"Do you think they'd have copies of old faculty CVs on file there?"

"It's doubtful." Vicki smiled. "What are you looking for?"

"Just some background on Dr. Deery."

"You might find some old course catalogs on file at the library. Usually the catalogs tell where they earned their degrees. At least that would give you a starting point."

"Thanks, you've been a big help."

Sarah was only being polite. She'd collected some small leads, but not the smoking gun she was after. Maybe Doheny Library would yield better results.

Chapter Thirteen

When Sarah pulled out of the parking garage at University Park Campus, her mind was fixed on what she'd learned over the space of a couple hours at Doheny Library. The driver of the BMW that almost took a broadside greeting from her front bumper didn't care what had distracted her. His hand gestures and blaring horn made it clear that he was pissed.

The BMW driver's ire was Sarah's wake up call. Her eyes stayed peeled to the road as she merged onto the freeway and found her groove in the flow of traffic. Her GPS already started guiding her to Jackson Andrews's office based on the details she input just before leaving campus.

According to the 1940 *El Rodeo* yearbook, old man Andrews and Martin Deery belonged to the same fraternity. In the 1963 edition, Sarah learned that the younger Jackson Andrews joined the same fraternity chapter years later. But any mention of Tyrone Wallace eluded her, assuming there'd been something for her to find.

Sarah's imagination would have easily pieced together a conspiracy that implicated the Jacksons in the deaths of both Dr. Deery and Professor Moran. But one piece didn't fit yet, or maybe it belonged to another puzzle. The troublesome piece was Grandpa Lake, who was probably the same as Lake Matthews. The year after Deery started teaching at USC, Lake Matthews wound up dead in Pasadena, California. And from what she read in the old course catalogs, Dr. Deery earned his undergraduate degree at Wicomico Teachers College in 1940. The fall after he completed his doctorate at Johns

Hopkins in Baltimore, he joined the USC faculty.

Deery might have met Grandpa Lake back in Wicomico County at the teachers college. And if Grandpa Lake had been in L.A., he could have crossed paths with both Deery and Moran there. After all, Moran had those clippings about Lake Matthew's murder and about Deery's suicide.

As Sarah approached the Solano Avenue Exit from the Harbor Freeway, a strange impulse came over her. She got off the freeway and followed surface streets until her car came to a stop in a secluded part of Elysian Park. The park bordered the Echo Park neighborhood, a largely low-income Latino community that suffered from depressed real estate values and higher than average crime rates. During the time when Grandpa Lake may have hung out in L.A., Echo Park was an enclave for intellectuals, liberals, socialists and communists – targets of McCarthy era suspicion and persecution.

Without any idea about why she had driven there or why she might place such a phone call, Sarah dialed directory assistance and asked to be connected to the main switchboard at Wicomico Teachers College. When the receptionist answered, Sarah went into automatic mode. "Hello, my name is Sarah Morgan. I'm doing a piece on the College's history department, and I would like to talk with someone who could give me some background on former faculty members. I'm particularly interested in people who taught back in the 50s."

The receptionist bellowed an immediate response. "Well, dear, you're in luck. I happen to be working a little late today, and I'm as historical as anyone around here. Maybe I can give it a shot. Are you interested in any names in particular?"

"Well yes, does the name Lake Matthews ring a bell?"

"Oh sure. Now it's not like every young buck makes a lasting impression. I mean most of them just use this place as a stepping-stone for their careers. But this one was an exception. Those sad eyes of his really got to you. It was tragic though, the way the poor fellow went off the deep end when his girl dumped him. She was a lot younger, but that was only part of it. A lot of couples had problems back then on account of arguments over the professor's wife who died from a botched abortion. And Matthews was awful temperamental, even without the extra stress. Just the same, they broke up and he left town."

With her next question, she took a stab in the dark. "How about Martin Deery? I know he attended classes there in the late 30s."

"Actually, he was my uncle, and he kind of took Matthews under his wing. Matthews went out to see him after the thing with his girl. Poor Uncle Martin. The rumor was that he killed himself. My daddy says it was a big waste of a life. He was the brainy one in the family. After he taught a couple of years here, he went to finish his doctor's degree at Johns Hopkins, and he taught at USC on the west coast for a few years after that."

"You said Dr. Deery killed himself?"

"Yes, but Matthews is dead, too. He died a few years before Uncle Martin. It was while he was back there staying with my uncle. They never figured out what happened."

If Sarah hadn't been parked when the receptionist's story sunk in, she would have collided with someone or something out on the freeway. Her heart raced and her head started to spin. Everything became a blur. Grandpa Lake and Deery were definitely connected. And solving the mysteries behind their deaths had become as important to her as finding Lincoln's diary and proving her own innocence. In fact, she began to wonder if all three deaths – Deery, Moran and Grandpa Lake – weren't related somehow.

"Ma'am, are you still there?"

Maybe the voice calling out to her from her phone snapped her back to the moment. Or possibly the shock of what she had just heard wore off, allowing her to refocus on the here and now. Whichever it was, Sarah looked out the windshield and her heart jumped up into her throat. Her mouth flew open and her eyes grew wide enough to distort every feature of her face. Sarah lofted the cell phone onto the passenger seat and started groping for her keys. Hopefully, they were still in the ignition.

Swaggering toward her from the cover of a neglected avocado orchard were three bronze-shouldered figures. Their muscles bulged out from their skintight, sleeveless shirts. All three wore baggy pants belted low around their pelvic bones, and one wore a bright bandana under a Dodger's baseball cap. They appeared to be wielding weapons of some sort, and the closer they got to her car, the faster they moved.

Sarah's heart slid from her throat to its rightful place in her chest. The motor was still running, allowing her to jerk the car into reverse and hit the gas hard before the would-be assailants lunged for her door handles. Just outside their reach, she wheeled a u-turn and sped through the park, wondering how and why she'd wound up there.

Once Sarah caught her breath, she reached over to the passenger seat to pick up her phone. With her heart still palpitating, she touched the navigation icon and waited nearly to the end of her patience for it to display the map to Andrews's office. In a few moments, the GPS began guiding her out of the park.

Turning   onto   Solano   Avenue,   Sarah reprogrammed her destination using the voice command, "Giddings Alley, Pasadena, CA." It was the place Grandpa Lake's body turned up more than five decades before. Maybe it was her imagination, but what had to be Grandpa Lake's voice was echoing in her head, calling her to the last place on earth he drew breath. Did he have something urgent to tell her? Of course, reason told her there were no such things as ghosts. Not only that, but young, single women had no business walking the streets of Pasadena alone at dusk. But none of that mattered to her. Something kept insisting "Giddings Alley." She shook her head as if trying to juke off the competing voices.

About twenty minutes later, parked at a gas station on the corner of Colorado Boulevard and Hill Avenue, Sarah couldn't stop the questions about Grandpa Lake from swirling in her head. Pasadena's only block of Giddings Alley ran parallel to Colorado Boulevard just yards away. On the other side of the gas station, the vacant showroom of an abandoned car dealership looked old enough to have been around when Grandpa Lake encountered his killers.

Sarah wasn't into channeling spirits or other weird stuff. But sitting in her car, she closed her eyes and tried to feel his presence. What went through Grandpa Lake's mind on Giddings Alley on that night after Christmas in 1955? Sarah took a series of deep, rhythmic breaths. Maybe clearing her mind would help her feel some vibes that Grandpa might have left behind.

But nothing came to her.

She looked through the windshield, training her eyes on the alley just in front of her. That grimy asphalt once bore stains from bloody pools that collected around his body. How long was he conscious? What kind of pain did he feel? Was he feverish or shivering cold, or both? How long did he lie clinging to precious seconds, hoping each one wouldn't be his last? What went through his mind as the fire in his chest told him he didn't have the strength to take another breath? The sound of harps from her phone interrupted her trance.

"Hi, this is Sarah."

"Jackson Andrews here. Is everything going okay?" he asked.

"Yes, I'm just running behind," Sarah apologized.

"Not a problem. Why don't I meet you at the restaurant? I can get started with a cocktail."

"Okay, I'll need some directions."

"I'll text you the name of the restaurant and its address. You can plug it into your GPS, right?"

"Sure."

"Where are you now?" he asked.

"Um – I'm somewhere on Colorado Boulevard, I think." He didn't need to know exactly where.

"You're probably not far, then. I'm sure the GPS will get you there just fine."

Sarah tapped End Call and waited for Andrews's text. After a few moments, when no message alert appeared, she eased the car door open. A cool wisp gave her a shiver as the sun pulled back its warmth from the dusk settling over Giddings Alley. Lights glared down from the Pasadena City College parking lot across the street, helping to ease her jitters. She took short, calculated steps toward the alley, the way a hunter creeps up on his prey.

Peering over the low retaining wall at the edge of the gas station parking lot, Sarah looked down the alley toward the distant cross street. Nothing eerie, suspicious or enlightening caught her eye. She only saw a solitary pedestrian strolling toward the other end of the alley and a handful of cars cruising past the intersection. Andrews's text message alert broke her concentration.

The restaurant was only a few blocks away, much easier to find than an open parking space. Arriving before Andrews gave her time to plan how to approach him about the things she learned on her visit to USC.

Her planning and rehearsing turned out to be useless exercises, though. After enduring a tedious ritual of perusing the menu, listening to Andrews's critiques of the recipes, meaningless banter, sipping wine – his selection didn't measure up to his raves about it – and swallowing mouthfuls of salad at just the right moment to get a word in edge-wise, Sarah recognized that Andrews had hijacked her agenda.

"The old man tells me you think the Sons of Freedom might have had it in for Dr. Moran."

"I just asked him a question. I didn't accuse anyone of anything," Sarah protested.

"Even so, he took offense." Andrews looked past her.

"Sorry, I didn't mean to offend him." Sarah leaned over the table and tried to commandeer his field of vision.

He looked at her. "Well if you're interested, I can point you in a more productive direction."

"I don't care what rocks I have to look under."

He cocked his head to one side. "You might consider exercising some discretion."

"Why? How much more trouble can I get into?" Sarah looked down at her plate.

Andrews smirked. "I almost envy your naïveté."

She leered back at him.

He shook his head. "I'm just saying that you

could upset some powerful people who don't care whether they play nice or not. They don't have to. That's how they got to be powerful in the first place."

"Go ahead." She egged him on, staring harder.

"Okay. You insist that Lincoln's diary is real and whoever killed Moran did so when they were trying to steal it. So, maybe I can give you a lead on someone who's been in the market for purported Lincoln diaries in the past."

"I'm listening."

"Lincoln desperately wanted the transcontinental railroad to succeed. Even in the middle of the war, he pushed hard to get the railroad launched. His former client, Thomas Durant, headed the Union Pacific Railroad. He was supposed to build the eastern half of the new line. When Lincoln found out Durant had only laid forty miles of track in eighteen months, and on top of that, he'd been bilking his investors as well as the government out of millions, he fired him and hand-picked a political ally to run the railroad."

Sarah looked away. "Thanks for the history lesson, but what does that have to do with finding the diary?"

"Patience, I'm getting there."

Sarah looked back at him and frowned. "Okay, go on."

"Other railroad tycoons supported Lincoln as well, but they didn't necessarily agree with everything he wanted to do. They put up with him because the railroad made them a ton of money. So when he dumped Durant, it scared them. They worried they would be next."

"So you're saying they exploited Lincoln's depression as the war wound down and helped him plot his own assassination?"

He laughed. "No. But some of them might have

joined a conspiracy to kill him, and Lincoln could have recorded his suspicions about them in his diary."

"Interesting, but I could use more specifics."

Andrews looked over both shoulders before he continued. "Well, it could be that Lincoln learned somehow that the other railroad men were plotting to kill him."

"So you're agreeing that someone who's descended from the old robber barons would kill to get their hands on the dairy."

"Only suggesting. We're talking about some enormous wealth and prestige, but more importantly, some huge philanthropic institutions could be impacted. Charities are deadly serious about their reputations, if you get my drift. They get neurotic about anything that might turn off big donors."

Sarah leaned back in her chair. "That still doesn't add up to murder. Does it?"

"They don't like messes, and sometimes murder is an effective way to clean up a mess, or to prevent having to clean one up." Andrews nodded his head up and down, twice.

"So which robber baron's heir approached you about acquiring a Lincoln diary?"

Andrews leaned across and whispered something.

Sarah's eyes widened.

Andrews sat back in his chair, studying her face.

Sarah stared back at him. Her eyes were glazed over.

Andrews warned, "Don't you dare tell anyone you got that from me."

Sarah couldn't speak.

"I'm serious. This conversation never took place."

She blinked, trying to rattle her circuits back to functioning order. "Oh – uh – yes, I understand."

While Sarah remained seated, still reeling from Andrews's revelation, he paid the bill and got up to leave. But once he had taken a few steps toward the door, he looked back at her. After a moment, he returned to the table and rested his hand on the back of her chair.

She looked up at him and started to stand.

"Are you going to be okay?" Andrews's tone was warm.

"I'm all right. Just a little stunned." A faint smile found its way onto her face.

"I'll walk you to your car," he offered.

"I think I'll take you up on that." Sarah stood and took a moment to steady herself. She had one more question. "Oh, I just remembered something I meant to ask."

"What's that?" Andrews asked.

"Does the name Tyrone Wallace mean anything to you?" She watched his face.

Andrews didn't flinch. Her question failed to agitate the veins in his face or neck even a smidgen, and it didn't leave the slightest trace of a new crease anywhere on his face. He shook his head. "Sorry. It doesn't register."

Chapter Fourteen

Standing at the threshold of her motel room, Sarah's heart all but stopped. Her suitcase was open and turned upside down on the bed with both sides sliced through. The bed linens and her clothes were scattered over the floor. The dresser drawers were either hanging out to the point they could easily fall off their tracks, or they were strewn around as if they'd been yanked out and tossed aside. The cheap imitation paintings and posters from the walls were in a heap on the floor, and the mini bar had been forced open and emptied. Whatever the burglars wanted, they couldn't have missed it. But how in the world did they get in?

Turning on her heels, she made tracks for the front desk. Her exhaustion yielded to an adrenaline rush that demanded an explanation for the brazen invasion of her paid-for private space. The motel staff was going to suffer for its incompetence.

When the night manager overheard her complaints at the front desk, he bolted from the back office to give Sarah his full attention. He only turned from her long enough to give the security guard a verbal lashing, including a promise that heads would roll. Sarah's demand that he call the police to investigate sent him to a phone instantly. He didn't even notice her dialing someone on her cell phone as well.

Everyone nearby learned what Sarah could be like when she lost her temper. Refusing any constraints of reason, she unleashed all the pent up resentment from every offense she'd suffered in the past. The night manager didn't deserve the totality of her accumulated wrath. He just happened to be next in line and suffered for everyone who'd gone before. And after her eruption, every ounce of her spent anger got gathered up and stuffed back into her memory banks to be reused on some future victim. In fact, all her venting didn't purge her of the tiniest measure of hostility. The guilt and embarrassment she felt from her tirade only stoked her ire all the more.

When the first detective on the scene turned out to be Hetherington, Sarah began complaining to him, "Well Detective, now maybe you can pretend to do a real investigation."

Hetherington brushed past her, not giving her the briefest glance. He went straight to the night manager and displayed his badge, introducing himself as "Detective Glen Hetherington, Homicide Detail."

The manager stammered out his own name in response, all the while shifting his eyes back and forth between the Hetherington and his irate customer.

Detective Hetherington turned and gave Sarah an icy stare, insisting, "The first thing I'm going to do is figure out whether I'm being played."

Sarah returned his glare with one that could bore through granite. "Give it a rest."

The detective held his tongue. He must have known that aggravating her any more would just make his job impossible. "Why don't we go up to the room? We might figure out what they were after."

Sarah softened the edge on her voice. "Okay. It's still Room 415. But we know what they wanted."

Hetherington turned to the security guard. "You'd better come along. I'm sure I'll have some questions."

The night manager followed close behind. "I'll join you, if you don't mind."

As they rode up the elevator, Sarah kept her arms folded tight against her chest, her eyes were straight ahead, and she clamped down tight on her molars. Standing next to her, Hetherington wore an impatient scowl while he kept his eyes trained on the display that counted off the floors. When they got off the elevator, the manager, who spent the entire ride glancing back and forth between the two of them, answered his cell phone. "Send them up to Room 415." He turned to Detective Hetherington, still baffled at why a homicide detective had responded to a reported break-in. "The others are on their way up," he reported.

At the threshold of her room, Hetherington peered inside, and without looking at Sarah, he asked, "You want me to believe they were looking for your grandmother's journal?"

"I just want you to see the truth." Sarah lacked the patience to mince words.

"What's the truth?"

"Obviously, someone knows about my grandmother's journal. It's the only thing that points to Lincoln's diary. And they can't afford to have evidence out there that undermines whatever plans they have for it."

"Funny, I'm thinking someone must believe you got lucky and found Lincoln's diary – which you lifted after you clubbed Moran in the head."

Sarah sneered. "You're just looking to take the heat off your powerful friends, and I'm an easy scapegoat."

Detective Hetherington lurched back. "What?"

He was still warding off Sarah's evil eye when the Robbery Detail arrived. "Hetherington, what are you doing here?" asked the lead robbery detective "No one said anything about a body."

Hetherington snarled. "Someone called in a tip on

a case I've been working. Looks like a false alarm, though. Anyway, I'll get out of your way. Just let me know what you find here."

Detective Hetherington gritted his teeth as he brushed past Sarah. "I'll be seeing you soon."

Sarah called after him, "Be sure you have some real evidence before you waste anybody's time." She didn't buy his effort to intimidate her. He would have arrested her already if he thought he could make it stick.

The robbery detective looked at Sarah. "You two aren't friends."

"Gee, you're some detective." She rolled her eyes and pretended to ignore him as she surveyed the room again.

"Any idea who would have done this?" The detective drew a pen out of his shirt pocket.

She glared back at him. "Besides your buddy who just left us, I'm only aware of two people who know where I'm staying. And both knew I'd be gone all day today. One of them wouldn't do this kind of thing. The other, he might have hired it out. But there are others who might be watching me close enough to have figured out I was gone."

The robbery detective looked sideways at her. "Why do you think someone's watching you?"

"They think I have something they want, and they're framing me for murder."

"Ah, that's why Hetherington dropped by."

"I called him. I wanted him to see that someone really is after my grandmother's journal."

"So, you called him over to see this?"

"Well, breaking into a motel room is pretty suspicious behavior if you ask me."

"I see." The detective slipped on a pair of latex gloves and ran his hand along the doorjamb and the edge of the door. "Tell me again, who knew you were staying here?"

"Jackson Andrews, a dealer in rare books. He's out in San Marino, and I had dinner with him tonight. And there's Elliot. I don't know his last name. He's a research assistant at the University of Redlands. He's been trying to help me figure out who killed Professor Moran."

"I see." The detective inspected the door latch from various angles. "No forced entry."

"So they had help from someone who works here," Sarah prompted him as she rolled her eyes. "Check the security cameras."

The night manager fidgeted with his cell phone and looked over at the detective, avoiding eye contact with Sarah. He turned his back to her so he wouldn't see her reaction when he whispered to the detective, "The cameras on this floor have been out of commission since late this morning."

"Sweet!" Sarah clenched her teeth.

The robbery detective tried to diffuse her irritation. "Who do you think is watching you?"

"I'm not sure exactly. At dinner tonight, Mr. Andrews told me about some people who want to suppress the diary." Sarah hesitated. "But I didn't get anything specific from him." Even though Andrews gave her more details than she let on, she figured laying the blame on some vague person who's connected to Stanford University would sound ridiculous. "Whoever they are, they know about my grandmother's journal and they're trying to get their hands on it."

"Why is your grandmother's journal so important?"

"Because it talks about the diary."

"What diary?" he asked.

"Lincoln's diary."

The detective shook his head. "I'm sorry. I'm confused. Are you saying that someone wants your grandmother's journal because it mentions a Lincoln diary and they don't want people to know what either of them says?"

"Yes." Sarah nodded her head.

"Who wouldn't want people to know what's in Lincoln's diary?"

Sarah crossed her arms. "People who might be embarrassed by revelations about their ancestors."

"Wait, this isn't one of those 'Lincoln was gay' things is it?"

"No." Sarah shook her head. "The diary talks about Lincoln's depression and it might say he planned his own assassination with help from people who were supposed to be his friends."

"So, you're saying Lincoln was a nut case?"

Sarah shook her head again. She wanted to go through the litany of possibilities, all the people who might want the diary and why, but that would only confuse the drone. She rolled her eyes and sighed, "I don't know all the details."

"So what is it again that your grandmother's journal has to do with this?" The detective scratched his head.

"She talked about Lincoln's diary in her journal. She wrote about how a lawyer delivered it to her after my grandfather died." Sarah stared hard into the detective's eyes. "I think Detective Hetherington knows what I'm talking about."

"Look, Ma'am. We're going to do our thing here, just as thorough as we always do. When we're done, we'll file a report and someone will contact you."

Sarah sneered. "So you're just going to sweep it under the rug."

"No Ma'am. We're going to do our jobs. But I can't promise we'll break any speed records. We're busy protecting people's lives and property."

Sarah motioned around the room. "Well I have a life, and this is property."

"Yes, but your life doesn't appear to be in any danger, and we'll do our best to get your property back. By the way, what did they take?"

Sarah pressed the heel of her hand against her forehead. "They didn't find what they wanted."

"I thought you said something about a journal."

Sarah half laughed. "Detective Hetherington has it. He took it as evidence."

"I see. Well, why don't you go down to the bar and get a drink or something while we do our job? I'll send word as soon as we finish. Maybe these nice people here can get you set up in another room." He gestured toward the night manager.

Sarah threw up her hands. "Fine."

When she and the manager got to the front desk, he coded a new key for her. He promised that housekeeping would deliver her belongings to the new room as soon as the investigators wrapped up their work. Sarah forced a grin and acknowledged his apology with an unintelligible reply.

He almost coaxed a smile out of her when he offered to cover her bar tab for the evening. Sarah pointed across the lobby to a window that looked out onto a semi-private gazebo. "I'll be out there. A glass of wine will be fine. Make it white and chilled."

As she waited for the server to deliver her drink, Sarah held back her tears. But after he served her and disappeared back into the lobby, tears started pouring out of her like a monsoon. Running away was starting to make a lot of sense. Under her sobs she muttered, "Damn the damned diary and forget all the rest. Just leave me alone."

It was on her third trip to the front desk to check on the investigators' progress that the clerk said her things had been delivered to her new room. That was when she noticed she hadn't touched her wine since the first sip. It had gone flat and lost its chill.

At the bar, her server brought her a fresh glass. After eyeing it for a few seconds, she ordered another. With a glass in each hand, Sarah sipped her way back to the gazebo and started to relax, no longer in a hurry to settle into her new room. The fresh wine was crisp, fruity and familiar. What more did a girl need?

Chapter Fifteen

Sarah's cell phone rang just before nine o'clock. A faint smile slipped across her face. She'd gotten dressed hours before, unable to sleep, thanks to wine induced indigestion and panic over forgetting what time Elliot was supposed to come by for breakfast. Playing Sudoku on her phone kept her busy in the meantime. Her excuse for settling into a rut was that her brain needed a rest.

At breakfast, Elliot teased about her appetite – she attacked every morsel like a stray dog that hadn't eaten in days. And about her ordering Joe's Scramble – fried potatoes, onions, sweet peppers, cheese and eggs all tossed together – he said he couldn't picture her eating like that very often, not with her slim figure and gorgeous complexion. Her battered ego wanted to argue, but she chose to indulge in his flattery – at least for a moment. However, anxiety soon took over, and she unloaded about the mess her life was in – how it depressed her to be so overwhelmed. He told her he admired her stamina and determination. It struck her that if there'd been more people like him in her life over the years, it wouldn't have been necessary to build up layers of aloofness for protection.

"Most people would have buckled by now." Elliot told her.

She looked down at her empty plate. He sounded genuine. Being with him was like curling up with one of Grandma's old quilts. And with him watching her back, she could take on the world. Reaching across the table and giving his hand a squeeze would deliver the perfect signal to let him know her thoughts, but that might be too aggressive for his taste. After all, this guy was a throwback to another generation, a time when men were wise, dependable, chivalrous and strong.

Elliot broke her silence. "So Andrews thinks you've touched a nerve with some pretty powerful people?"

"Yeah, I guess so." Sarah caught hold of his gaze. His eyes overflowed with confidence.

"Do you think they were behind what happened last night?"

Sarah hung her head. "I could be wrong, but I just can't see either of the Andrewses being able to get security to let them in. After all, whoever got access to a pass key must have had a lot of influence."

"So you think it's someone with a lot of weight to throw around?"

"I'd say Stanford is a pretty heavy name." Sarah looked at him again.

"Is that the name Andrews gave you?" Elliot furrowed his brow.

"Yes."

"That could present a challenge. How do you plan to go up against guys that big?"

"I don't know. I guess I could look up the name Stanford in the phone book." Sarah half laughed.

"Well, Leland Stanford didn't have any heirs. All of his money went to the university that was named after his son who died fairly young."

Sarah laughed aloud. "So, why would Andrews send me off in that direction?"

"Maybe he's really trying to be helpful. After all, the university would have a lot at stake if the diary connected Stanford to Lincoln's murder. They wouldn't want to be tied to anything messy, remember?"

Sarah shook her head. "Elliot, this is way over my

head. I'm just a contract linguist. I translate things, and occasionally I interpret for dignitaries. Sometimes, I sit in and observe interrogations."

Elliot grinned. "Well, maybe we can lay a trap."

"We?" Sarah smiled.

"Sure, I can ride shotgun for you."

Sarah's smile broke into a grin and everything inside her felt warm. "How would we set a trap?"

"We could use your grandmother's journal as bait. Who else knows about it?"

"Just us, the Andrewses and Detective Hetherington."

"Great. So we know that anyone who wants your grandmother's journal must be linked to the Andrewses, and if they aren't looking for the diary as well, they must be connected to Moran's murder."

Sarah's smile dissolved. "Wait. That phone call – the one with the garbled voice. He asked for the journal, but said nothing about Lincoln's Diary. That had to be Andrews."

"Okay. We just have to wait for him to call back. Set up a rendezvous and nail him."

"But, I don't have Grandma's journal."

"Oh. Where is it?"

She lowered her head. "Detective Hetherington took it as evidence."

"Ah –" Elliot nodded.

"And who knows what it says. I didn't get a chance to –"

Elliot leaned across the table, his eyes widening. "So you don't know what's in it?"

"I've read parts of it, parts about my father and grandfather. But there's a lot I didn't get to read. Why?"

Elliot leaned back in his chair. "Oh – I'm just

surprised, that's all. I had the impression you'd read it all."

"No."

Elliot leaned forward and planted his hands flat on the table. "Okay, we can still pretend that you have the journal. No one knows you don't, right? I mean, we're the only ones who know the cops have it. Even if Andrews hired someone to break into your room last night, you can just say you took it with you to L.A. So all you have to do is call the younger Andrews and tell him what happened last night, but be sure to let him know that you had all your valuables with you, including the journal. Dangle it in front of him like bait."

Sarah's face beamed. "Hey, thanks for being a friend."

Elliot smiled and reached across the table. He laid his hand on top of hers. "Just call me a sucker for strong, sexy women."

Sarah smiled back, turning her hand over so their palms touched. They laced their fingers together, making her heart flutter and her internal temperature rise. Her breath dissipated. There wasn't enough of it left to squeeze out another word. And even though neither 'strong' nor 'sexy' fit her self-image, knowing he thought about her that way made her glow.

Once Elliot headed off to cover Moran's classes, her emotional horizons clouded over, and her mood turned pouty. Later, after her phone call with Andrews, there wasn't a hole deep enough for her to crawl into. Elliot was going to think she was an absolute flake. She'd gone farther than he'd told her to and got carried away trying to figure out the connection between Lake Matthews and Professor Deery. She just couldn't help herself.

Andrews laughed at the rumor that he had slept

with Deery. He said his grades in Deery's class were ample proof they didn't have any such relationship. Besides, as Andrews explained, he had the opposite kind of reputation. His crowning achievement in college was creating a secret society that went by the acronym NFL. It had nothing to do with football, but everything to do with keeping score on how many different girls its members could lay.

The conversation wasn't a complete bust, though. Sarah learned from Andrews that Professor Deery had once been on the hunt for undiscovered Lincoln documents, and Andrews's father handled a few transactions for him. Apparently, Deery was involved in some Lincoln research, as well. Maybe it was while Moran studied under Deery at USC that, as a graduate student, he caught the bug to pursue the assassination conspiracy angle.

Andrews also recalled that his father and Deery roomed together at USC for a short time. After that, they shared a bungalow near Pasadena City College so Deery could be closer to his friends in Echo Park. But the relationship between Deery and the elder Andrews imploded over Deery's sexual orientation and political leanings. Apparently, old man Andrews once described Deery as being 'queer' in a variety of ways. After Andrews's father moved out, Deery continued to live in the bungalow, even as the neighborhood went to pot. Deery was living there when he died.

Nevertheless, Andrews said his father almost fell apart when Deery killed himself. Of course, the professor's death had a silver lining. Andrews's final grade in Deery's class went from an F to an A because the university felt his students had endured enough trauma.

After a few minutes of wallowing in self-pity, Sarah pulled herself out of her funk and headed to the motel parking lot. She paused after rounding the corner of the building, hoping to savor a view of the mountains in the distance. Mountains so stark and majestic didn't exist around the Chesapeake Bay. A scowl settled over her face when she couldn't find the rugged peaks where they'd been the previous morning. They were shrouded by a morning haze, the same grayish-brown soup that had given the air a warm and acrid taste on previous afternoons. Based on what she'd been told, the day would get hotter and smoggier before it was over.

When Sarah slipped behind the wheel of her car and looked through the windshield, she smiled. Maybe the day would be bearable after all. A note was pinned under her windshield wiper. Her heart told her it was from Elliot.

But her heart was wrong. When she opened the car door and reached around to retrieve the note, its block letters, apparently cut from newspaper headlines and magazines captions, screamed at her, "*DO WHAT YOU'RE TOLD AND NO ONE GETS HURT.*" Her eyes locked as she collapsed behind the steering wheel and tried to catch her breath. It was as if someone had snuck up on her and bounced a medicine ball off her gut.

Not expecting he'd help, but out of stark fear, Sarah dialed Detective Hetherington. As the phone continued to ring, her heart sank knowing he'd just count it against her. Her heart was right. Hanging up would have been the better option.

"I'm sorry, Sarah, but it sounds like you're just trying to throw us off again. We call that obstruction."

"Are you serious?" Sarah begged.

"Look, last night you said someone broke into your room, but there was no forced entry. Our crime scene guys didn't find anything suspicious, no fingerprint matches, no trace evidence that's helpful. And now, there's a cryptic note on your windshield, probably no fingerprints, no witnesses. You could be making up this whole thing."

Sarah protested. "But all this happened after I dug up a bunch of stuff you've overlooked."

"Such as –"

"Such as the fact that some very powerful people think I'm standing in the way of whatever plans they have for Lincoln's diary." Sarah raised her voice a few decibels. "I'm talking about people who are used to getting their way."

"And who would that be?" Hetherington scoffed.

Sarah's tone softened. "I'd rather not tell you over the phone. Can I come to your office?"

"Sure, why not? I love wasting time."

"Is now okay?"

"Fine."

His tone turned Sarah's face hot without her having to wait for a sweltering mid-day sun. Not even the MAX setting for the car's air conditioning could cool her off. But in spite of her emotions, her brain tried to organize the hodgepodge of information she had been collecting into a compelling story for Detective Hetherington. Mind over emotion – the same iron will that earned her a good bit of success on the lacrosse field. She liked to think that willpower and discipline were her strong suites. Including good habits like glancing back and forth between the road ahead and the rearview mirror as she drove. In her present situation, it could mean survival. But somehow, the third car in line behind her had escaped her notice until she started to turn into the Sheriff's Headquarters parking lot.

Her shoulders tightened as the mystery car drove past the parking lot entrance. She ground her teeth wondering if she'd missed seeing it for several miles. The car looked like the one that bolted out of Moran's driveway the day he was killed.

She tracked the car after pulling into a parking space that faced out toward the street, but never got a good view of the driver. Her stalker slowed down about a hundred feet beyond the far end of the lot. Was he going to park down the street and wait for her to finish her business with Detective Hetherington?

Just as she turned off the ignition, her cell phone rang.

"Hello."

"Sarah." The voice sounded garbled just like before, like someone talking underwater. It was hard for her to tell, but a hint of the younger Andrews's voice might have been buried in all the distortion. "I told you, no police. Just wait for our call and do what you're told."

The caller hung up. In her call log, the number registered as "Unknown" with no more details than had shown up on the display. Another flimsy story for Hetherington.

Right again. Hetherington didn't believe any part of her story. Everything had an explanation. And yes, he knew about Deery's suicide. The fact that Lake Matthews was her grandfather made him more suspicious, not less. He already told her he had known about a Lincoln diary. The note they found on her grandfather's body mentioned it. He never found any proof that Deery ever tried to buy a Lincoln diary. Sure, the elder Andrews and Deery knew each other. But so what? Andrews, Jr. certainly wasn't gay. As for the powerful people she claimed were stalking her, he laughed. He said, "It makes good TV, but for the most part, powerful people stay powerful by keeping their noses clean."

Sarah's brain went into tilt mode like a malfunctioning slot machine shutting down and triggering an alarm. An electrical impulse in her head complained something wasn't right. No matter how hard she tried, Hetherington wouldn't believe her. Why wouldn't he at least try?

He was a bit helpful, though. According to Hetherington, in case she hadn't noticed, there were a lot of light colored late model sedans in Southern California. Light colors reflect heat. Dark colors absorb heat. Just try getting inside a black car that's been sitting out in the glaring sun on a hot summer day.

Hetherington also told her it wasn't Moran pulling out of his drive the morning he died. He drove an SUV not a sedan. When Sarah protested she saw someone leaving the scene, and that person must have been the killer, Hetherington rolled his eyes. Once again, he accused her of making up stories to throw off the investigation. No one reported seeing a second light colored sedan. They only reported seeing her speeding away.

"But I wasn't speeding," she insisted.

As Sarah walked out of the Sheriff's Headquarters, the same hollow feeling visited her that she used to get from arguing with Mom. The feeling of getting sucked into a black hole and not being able to stop the downward spiral.

Chapter Sixteen

Her dress looked frumpy enough. Hopefully, Reverend Davis would approve. Elliot had directed her to the Salvation Army Thrift Store where she found it. Though there wasn't a chance he'd get to see her in it.

Sarah had little problem carrying off the drawl and southern charm. Growing up around people who talked and acted that way made it easy. Of course, Mom wasn't like tat, and neither was Grandma Cassie. But Maryland, being a border state, had plenty of people who preferred the old southern ways. It occurred to her that Lincoln's biggest miracle was surviving as long as he did, sandwiched between the Confederacy's capital and Maryland's underground of Southern sympathizers. He virtually spent his entire presidency behind enemy lines.

The hardest part of getting ready to meet Reverend Davis was memorizing a few *Bible* verses to salt their conversation. Peppering wouldn't be Biblical, even if it did describe the aggressive approach of many believers she'd encountered. Sarah learned from watching religious cliques in high school and college that the hardcore types glommed on to anyone who talked and looked like them, especially if they had money or status, unless they asked too many questions. If you wanted to sound especially holy, quoting from the "Good Book" was crucial, the *King James Version* of the *Bible* that is.

To make things a little easier, Sarah downloaded an interactive edition of the "KJV" onto her cell phone. It was complete with a search engine and commentary. She remembered enough of the religious banter that got thrown at her in school to make good use of her fancy research tools. Back in high school, kids probably meant well, but getting 'saved' wouldn't have filled the hole in

Sarah's heart. Not when what she really wanted was an earthly daddy who loved her.

As Sarah wound her way through the canyon toward Crafton Hills, the sight of neglected orange groves and struggling avocado orchards made her wonder how any place could be so devoid of beauty. The breeze that whisked through the rows of dead and dried-out branches whispered something that sounded like "You can't afford to blow this one."

After overshooting the drive up to the Davis family compound she had to make a U-turn and come back at it from the opposite direction. The driveway didn't angle to the street in a manner that made left hand turns easy, so the maneuver required coming to a near stop. That wasn't easy with the tailgater on her rear bumper as she cut back hard onto the uneven concrete. A series of switchbacks led up to the main house, passing prickly cacti, dried out sagebrush, spindly yucca plants and tangled masses of greasewood. The late morning sun beat down on her the twenty yards from her car to Davis's front door.

Reverend Davis greeted her, cheerful and bright like a desert sunrise. He slurred his syllables as if his tongue was chasing them between and around his loosely fitted dentures. It was hard to tell whether he was authentically southern, or if he had just perfected his drawl over years of fitting in with the brethren. He surprised her by not being older. He appeared to be comfortably south of sixty, energetic and agile, sporting a souvenir T-shirt from an ironman competition. The caption under the shirt's logo suggested God only cared about the Reverend's success – all the other competitors were like extras on a movie set.

Davis led her through the entry hall into the inner

sanctum of his sprawling single story, low ceiling ranch home. Before they were seated, he offered her a glass of sweet iced tea "... made the southern way, as it should be."

Sitting across from her host, angled toward his plush armchair, Sarah postured herself a bit forward in the straight back wooden chair he'd offered her. Her spine tracked its lines. She smoothed her skirt over her knees and kept her calves pressed together while she drew her ankles back to one side. Her half-inch heels underscored her deference to his ego.

"Thank you Reverend, for seeing me on such short notice."

"I don't normally meet with young ladies alone, but your situation sounded urgent, and I certainly wouldn't want you to form an impression of the Sons of Freedom based solely on your encounter with that old devil Andrews."

"I understand. He made me feel very uncomfortable."

He smiled. "What can I do for you Miss Morgan?"

"Well Reverend Davis, I am eager to place the Lincoln diary in a proper home, as soon as it's returned to me, of course."

"The idea of a private Lincoln diary is hard to imagine. But if one exists, it should be protected from pinhead academics who would twist it for their liberal purposes." Something about the way he spit out the word 'liberal' gave her the impression it was a disgusting thing to be.

"My thoughts exactly. So you can see why it horrified me to learn my poor mother, distressed as she was in her final days, allowed herself to be swindled out of it by the likes of Professor Moran."

"Well I'm glad to see you're considering the Sons of Freedom as the beneficiary of your gift."

"Yes, but I want to be sure it will be used as it should be. Please tell me about the organization and what your people would intend to do with the diary."

"I can certainly give you the assurance you are looking for, dear child. But first, can you tell me what the diary says?"

"Unfortunately, I haven't had the opportunity to study it – er – thoroughly, I should say. Most of what I know I've read in my grandmother's journal. My grandfather used to read her passages from the diary, and she recorded her impressions of the things he read."

"And where is your grandmother's journal?"

Sarah's chest went hollow as if it had been sucked clean by the force of a black hole that flew past her out of nowhere. The journal was supposed to be Andrews's bait. She stammered out another lie, hoping to minimize any damage from her faux pas. "Oh it's locked away safely in my motel manager's safe." The detail about the safe would help her know whether an attempt to get at Grandma Cassie's journal came from Reverend Davis rather than Andrews. "But please answer some questions for me. I need to understand what kind of people I'm dealing with. Not that I put much stock in such gossip, but I'd be remiss if I did not make every effort to know the truth. There are rumors that someone from the Sons of Freedom may have been responsible for Dr. Moran's murder. Could that possibly be true?"

"My dear, that is a highly inflammatory accusation."

"I assure you, Sir, it's not my assertion. But prudence dictates that I make a diligent inquiry, and justice dictates that I give you every opportunity to set the record straight. I desperately want to believe that it isn't true."

Reverend Davis cleared his throat and furrowed his leathery brow. His lips contorted as if he was about to spit out another disgusting word. "Dr. Moran was a degenerate. A traitor. When people like that die, humanity is better off. I can only imagine the celebration that took place in heaven."

Sarah recoiled. An all too familiar twinge pinched her throat. Did this guy never hear John Donne's "No man is an island ... any man's death diminishes me ...?"

Davis continued, "While I don't condone lawless acts, people must understand that patriotism requires sacrifice and treason demands punishment."

Forget John Donne. Sarah was ready to leap out of her chair and stuff the Reverend's self-righteousness down his throat. She had little patience for people who used their ideologies to justify dictating how other people should live. Liberal or conservative, it didn't matter to her. But she restrained herself. "I certainly hope you didn't intend for that to be a confession of some kind."

"Absolutely not. I only meant I could understand how someone might do such a thing. There aren't enough patriots left in this country, people who are willing to defend its honor and answer God's call to spread the blessings of liberty around the world. But to put your mind at ease, no one affiliated with the Sons of Freedom would have killed Dr. Moran, no matter how much he may have deserved a traitor's death. We are law-abiding men, first and foremost. Otherwise, there'd be a mountain of corpses in our wake. And Moran would have been low on our list. We'd be too busy cleaning up Washington to bother with the likes of him."

Staying longer would have allowed her to get deeper into the Reverend's head. But, the instinct to flee his vitriol overpowered her judgment. In fact, the atmosphere under that low hung ceiling pressed down on her from the moment they walked through his front door. She just had to get out of there.

It was clear to her that he wanted Moran dead, but not enough to go out of his way to kill him. On the other hand, maybe he protested too much for a man with clean hands. Why did he only show a passing curiosity about the diary's whereabouts while he asked her specifically where she kept Grandma Cassie's journal?

When Sarah left Davis's compound, her internal weather forecast had turned gloomy again. Her appetite was gone, mostly because of the hostility that oozed out of the Reverend's pores. The only eating that could appeal to her at that moment would be something familiar, nothing Mexican or Thai. But California didn't have a much normal food. At least not anything that jumped out and waved a sign saying here I am. Eventually, she recognized a chain restaurant that served soup and salad. A sit-down place. Somewhere to make herself obvious, leave a big tip and get a receipt. Just in case.

After lunch, Sarah's sugar levels and her mood modulated enough that no one around her was in any danger of physical harm. Getting out of that frumpy dress also helped. But as gray clouds kept gathering over her emotions, keeping busy was critical. With that in mind, her next stop was the Lincoln Shrine.

When Sarah asked to see the curator, one of the Shrine's docents directed her to the administration offices in the library across the courtyard. Her disposition didn't improve in the slightest on learning that Dr. Burgess kept regular office hours in the main library building and that he arrived on campus by nine o'clock every morning.

Knowing those details a couple of days earlier might have kept her out of her current mess. It could have been her alibi. Her frown turned to a scowl when the receptionist told her that Dr. Burgess had just left for the rest of the afternoon.

But her luck wasn't as bad as she thought. Moments before Sarah arrived at the administration office, Dr. Burgess had slipped past the receptionist, returning to his office to retrieve a file. As he headed back out to his car, the receptionist caught his attention and told him Sarah wanted to talk about donating some artifacts to the Shrine. The curator apologized for being in a hurry and offered to give Sarah a few seconds if she didn't mind walking with him to his car.

As they approached Dr. Burgess's car, Sarah finished explaining that, while making an inventory of her mother's estate, she discovered a number of Lincoln artifacts, including documents that referenced the existence of a private Lincoln diary. The curator spun around and smiled, engaging her with full eye contact. He told her his next appointment would forgive him for being a few minutes late, especially if he needed the time to explore an opportunity as promising as hers.

Sarah's expression changed as dramatically as Dr. Burgess's mood had. Both breathing and swallowing became a struggle for her. The curator's car was a late model, light colored sedan just like the one that bolted out of Moran's drive, and the one that followed her to the Sheriff's Headquarters.

She stuttered and forced a smile. "I wouldn't think of holding you up from anything important. I'm in town for several more days. I can come back."

"Believe me, I can take the time."

"No, I insist. You go. I'll call you tomorrow." She extended her hand and offered him a firm handshake.

He looked at his watch and smiled. "Okay, I'll look forward to your call. Here's my card."

Sarah turned and started back to the spot where she'd parked her rental car, taking a few steps before Dr. Burgess called after her. "Say, how would you like to meet some of the world's biggest Lincoln aficionados?"

Sarah stopped in her tracks and wheeled around, unveiling a nervous grin. "When?"

"Meet me at the entrance to the Shrine – tonight at ten o'clock sharp."

"It's a date, thanks."

Sarah walked away from the curator, surrendering to an impulse. For sure, Detective Hetherington wouldn't follow any leads that didn't point in her direction. But maybe stalking Dr. Burgess for the rest of the day would lead her to some valuable clues. After all, he owned the right car.

Chapter Seventeen

Sarah kept her eyes peeled on Dr. Burgess's car, reading his license plate number into her phone's voice recorder as he passed her on his way out of the staff parking lot. Detective Hetherington had seared into her mind that there were more than a few light colored sedans in Southern California. But not all of them belonged to people who had a connection with the dead professor. The license number would let her confirm that she'd caught up with Dr. Burgess's car if he got away from her in traffic.

Sarah lost visual contact with her target as he turned right after a couple of blocks. And her car was still a short sprint away in the opposite direction. But more than likely, he'd head toward the freeway, probably planning to take the westbound entrance at Orange Street. Based on what she'd seen on maps of the area, there weren't many destinations to the east except for Palm Springs, about 50 miles away. He'd probably be following the same route her GPS had calculated on the morning Moran was killed. So if the gauntlet of traffic lights along Orange Street cooperated, catching up with him wouldn't be a problem..

A few minutes later on I-10 just before the I-215 interchange, Sarah was sure she'd caught up with Dr. Burgess. Driving a car at 85 mph was not her style, but as Grandma Cassie taught her, "Focus on what's important, and always go one step beyond what you think you can do."

Sarah wasn't speeding for the joy of it. It was about catching the bad guy, saving a life – her own. Of course, as she was saving her life, a the nagging voice in her head warned her to watch out for the state patrol. It wasn't clear to her how the particular phenomenon worked, but her fear was that the highway patrol would be Johnny-on-the-spot to nab her exactly when her speedometer registered one tick mark past the posted speed limit. And they wouldn't be willing to overlook her infraction.

Her conscience took a back seat as Sarah swallowed her sense of guilt and goosed the accelerator. At the point when there were only a couple of cars between her and the light-colored sedan, she slipped in line and shadowed him until he exited the freeway at Sierra Avenue. Rolling up behind him at the end of the exit ramp, it occurred to her to hide her face by flipping down the visor.

However, in the moment it took for her to handle the visor, he turned onto Sierra Avenue before she checked out the license plate. A couple of cars sped past her at the intersection before it was safe to pull into traffic to tail him. With a couple of cars between them, his route took them through a small commercial district that belonged in a time capsule from the 1950s.

A few blocks later, the area's old-town charm gave way to newer construction, including a modern campus with a design that suggested something of substance went on inside. Sarah followed the light-colored, late model sedan as it made a right turn into the campus parking lot. A conspicuous sign along the building's roofline read "Steelworkers Auditorium." The signage at the entrance had indentified the complex as the "Lewis Library & Technology Center." That gave her hope.

But the man who got out of the car wasn't Dr. Burgess. Sarah's heart sank. Chasing the wrong car for more than twenty minutes was the height of stupidity.

Without agonizing over the urge, she picked up her phone and dialed Elliot. Who else could she count on for encouragement?

When Sarah asked Elliot if he was free to talk, he asked if everything was okay. She said, "No. I need someone to lift my spirits." When he asked what had happened, he accepted her excuse that it wouldn't be easy to explain over the phone. Besides, a latté would do her a lot of good. They agreed to meet at the Starbucks on Orange Street in about half an hour.

On her way back to Redlands, listening to Angela's voice mail – "Just wanting to touch base" – grated on her nerves. Sarah bit her lip and tapped the Return Call icon. As the phone rang, the thought rattled around in her head, "Why can't the phone company make a commercial about giving people space? Some of us just don't feel like being reached out to and touched all the time."

Sarah and Angela exchanged meaningless banter until Sarah pulled into the parking lot behind Starbucks. Sarah wasn't about to clue Angela in on everything that had happened. Letting her come out to stick her nose into things would just aggravate the situation. One more critic wouldn't do her any good. Support was what she needed most.

Sarah found Elliot sitting outside Starbucks, soaking up some UV rays while he waited for her. Even though it was the coolest day of her trip, the sun weighed her down.

After hearing where she'd been, Elliot grinned. "You were out at the Lewis Library?"

Sarah's face yielded a reluctant smile as she nodded her head.

"It's a terrific facility, isn't it?" Elliot's eyes gleamed.

"I didn't go inside." Sarah peeked at him. Her smile had faded.

"Too bad. You missed one of the coolest libraries I've ever been in. Whoever designed it must take learning seriously, especially when it comes to kids."

"It's nice from the outside." Sarah looked up at him and tried to mimic his grin.

"What were you doing there?"

Sarah shook her head. "I thought I was following Moran's killer."

Elliot choked on his latte. "You were what?"

She gave him a cold stare. "I saw the killer's car at the Lincoln Shrine."

Elliot's smile evaporated. "How do you know what kind of car the killer drove?"

"I saw him speeding out of Moran's driveway the morning of the murder."

"You were there?"

"I only drove by to be sure I could find the place. After that, I went down the hill for lunch."

Elliot sat back in his chair. "Why didn't you tell me?" He folded his arms across his chest. "Have you told the police?"

Sarah shook her head. "Yes, but they don't believe me. They say I'm making up the story to throw them off. I stopped to ask directions from an old couple who were out walking, so Hetherington has witnesses who put me at the scene."

Elliot unfolded his arms and leaned over the table. "Did you actually see the killer?"

"No, he was going too fast."

"Are you sure the killer was a guy?"

"No, not really." Sarah looked down.

"Did you get the license plate?"

She shook her head.

"Was there anything special about the car?"

"No, it was a light-colored sedan – a Toyota, I think. But Detective Hetherington says everybody out here drives those."

Elliot grinned. "Well, everyone except people who drive BMWs or black Mercedes or SUVs."

She stuck out her tongue.

Elliot sat back. "Sorry."

They looked away from each other and neither of them spoke for a moment.

Finally, Elliot asked. "How do you know the light-colored sedan you saw at the Shrine belonged to the killer?"

Sarah looked up at him. "Well, I decided that it doesn't matter if everyone in Southern California drives a light-colored sedan. It only matters that someone who knew Moran drives one."

Elliot shrugged his shoulders.

Sarah leaned across the table. "The Shrine's curator drives a late model light-colored Toyota. I watched him drive off and tried to follow him."

Elliot leaned forward. "So he's who you followed to the Lewis Library?"

"No." She hung her head. "I lost him and wound up following a car that just looked like his."

Elliot leaned back in his chair again and frowned. "I don't see him as the killer."

"Why not? He must have despised Moran for trying to smear Lincoln's reputation."

Elliot's eyes brightened. "As a matter of fact, you're right. The two of them used to get along just fine, but shortly after Moran bought your mother's document, they had a pretty bad argument."

"What about?" She straightened up.

"I'm not sure. I just know that Dr. Burgess stopped by Moran's office a couple weeks back, and when I showed up they were yelling at each other. I didn't hear what they argued about, and Moran wouldn't say."

"So do you think I'm on the right track?" Sarah scanned his face for confirmation.

"Could be. We just need to figure out how to prove it."

Sarah smiled. 'We' was the best word in the English language at that moment.

Elliot cocked his head. "By the way, did you call Andrews this morning?"

"Yes, but right now I want to focus on Dr. Burgess." She looked away.

"Well, if Andrews takes your bait that would rule out Dr. Burgess." Elliot checked his watch.

Sarah fidgeted.

After a bit, she looked back at him and grinned. "I suppose you're right. But Andrews doesn't seem the type to drive a light-colored sedan, unless it's a Mercedes."

Elliot grinned back.

Sarah glanced down at her empty cup and gave it a shake.

Elliot slid his chair back. "Can I walk you to your car?"

She smiled. "Thanks, I'd like that."

As they walked along the side of the coffee shop toward the parking lot, Sarah leaned into Elliot. Their hands almost touched when they turned the corner and headed toward her car. She caught her breath. Her body tingled all over. It took her a moment to regain her composure and look at him, trying to catch his eye.

Elliot startled her when he pulled away and

shouted, "Hey! Get away from that car." He was pointing at her rental car and at a burly hooded figure who was jamming something down inside the door along the window track. Elliot broke and ran toward him.

The man turned, saw Elliot and bolted.

Elliot sprinted after him.

About a block away, the hooded figure jumped into the passenger seat of a waiting sports car.

Elliot bent over at his waist, gasping as the car sped away.

Sarah ran up to him and put her hand on his shoulder. He was still gasping for breath.

"Are you okay?" She leaned over with her ear close enough to his lips that she could have heard him whisper.

"Sorry, I didn't get the license plate." Elliot wheezed.

"That's okay. At least you didn't get hurt."

They exchanged smiles.

Elliot started to stand. "I think Andrews took your bait."

Sarah helped him up. "Well, I have a confession to make, actually two."

He put his hand on her shoulder. "Okay."

She sighed. "I slipped and mentioned Grandma's journal to Reverend Davis. And worse, even if Andrews did send that guy, I can't be sure he's after Grandma Cassie's journal."

"Why not?"

"When I called Andrews, he might have gotten the idea that I was trying to connect his father to my grandfather's murder." She held her breath, bracing for his scolding.

Elliot ran his fingers through his hair. "How could his father have been involved in your grandfather's death?"

"Well, his father knew someone who my grandfather may have lived with out here in L.A."

"And how does that connect him to his murder?"

"He doesn't know that's all I know. But an old *Bible* verse says something that a guilty man flees even when no one is chasing him. So if I am onto something, Andrews's imagination can fill in any details that I didn't give him. And it's anybody's guess what he thinks might be stashed in my car."

"I see."

Sarah studied Elliot's face trying to read whatever thoughts were swirling behind his ocean blue eyes.

After a disquieting silence, Elliot started to chuckle. "So we think Andrews has something to hide and that makes him a possible murder suspect. We just don't know how many people or who he might have killed."

Sarah shrugged.

Elliot shook his head. "At least we're not going backwards."

Sarah touched his wrist. "But let's not let Dr. Burgess off too easily."

Elliot smiled. "I agree. Let's not eliminate him just yet. We have a long way to go to prove that Andrews is our man, so a backup suspect might come in handy."

She folded her arms across her chest. "Are you thinking it's just a coincidence that Dr. Burgess drives a car just like the one I saw speeding away from Moran's place?"

"Maybe." Elliot rubbed the back of his neck. "If old man Andrews did kill your grandfather, he easily could have killed a second time. But at his age, he would have needed an accomplice to do Moran. So either he hired someone who was smart enough to drive a nondescript vehicle, or his son rented a car to do the deed."

"Maybe Deery did the old man's dirty work the first time. I don't see the old guy as the kind who likes to get his hands dirty."

"That's the kind of idea that could grow on me. A consistent MO means we only have to sell the story once."

Sarah looped her hands around Elliot's elbow and smiled at him. "Hey, are you hungry?"

Elliot looked at his watch. "Man, I lost track of the time. I'm late for dinner at my aunt's."

"Oh –" Sarah's smile faded.

"Look, I'd invite you to come along, but Aunt Agnes·doesn't like surprises."

"I don't want to get you in trouble. You'd better go." She let go of his arm. "I really appreciate all your help. You're literally a life saver."

Elliot took her hand. "Look, how about a rain check?"

Sarah smiled. "My social calendar is pretty empty. I'm sure I can be free any time you're available."

Elliot smiled back. "I'll call you in the morning."

"Sure."

Later that evening, Sarah remembered her 10 o'clock appointment at the Shrine with Dr. Burgess and his Lincoln aficionados. With something to occupy her time, she found it easier to swallow the idea of playing second fiddle to Aunt Agnes.

Chapter Eighteen

A tall strapping man with jet-black hair leered at Sarah from across the Lincoln Shrine's basement. Two 60-watt bulbs hanging from the ceiling provided the meager lighting through which she noticed him whispering with both the elder Andrews and his son. She learned from Dr. Burgess that the man's name was Henri Rothschild, of the French banking family. He was an older version of the courier who had delivered Moran's check – maybe ten years older. Dr. Burgess identified two other men who were huddling with Rothschild and the Andrewses. They were John Easley, Moran's attorney, and Dr. Zografas from the Huntington Library. If she threw Dr. Burgess into that mix for good measure, Sarah had the makings for a bone chilling conspiracy.

According to Elliot's research, the Rothschild family controlled most of Europe's governments during the 19th century. Their leverage came from buying up government bonds at depressed prices during wartimes and using peacetime profits from the bonds to finance reconstruction projects. The Rothschilds' illusion of generosity compounded the politicians' dependency on their money. The strategy reminded her of how drug dealers hook kids to become customers The French bankers had planned a similar power play to seize economic control of the American continent during the Civil War, but Lincoln stopped them cold. It was anyone's guess whether the family played a role in his assassination.

Elliot had speculated that the Rothschilds could have attempted to manipulate Lincoln into committing suicide when he was severely depressed near the end of the war. Elliot went giddy over the possibility that Lincoln could have described some of the Rothschilds' schemes in his private diary.

When she had first arrived at the Lincoln Shrine that night, her spine was tingling with apprehension. The neighborhood's vacant streets and the darkened windows at the nearby library reminded her of blind alleys in Baltimore's toughest neighborhoods. It didn't matter where your were. Dark is dark Even in suburban Redlands.

With no immediate sign of her host, Sarah had peered through the darkness after stepping out of her rental car. A chill kissed the back of her neck despite the residue of heat that still lingered from the warm afternoon. Not until arriving at the heavy wooden doors framed by the massive granite arch did she make out the form of a figure standing in the shadows dressed in a dark cloak.

Dr. Burgess's "Good evening" echoed off the Shrine's limestone façade.

After Sarah stammered back a cautious response, Dr. Burgess joked that it was easier to enforce security when trespassers couldn't see where they're going. His snickering jarred her already raw nerves like the zing of a dull knife slipping across the surface of a plate of cheap china.

Once Dr. Burgess directed her through the entrance, she noticed a solitary candle illuminating the Shrine's vestibule. The sight of the lonely candle in that hollow, empty hall numbed her bones. At that point, it didn't look like there was any kind of meeting going on. A nagging voice in her head kept reminding her of Christians being thrown to the lions.

Sarah had struggled with swallowing when Dr. Burgess opened a secret panel in the wall behind one of the display cases. The opening revealed a stairwell that descended into a musty cellar. When they reached the foot of the stairs, Sarah caught the echoes of indistinct murmurings, hoping they were human voices.

The air tasted almost dead as she and Dr. Burgess picked their way through a narrow tunnel into a hazy catacomb where she counted maybe a dozen black-cloaked figures, some of them wearing hoods. That's when Henri Rothschild abducted her attention.

Dr. Burgess leaned toward Sarah and whispered. "The word has gotten out about your Lincoln diary, and everyone here wants to make a pitch for it."

Sarah gulped. She didn't remember ever commanding so much attention, unless it was from Grandma Cassie.

Dr. Burgess continued to whisper. "When we originally called this meeting, we thought we'd be strategizing how to get the diary away from Dr. Moran. But obviously things have changed with him dead. Now, you're the one everyone's focused on."

Sarah took a half step backward. "Look, I didn't kill him if that's what you're suggesting."

"Absolutely not, but if you had, some of these folks would offer you a medal."

Sarah glared at him. "Would you be one of them?"

He smiled. "No, I'm not exactly a carnivore."

Sarah scanned the others huddled in clusters around the catacomb.

Dr. Burgess leaned closer to Sarah. "Andrews over there told me about your grandmother's journal. He says it cites some of the diary's entries."

"Actually, my grandmother only believed it was Lincoln's diary." Sarah's chilled flesh turned clammy.

Lying wasn't her strong suite, but if all those people were going to hound her for Grandma Cassie's journal, she didn't want to acknowledge its importance. "But, I suppose I'll be able to find some experts who can prove whether the diary is authentic."

Dr. Burgess smiled. "I suppose so. And the good news is that you have a basement full of experts who are eager to do just that."

"I didn't come prepared for anything of this sort. I'm still in the process of getting the diary back." A cold sweat collected along her hairline.

"I see." Dr. Burgess cocked his head as he studied her face. "Exactly who has the diary?"

"Detective Hetherington. He's holding it as evidence." Sarah changed the subject to stop him from pressing the issue. "Tell me more about Mr. Rothschild."

"Henri Rothschild is a part of the famous family of French bankers. He was in the area on other business and when he heard about our meeting he decided to drop in. An uncle of his normally represents our European chapter. "

Sarah gulped. "You're international?"

"Sure. We even have a chapter in the heart of Africa. It's amazing. Even some of the remotest tribes in the world know about Lincoln. Heaven knows how they've heard about him. But he's a symbol of liberty and human rights all over the world."

"And Europeans care about what's in Lincoln's diary?"

"They're concerned that a bunch of pseudo-scholars could misrepresent any vague references Lincoln might have made about them when he was under stress. You know, kind of like the Nixon tapes." Dr. Burgess smiled.

Sarah sneered. "Like entries that would suggest

our allies tried to take advantage of us when we were back on our heels?"

"It doesn't serve any constructive purpose to create an international incident over spilled milk."

"You're not trivializing the Civil War or Lincoln's death are you?" She wanted to pull her question back. Her nerves were too fragile for confrontation.

"No, of course not. I'm just saying that inflammatory rumors about the past don't serve the present."

"So they are hiding something." She stared at him.

"I was being purely hypothetical." He took a deep breath. "Would you like to meet him?"

"Honestly, I'm pretty tired. The past few days have been exhausting. If you wouldn't consider it rude of me, I'd prefer to get some rest. My attorney can handle whatever details any of them might want to pursue. I'm meeting him first thing in the morning, you know. And he'll get pretty – ah – aggravated if I'm late or don't show up. He actually didn't like the idea of my coming here tonight." Of course, Dr. Burgess had no way of knowing she had told a bald-faced lie.

"I think they'll understand. Do you have your attorney's name and number?"

"Not on me. I'll call you in the morning – from his office." Sarah held her stare and maintained a steady grin.

"Yes, do that." Dr. Burgess motioned to a young woman who hurried to his side.

"Ellen will show you out. I'll offer your regrets to everyone."

As soon as Sarah and her escort started for the

tunnel, Henri bolted from the Andrewses's clique and rushed over to confront her. Sarah stopped and braced herself.

"Ms. Morgan, excuse me." He spoke in a thick-tongued French accent, more pronounced than the courier who delivered the check from Dr. Moran's attorney. His voice was a lot more like her first mystery caller.

"I'm sorry, but I really have to go." Sarah's voice was pitched.

"I just want to be sure you understand. I didn't come all the way across the ocean to return home empty handed."

"Excuse me!" Adrenaline raced through her entire body.

"I don't mean to offend you. Please excuse my sloppy English."

"Who do you think you are, threatening me?" Sarah stared hard at him.

"Again, I apologize." Rothschild's tone mellowed.

"Apologize for what?" she demanded. "For being rude now, or for your threatening phone call earlier?"

"I'm not sure I know what you mean. I've never spoken with you before tonight. I represent the Rothschild Bank and we are strictly business people ... civilized people – bankers. I only mean to point out that we have the resources to acquire anything we want."

"And you want the diary because?"

"Actually, we want your grandmother's journal as well. I understand they compliment each other. They're, how do you say it, a package."

Sarah scanned through an array of mental images, focusing on her encounters over the past few days. A vision of the sedan bolting out of Moran's drive flashed to the front of her mind – a vague silhouette of its driver.

Was his face long and square-jawed like Henri Rothschild's? She remembered. The driver was tall enough that the car's low profile obscured her view of his head. She didn't get a good look at the driver's face, but it could have been Henri Rothschild.

Her stomach roiled, her shoulders knotted and her knees felt like sponges. It was the second time she found herself standing no more than eighteen inches from someone who could be a killer. Sarah sputtered, "Grandma Cassie's journal isn't for sale."

"I'm sorry to have upset you. I only wanted you to understand that my partners and I – how do you say it here? We are committed."

Subduing a flash of nausea, Sarah threw her shoulders back and bit her lower lip. "And I hope I've given you the impression that I'll make my own decision in my own time."

As Sarah and Henri Rothschild exchanged glares, the basement started to tremble. Within a moment or two, it began to sway. Sarah lurched forward into Rothschild, struggling to stay on her feet as the concrete floor rolled underneath her. But despite her best efforts, she tumbled to the ground as a deadening bang buffeted her ears, and the basement went dark. Twice it went dark. The first darkness followed the flickering of overhead lights and was accompanied by chaos. The second darkness ended in total silence. It followed a dull thud behind her ear and an explosion of pain that shot through her head.

Unaware of how long she'd been lying unconscious on her back, Sarah eased her head side to side on a makeshift pillow of sports coats and suit jackets. Without warning, a pungent odor attacked both nostrils, jerking her wide-awake.

A woman smiled down at her. "You'll be fine

Sarah, although you might have a slight concussion."

Sarah blinked a couple of times to chase the fog out of her head. As her eyes focused, the entry doors to the Lincoln Shrine took shape, as did the limestone tiles of its façade reflecting flashing lights from emergency vehicles parked out on the street. The woman who had spoken to her was wearing an Emergency Medical Technician uniform.

"What happened?" Sarah murmured.

"You must have knocked your head on something during the earthquake." The emergency technician secured a bandage covering an abrasion just behind Sarah's left ear.

As Sarah recognized more of her surroundings, she noticed that several of the Lincoln aficionados were milling around, though they had abandoned their cloaks, likely leaving them downstairs in their eerie meeting place. Conspicuously, Rothschild and the rest of the Andrewses's clique were gone.

Dr. Burgess chimed in, "The quake only knocked out some electricity and shook a few unsecured items off of their shelves, but other than that it was a minor one."

Someone in the background added, "Minor, but definitely close."

The emergency medical technician looked up at Dr. Burgess. "An ER trip isn't mandatory, but one of you should drive her home and be sure she checks in with her doctor in the morning."

"We can manage that," Dr. Burgess replied.

Sarah waved him off. "Won't be necessary. I can take care of it from here." She rolled to one side and propped herself with an elbow. Her head felt steady enough despite the pain.

"Are you sure?" Dr. Burgess asked.

"Positive," Sarah replied as she drew her knees

under her body and pushed up off the limestone tiles.

"I'll check with you in the morning, just to be sure," Dr. Burgess insisted as he helped her to her feet.

"I'm fine, really." Sarah took a couple of wobbly steps.

"I'll call just the same." He wouldn't let it go.

"Don't worry. I'm not going to sue." Sarah's head throbbed more intensely when she tried to smile.

Sitting behind the wheel of her car, Sarah couldn't believe she'd escaped the catacomb in one piece. Who'd ever heard of a hooded society that welcomed outsiders without wanting something from them, usually their lives. Hopefully, the throbbing in her head would dissipate before it hit the pillow.

Chapter Nineteen

The sound of harps on her cell phone ignited the stinging from under Sarah's bandage. She rubbed the sleep from her eyes and blinked to read her phone's display. "Unknown." But then again, Dr. Burgess did say he'd call.

She eased her head from side to side as if nursing a hangover and answered, "This is Sarah."

A voice gurgled from the phone. "In 30 minutes be at the Redlands Bowl. Park on the street across from the Lincoln Shrine. Walk down the center aisle to the stage. On the ground in front of the stage, you'll see a backpack full of cash. Don't bother to count it. It's the best offer you're going to get. Just take it and leave the journal in its place. Get back in your car and drive to your motel. By checkout time, Hetherington will be off your back. Come alone, or else. We know how to find you." The caller hung up.

Panic. Sarah sat up and checked the time. One o'clock in the morning. She'd only been asleep for an hour. Flopping back onto the bed, she covered her face with a pillow and muttered, "I don't have the damned journal!" New waves of pain rippled through her brain.

After lying in bed for a bit, she threw the pillow aside and sat straight up. Her head throbbed in protest, but there was no time for pain. She'd already wasted ten minutes sulking.. Sarah pulled on a pair of jeans and started pushing her head through her half-buttoned blouse. As the blouse raked over the abrasion behind her ear it was as if stingers from a swam of angry wasps were buried in her flesh.

She argued with herself, remembering the episode at the Lincoln Shrine just a couple hours earlier. "This is insane. What am I doing? I'll get myself killed if I show up. This guy kills people for real."

Sarah sat back down on the bed and buried her head in her hands. Murder wasn't just a sensational event, something that glued viewers' eyeballs to their TV's and readers to their novels. Murder was final, and getting murdered could happen to her.

Taking slow rhythmic breaths – controlled breathing always helped her focus – Sarah picked up her phone and thumbed through her Contacts. Her thumb hovered over Elliot's name. Was Aunt Agnes an alias for some co-ed named Amanda? But it didn't matter. It wouldn't do for Elliot to see her in this state?

She scrolled on to Hetherington's name. "What's the use?" Calling him would just be another strike. She flopped back on the bed and hid under the pillow again. Almost instantly, tears filled her eyes.

After a good ten minutes of sobbing, she threw the pillow aside and bolted up out of bed. Depressed or not, there was only five minutes to pull a disappearing act. Sarah tossed a handful of clothes and toiletries into her bag and raced downstairs.

An old boyfriend – he was a football coach – liked to say, "You're not down until your feet stop moving." Nothing else about that relationship was memorable, but recalling his pep talk propelled her through the motel lobby and out to the parking lot.

When Sarah turned onto Waterman Avenue, her mind was set. West. The airport was to the west. As she merged on to the freeway, thoughts were spinning through her head, and they weren't following any discernible pattern. Her heart felt a pinch at the thought of going home. But running would just make her look all the more guilty, especially in Hetherington's mind.

A bit later Sarah recognized the exit sign for Sierra Avenue, but passed. Hiding out in a small town so close to Redlands didn't provide any sense of safety. At the Ontario International Airport exit she kept driving. There had to be a better place to trade her rental car for a different model. The airport's rental desk would be closed at that hour. Besides, the airport was the first place they – whoever they were – would check when they figured out she was going to be a no-show.

Sarah snapped her attention back to the taillights in front of her. It would be easier to get lost in a crowd, and L.A. was a big place. Even at half past two o'clock in the morning, the westbound lanes of Interstate 10 were crowded, and everyone was driving like there was a full moon out. But that was okay. In spite of the crazies, heading west offered the best cover. The more people, the less it mattered where she was. Staying lost was her goal.

About ten minutes later, Sarah's eyes locked onto a freeway sign pointing toward Pasadena. Something pulled at her, drawing her toward Giddings Alley. She took the exit to the Orange Freeway, eventually merging onto westbound I-210.

As Sarah approached the Irwindale Avenue Exit, an all-night diner just off the freeway caught her attention. Hopefully, she'd put enough distance between her and the chilling prospect of death that stopping for a rest and something to eat would be safe. Besides the draw of Giddings Alley wasn't yanking on her with any sense of urgency. It was content just to have her in its sway. So her fatigue and her churning stomach advanced to the top of her priorities.

Once she parked her car in direct line of sight of a window booth, Sarah peeled her stiff, aching fingers off the steering wheel. With her car in full view, she'd be in position to react if anyone approached it, even if that meant bolting out the back door of the diner on foot. Brilliant ideas like that kept popping up in her head, even in her sleep-deprived state. Only one hour of sleep in the last twenty, not to mention it would be a while, maybe another twenty, before she found a safe bed to sleep in.

Sarah forced her eyes wide open as she slid into the window booth that overlooked her parking space. Remaining vigilant would be critical until her escape plan came together. Canada loomed a couple days drive to the north, but it got cold there in the winter, much worse than Maryland's Eastern Shore. A warm climate and a beach sounded better. Sleeping in a rustic bungalow and taking morning dips in the ocean had always been one of her dream vacations. She could see herself spending the day combing the beach barefoot in a sarong. And the Mexican border was only a couple hours away.

But her Mexican daydream collided with the reality that Hetherington would probably believe she was running from him, and he'd alert the border patrol to watch for her. In fact, all he'd have to do was put a trace on her passport. And anyone who had the necessary resources and motivation could intercept the web traffic on her cell phone. Henri Rothschild had access to resources like that, and maybe the Andrewses did, too – especially if they were in tight with someone at The Huntington. Getting lost in L.A. still looked like her best option.

Three cups of coffee, a Grand Salami Breakfast, two large orange juices, and one tall glass of water later, Sarah checked the time on her phone's display. It was almost nine o'clock. Still fatigued, yet somewhat refreshed, she drew a deep breath and let it out slowly. Staring out the restaurant window during the twilight hours she noticed the subtle changes that fell across the landscape as the sun crested a nearby ridge. The sky's evolving hues and the sun's gradient angles of light altered the texture of everything from distant boulders to close-up twigs on scraggly bushes. Even though L.A. teemed with the frenzy of modern urban life, its outskirts remained the habitat of leathery-skinned lizards that skittered in and out of shadows. The Basin was still in essence a desert, enchanting at dusk and twilight, not so much under the midday sun. Maybe there was a lesson for her in all of that.

Sarah asked the server for directions. It might be tricky finding a bank with access her accounts. But a supermarket that carried prepaid cell phones should be easy, and there had to be a place besides the airports to exchange her rental car. Apparently, all of that was a few miles down Foothill Boulevard – it actually became Huntington Drive just before the bank and car rental place. The knot in her shoulders unwound a turn when she realized the Foothill route led away from the freeway, deeper into L.A.'s patchwork of northern suburbs.

The server told her a convenience store up on Foothill carried prepaid cell phones. Foothill was the next left off Irwindale. When Sarah activated the throwaway phone, she used her old cell phone to move money from her bank account to her PayPal debit card. It might be safer for to use than a credit card. It was doubtful Detective Hetherington would think to put a trace on the PayPal account. On top of that, since there were no transactions in the last six months, it might not even show up if he searched the usual databases. Her final call on the old phone was to report her 'lost' credit card.

Sarah swallowed hard. Shutting off her old cell phone was like losing an old friend. Not that she had a lot of experience saying goodbye. Her relationships usually ended with nothing said. What she knew about all too well, though, were the hellos that were supposed to be but never were.

When Sarah got to the bank, she asked – in her capacity as trustee – to withdraw just under ten thousand dollars from Mom's trust account. Technically, it was her money, anyway, since Mom had passed away. Nine thousand nine hundred dollars fell just below the government's reporting threshold, and it would be enough that her PayPal card could be reserved for emergencies.

The knots tightened in Sarah's shoulders when the teller balked at letting her withdraw money from the trust account without approval from her branch manager – who was at lunch. The teller's maternal instinct kicked in, however, and she agreed to process the withdrawal when Sarah explained about her 'lost' credit card. Until the new card arrived, everything would have to be on a cash basis, including her motel. And spending a couple of nights on the streets of L.A. in her parked car with the doors locked would to too risky, being a young single woman. Of course there was always the risk that the replacement card wouldn't show up before her flight home. That meant the rental car agency would require her to pay cash to settle her account. Worse yet, if she had an accident in the meantime, the rental car company would demand the insurance deductibles be paid on the spot. It wasn't that she was a bad driver, but in L.A. traffic, anything could happen.

At the car rental agency, Sarah exchanged her light-colored sedan for a bright yellow economy coupe, explaining the cost of gas was killing her. After he flirted with her to the point she was looking to crawl under a rock with the local lizards to avoid any more harassment, the rental agent agreed to add the new charges to her old contract without running her credit card again. He also gave her a map and highlighted the route to Giddings Alley.

Chapter Twenty

Fatigue and lack of sleep tethered Sarah's feet to the sidewalks around Giddings Alley. It was worse than wearing ankle weights at the end of a five-mile run. Her eyes were pasty, demanding constant blinking to stay open, which created enough irritation to blur her vision.

By daylight, the neighborhood's intimidation factor dropped the way people told her evening temperatures were supposed to that time of year. There were no shadows at mid-morning from which night predators could pounce on their victims, the way they attacked Grandpa Lake. Nevertheless, someone wanted Sarah, and they probably wanted her dead. She could either fold, or pick herself up. The same as when her team was down two goals to none with the clock ticking off the final minutes of a lacrosse game. No one except her believed a hat-trick of miracle goals was possible. But she did it.

Sarah scoured the Giddings Alley neighborhood that had endured five decades of change since Grandpa Lake's murder, hoping to turn over some hidden trace of evidence. Maybe there'd be somebody at one of the community landmarks who'd known him, assuming there were any surviving relics of Pasadena's economic roller coaster that tracked all the way back to 1955. Possibly, someone would come forward whose memory stored some details of the night her grandfather died. After all, why else had Grandpa Lake beckoned there?

Her legs felt heavier and her shoulders drooped more as she walked down Hill Avenue toward Colorado Boulevard. Nothing looked like it might date back to the 1950s. At Colorado Boulevard, she turned right. The

City College campus to the left was overrun with so much new construction it offered little chance of finding anything historically significant.

But about two blocks down Colorado, something energized her. The building had undergone some modest cosmetic improvements, but the sign "Andy's Coffee Shop" looked as if it had been there since the beginning of time. Sarah crossed the street, not drawn by hunger or caffeine – she was beyond the point where that kind of stimulus would help – but she had new hope of digging up at least a tidbit about Grandpa Lake.

Inside Andy's Coffee Shop, patrons stood in line waiting to take their places at a row of booths along one wall, at a handful of bare-bones tables, or even at the horseshoe-shaped counter. Sarah opted for the counter, not wanting to take up a whole table others might need. As she slid onto a low-backed Naugahyde barstool, a menu, sans pictures, looked up at her from the chrome edged Formica countertop. The Mexican food on the menu caught her by surprise. A '50s style coffee shop ought to have more of an American flavor. But hey, it was Southern California.

She ordered scrambled eggs and wheat toast, to be polite, and asked the server how long the coffee shop had been at that location. The young Hispanic woman didn't know, but agreed to send the owner over after the morning crowd died down a bit.

Little Anthony and the Imperials Doo-Wopped in the background as Sarah studied the life-sized cut-out of Elvis in his signature gold lamé suit. The whole atmosphere brought a wistful smile to her face as she recalled Grandma Cassie groovin' to the Oldies and swaying to Doo-Wop tunes in her kitchen. Sarah's smile dissolved, though, recalling Mom sitting in a corner with her arms folded and her legs crossed, a scowl on her face.

Sometimes Grandma Cassie got fed up with Mom's moods, telling her to shake it off and move on. But, Mom never did.

When the owner, Yesenia, caught a break from the invasion of customers, she greeted Sarah with an energetic smile. But to Sarah's disappointment, Yesenia couldn't give her many details about the neighborhood's history. She'd only owned the place for a couple of years, but was hoping to bring it back to what it must have been like in its glory days decades before.

Poppy might help, though. He'd lived in the neighborhood for over fifty years. He always sat in the back corner booth with his family. Yesenia nodded over at the group seated there. They always came in about eleven o'clock and stayed for a while. Yesenia said she cleared the table when they arrived – literally. If people were sitting in Poppy's spot, they'd have to move. Yesenia knew Poppy would love to fill Sarah in on the neighborhood. And before Sarah could object, Yesenia made a b-line to Poppy's booth.

Sarah stared across the diner as Poppy turned and looked at her. He was a stoop-backed wisp of a man, with large, thick glasses and oxygen tubes laced over his big ears. He gave her a big-hearted smile and Sarah caught a glint in his eyes.

For the next hour, Poppy chatted with Sarah, painting a picture of the Giddings Alley neighborhood circa 1955. His daughter, Jackie, added a few anecdotes of her own. Sarah learned that a Ford dealership had been sandwiched between Colorado Boulevard and Giddings Alley since at least the late 1940s.

Poppy couldn't remember what took up the rest of the block back then, the part where the gas station and car wash stood. He had heard, though, that the Hill Avenue

Branch Library, across the alley from the car wash, had been there since the 1920s. Up until the College put in its lighted parking lots, the area would have been pitch-black at night, especially around the back entrance to the library.

Poppy shook his head when he told her that the neighborhood started going downhill in the early 50s. People stopped being the way neighbors should be. They started looking out for themselves instead of taking care of each other, and that was the end of the good old days – at least as far as Poppy was concerned. The alcove garden behind the library was unfenced in those days, providing a perfect cover for criminal activities.

Sarah took her opening to ask the $64,000 question. "My grandfather died on Giddings Alley over 50 years ago. His name was Lake Matthews. Did you ever hear of any murders around here back then?"

"As soon as I saw you I wondered if you might be his granddaughter. You have his emerald eyes. They always fascinated me. I've never seen another pair like them, until now."

"You know something about him?"

"At 94 years old you forget an awful lot. But I remember your grandpa as if it was yesterday."

"How? Did you know him very well?" Sarah's throat swelled as she choked back tears.

"Well, he wasn't around for very long, but I remember him because he volunteered with the Scouts at St. Anthony's Church. When he heard I'd been a scoutmaster back in Rochester, he pressed me pretty hard, trying to get me to help out. He said he couldn't do it all himself. I told him I thought he'd do a real fine job with the boys." Poppy adjusted his oxygen tubes. The loop had slipped off his left ear.

Sarah drew a deep breath and sucked her tears

back to where she could keep them at bay, at least for the moment. Being inches away from someone who knew Grandpa Lake flooded her body with adrenaline. She leaned closer to Poppy and peppered him with questions. "So you worked with him? Had he been a Scout before? Tell me what you remember about him." At some point, she looked over at Jackie, expecting to see traces of nostalgia in her eyes. Instead, Jackie was beaming. Her father radiated with life.

"No, I didn't work with him, but I did see him a lot in here. Seven-thirty sharp every morning he sat over there at that counter, maybe even on the same stool you were holding down – two eggs, crisp bacon and toast. He liked his coffee black and occasionally he splurged and had orange juice, too. We talked every day, but never for long. He'd come over and say "Hello" before he paid his check. I had to get to the shop by eight-thirty. He worked over at the college as a janitor, just biding his time, waiting for a teaching spot to open up." Poppy sniffed deep and took a long draw of oxygen.

Sarah gnawed the inside edge of her lip, waiting to hear more.

Poppy felt around the back of his ears to be sure his tubes were still where they belonged. "It shook us up pretty bad when he turned up dead in the alley. In fact, we'd invited him over to our place for Christmas Eve dinner and Mass, but he made some lame excuse. We liked having people over. Our big day was always New Years. We used to shuttle food and blankets up to the parade route where a bunch of us would sack out on the curb overnight, holding down our places." Poppy's eyes grew misty. "Your grandpa couldn't wait to see his first Rose Parade up close and personal. I really believed him when he said he'd be sure to make it that time. Those were the days."

Tears seeped up behind Sarah's eyes. She clamped down on her lower lip, trying not to cry. Poppy pressed his hand on hers. It was warm. She had expected his touch to be cold and frail.

Poppy locked onto her misty eyes. "Say, why don't you come by the house for dinner sometime? We don't cook like we used to. Marie isn't herself anymore. But I'm sure Jackie can scare up something decent." Poppy reached over and squeezed his daughter's forearm.

Sarah frowned. "I'd love to do that, but I'm only in town for a few days."

Poppy straightened his back as best he could. "Okay, it'll be tonight. That's how your grandpa missed out. He procrastinated. He passed up on Christmas Eve, but said he'd be there for New Years. But he never made it. We're not going to let you do the same."

Sarah grinned. "Okay then, let's do it tonight. What time and how do I find your place?"

Jackie wrote out directions on the back of a paper napkin and asked Sarah what she liked to eat.

Sarah said her tastes were pretty simple, nothing exotic.

Poppy reached over and took Sarah's hand again. "I lost one of my little girls. She was only twenty-eight. She was the most beautiful girl in the world."

Sarah squeezed his hand. "I'm sure you miss her very much, just like I miss both my grandpa and my father. But I lost them from the very start. I never knew either who they were."

Poppy's eyes misted. "Daughters need their daddies as much as daddies need their daughters. I was blessed with twenty-eight years of precious memories and you have none. I know it won't be the same, but maybe I can give you some of my memories of him to hold onto."

Sarah assured him she'd be at his house promptly at six.

He squeezed Sarah's hand. "You'd better be on time."

After Poppy and his family headed out the rear door of the coffee shop, Yesenia made her way over to the booth with another lead. She told Sarah to check out the library on Hill, just off Colorado. It was the same one Poppy told her about, across Giddings Alley from the car wash.

Chapter Twenty One

Sarah swallowed back tears and tried to picture Grandpa Lake, sprawled out dying on the grimy pavement behind the Hill Avenue Library. Did his attackers use the dumpster, or one like it, for cover before they ambushed him? Or did they pop out of the shadows half a block away, down by the used car lot, chasing him toward the library until they caught up with him and robbed her of her grandpa's hugs. She hoped some subtle detail would grab her attention and scream out, "I saw it happen." The lump in her throat grew into a gnarly knot as images of him dying all alone toyed with her head. He deserved better. Aloneness was her calling.

The library sat back from Hill Avenue, buffered by a neatly manicured lawn and forty-foot fern pines. A slight breeze could convert the grounds to an oasis in the heat of summer. Sarah grinned at the Spanish style adobe face, red tile roof, and mission design. Zorro might have borrowed books there over two hundred years ago. Grandma Cassie had a collection of old black-and-white Zorro episodes that she watched almost as often as she listened to her Doo-Wop albums.

Just a few steps inside, Sarah surveyed the white plaster walls covered with dark-stained shelves reaching halfway up to the mahogany beamed ceiling some fifteen feet above her head. Light from several tall arched windows on the exterior wall filtered over rows of time worn wooden tables and spread across the entry way to a librarian's desk. She approached the librarian and asked for information about the neighborhood's history, especially the period around 1950.

Pointing across the room to a small bronze faced man with a thin crown of silver hair, the librarian said,

"He's been in the neighborhood almost as long as the library. But he has a much better repository of local history in his head than you'll find on these shelves. His name is Juan. He's shy, but once you get him started he can talk about the area for hours."

Sarah whispered, "Thank you," and stepped, almost tiptoed, toward the table where Juan was reading a newspaper. She paused a couple feet from the table where he was sitting, and after a respectful silence said, "Hello, I'm Sarah." She continued watching him for a hint of acknowledgement.

He refolded the newspaper, making sure he maintained its original creases.

Sarah spoke again. "The librarian told me you might be able to help me."

He looked up at her. His eyes were dull.

She continued, "I'm trying to find out what this neighborhood was like back in the 1950s."

He looked down at the table, still not smiling. "Are you a teacher?"

"No, I'm –"

He interrupted. "A reporter?"

"No." Sarah caught her nervous chuckle before it left her throat.

"A cop?"

Sarah stammered, "Why no. I'm a – a writer."

"What do you write about?" He asked.

"Do you mind if I sit down?" Sarah pulled a chair back from the table.

"Sure, go ahead."

"You're Juan, right?"

"Yes, Ma'am."

"I want to write about how the neighborhood has changed – from what it was fifty years ago to what it is today." Sarah took a pad and pen out of her bag. "How long have you lived here?"

"You aren't going to ask me anything that will make trouble, are you?"

"Such as?" she pressed.

"Like complaining about the college buying up houses and stores and tearing them down."

"Has that been a problem?"

"Some people think so." He looked away.

"Do you think so?"

"I don't feel one way or the other." He continued to scan the room.

"How long have you lived around here?"

He looked down at the table. "Almost sixty years."

"Were you born here?"

He smoothed the newspaper with both hands. "I was left at the church when I was about seven. The priests raised me."

"Where's the church?"

He eyed the library's massive entry door. "The next block down Hill Avenue."

"So, do you still live with the priests?"

He kept staring at the entrance. "Yes, I take care of the gardens at the church."

"What's the name of the church?"

He looked straight at her, studying her eyes. "St. Anthony."

"So, what was the neighborhood like back then?"

"In the 50s?" He looked down at his hands.

"Yes, the 50s."

He looked back at her. "Everything was smaller – the college, the church, the shops. And there were more houses, but there were fewer people. We pretty much knew everybody."

"Not a lot of strangers?"

"Some." He shrugged.

"Did any stand out?"

He studied her eyes. "Sure you're not a cop?"

"No, I'm just curious what kind of people would hang around the neighborhood."

He kept focusing on her face. "College people mostly."

"City College?"

He smiled briefly. "Sure, and Caltech."

"Did you get to know any of them?"

His smile faded. "Not really, but there was one professor from USC. He spent a lot of time with the priests."

"What made him stand out?"

Juan looked down at the table.

"Was he a bad guy?" Sarah asked.

Juan looked away at a shelf of books.

"Did he hurt you?"

Juan looked back down at the table. "No."

"Did he hurt someone else?"

He kept his head down. "I shouldn't talk about this. The priests say that people's sins are between them and God."

"Did he hurt someone really bad?"

Juan shook his head. "The priest told me he couldn't talk about things people confessed."

"Did he hurt one of the priests?"

He bit his lower lip and looked away again.

Sarah saw a mist collect along the edges his eyes. She reached across the table and put her hand on his wrist. "Juan, tell me. Who did he hurt?"

Juan looked out the window. "What difference does it make? It was more than fifty years ago."

"Juan, my grandfather died on Giddings Alley just over fifty years ago." Sarah stood and walked around the table, planting herself in his field of vision.

Juan looked up at her. His face was contorted. "I'm sorry."

"My grandfather's name was Lake Matthews. My grandmother and my mother died not knowing what happened to him. That was a sin, too."

He shook his head. "The professor killed himself forty years ago. He got his punishment from God."

"Okay. If he's dead, we don't have to worry about his reputation anymore?"

Juan looked into her eyes. "It wasn't the professor who killed him."

"How do you know? Do you know who did kill him?"

"I can't break the priest's vow of silence. It would be a sin."

"Did you see it happen?"

He shrugged. "I just know it wasn't him."

"Did the professor know who did it?"

"I told you the professor's dead. He couldn't tell you even if he knew."

"Does the priest know who did it?"

"The priest died a few years ago, too."

"Juan, I need you to try to remember every detail that you can."

Juan shook his head. "I'm not sure there's anything more I can tell you."

"Juan, promise me you'll try as hard as you can. My life literally depends on it. Whoever killed my grandfather may have killed a second time. This time the police think I did it. If you don't help me, the real killer could get away with two murders, and I'll pay the price for both. Is that fair? Is that what you want to happen?"

"I don't know what I can do." The rows of creases on his face had multiplied.

Sarah reached out and cradled his calloused hands in hers. "Just try to remember. I don't want you to cause you any trouble, but you're the first person I've found who might be able to help. Just sleep on it. Can you meet me tomorrow for breakfast at Andy's Coffee Shop?"

A tired smile breached his face. "Machaca?"

Sarah smiled back. "Whatever you say."

"Okay."

"Oh – there is one more thing." Sarah glanced down.

"What is it?" Juan's question came out weakly.

"There's a name, Tyrone Wallace. Does it mean anything to you?"

Juan stared at the ceiling as if he was studying an invisible message carved into its beams. After a moment he looked back at Sarah. His eyes were blank. "No, Ma'am. I don't remember anyone by that name."

As Sarah left Juan at the library her legs found fresh energy. She had struck a mother lode of information about Grandpa Lake. It just had to be mined. That meant setting up camp near Giddings Alley for a few days. Her first stop was the City College bookstore to pick up a spare disposable cell phone and other supplies. Next, she walked back to the Starbucks on Hill Avenue where she'd left her car. The sight of it quieted the pulsing veins in her neck. No one had towed it away or broken in.

To make herself right with the world, or at least with the coffee company which had presumably suffered due to her violating the one-hour parking rule, she ducked in and bought a latté.

Chapter Twenty Two

Before showing up at Poppy's for dinner, Sarah checked in at the Vagabond Inn. It was just a block down from Andy's Coffee Shop on the opposite side of Colorado Boulevard. The clerk hassled her over leaving a credit card imprint. She lied again about her 'lost' card. He doubted her, but accepted cash to prepay a night's lodging. She refused to give him $100 more as a deposit for the house telephone and pay-per-view TV, arguing neither would get used.

When she got up to the room, Sarah fished Elliot's phone number out of her bag and dialed it on the disposable cell phone.

"Hi Elliot, it's me, Sarah."

"Where are you? Detective Hetherington is really pissed. He thinks you've gone fugitive."

"I guessed that would happen, so I can't talk long. But I really need your help."

"Can we meet somewhere and talk?"

She hesitated. "Okay, I'll call you when I get it figured out."

"Wait Sarah."

"What?"

"What's going on?" he pleaded.

"I went to the Giddings Alley neighborhood and found someone who might know who killed my grandfather. But I doubt Detective Hetherington will believe me just yet. I need to be sure I have solid evidence. And someone's after me in a real serious way. They want Grandma Cassie's journal, and they want it bad."

"Where are you?"

"We've probably talked too long already." Sarah

tapped End Call and strolled into the bathroom to drop the disposable cell phone in a sink full of water. It had given her one call to Elliot without her worrying that anyone would trace it. That was its job. The phone surrendered its last tiny air bubbles as she plopped down on the bed and started surfing the free TV channels.

At about half past five o'clock, Sarah clicked off the TV, freshened her sparse makeup and headed out for dinner at Poppy's. The thought of sitting around a dining room table like a family reminded her of watching reruns of *The Waltons* with Grandma. Sarah knew how family meals were supposed to work. She just hadn't enjoyed the experience often. Mom was rarely social. That left Grandma Cassie to share meals with. But Grandma wasn't usually hungry by the time she nibbled her way through cooking. Mostly, Sarah ate alone. Not much different from now, except now her approach to eating was more like grazing on whatever was handy, taking in just enough calories to kill her appetite. Back when she was growing up, Grandma made her clean her plate.

After Sarah turned north on Hill Avenue, she took a left at the third light and a right into an older, well-kept neighborhood. A few blocks later, Sarah parked in front of Poppy's 1960s vintage rambler. Jackie met her on the concrete driveway that ran along one side of the house. It passed under an awning which was not exactly a carport.

Jackie guided Sarah through a side door into the kitchen. A TV blared from the living room around the corner. That's where Poppy and Marie spent the bulk of their waking hours in matching recliners. Marie was a few years younger than Poppy, but pretty much out of touch with everyone else's world. Though it comforted her to know something was going around her.

The house was like Poppy, simple and not large.

When he heard their voices, he eased himself out of his recliner and dragged several feet of oxygen tubes behind him toward the kitchen. Jackie leaned into Sarah and whispered as she pointed down the hall, "He can get as far as the first bedroom without moving the tank."

Poppy shuffled up to Sarah and nudged her elbow to guide her over to a picture on the wall opposite the bedroom door. It was the first thing he saw when he got out of bed and headed to the bathroom. "She was a beautiful girl, only twenty-eight." He stared at the picture, neither smiling nor showing any pain or grief. "We miss her, you know." He looked up at Sarah.

"Yes, I can tell."

After a moment of silence, Poppy smiled and directed Sarah back through the kitchen to the dining table. "It's really good to have company again. I hope you like the food."

Everything about dinner was effortless, as if she was floating in a dream. In fact, being part of a family was a dream she only dared to entertain in rare moments of optimism.

Poppy might have read her mind. "Families are everything, but sharing them with friends is the best."

Sarah looked down at the table. "Yeah…"

Poppy continued. "I remember when I first came out here from Rochester, looking for work. I missed my girls. They stayed back home until I got settled. I was lucky. I found a job right away. In fact, I was offered four jobs."

Sarah smiled.

"Marie and the girls finally joined me. That made things a lot easier."

Sarah studied the lines time had carved on his face. Her smile faded. "It's good to be with the ones you love."

"The job was good, too, even if it took a while to work out some kinks. Some of the guys in the shop had careless streaks, and I was the quality inspector. One big guy threatened me the first time I rejected a piece he'd done. His size didn't scare me, though. I stood up and right in front of everybody I told him straight out, I had a job to do and nothing was going to make me go slack."

"I can see you doing something like that." Sarah grinned.

"Well, the next time he tried to test me I called the big boss over. I said to the both of them that it was my job to be sure everything that went out of that place was top drawer. And you know what the boss said?"

Sarah imagined that fifty years ago the fire in his eyes was no less intense than what it was right then.

"He said he wouldn't have it any other way. That was the last time I had any problems."

Sarah nodded, still smiling. "That's the way it should be."

"You know, Sarah, your grandpa could stand up for himself, too – when he was backed against a wall over something he thought was important."

Sarah looked down again. Her chest swelled, but she couldn't picture the object of her pride. The images she'd painted in her mind since childhood had been displaced by a grainy black-and-white clipping from a news article that reported his murder.

"He had this book – guarded it real close. Said some old woman gave it to him back during the war. She told him to learn from it and to protect it with his life. It was supposed to have belonged to Abe Lincoln, but it was never supposed to be put out to the public."

"You mean Lincoln's diary?"

"It was probably something of that sort. I never

read it. It didn't matter to me if it was or if it wasn't. As long as it worked for him, that's all that mattered. Your grandpa said something once about trying out a few notions he learned from it. He hoped, when he got his head straightened out, the girl he'd left back home would give him another chance. I suppose if it was something special like Mr. Lincoln's diary, he had a good reason to argue about it with that professor who used to drop by Andy's Coffee Shop now and then. Your grandpa and him went at it pretty hard just a few days before he got killed."

Sarah gulped. "What makes you think the professor was after the diary?"

Poppy looked at her hard. "Your grandpa said he'd hassled him over it before. Tried to buy it from him. But your grandpa told him. 'No sale.'"

Sarah's eyes pleaded for more.

Poppy continued. "Well anyway, there were stories after your grandpa died that some big shot had wanted the diary. Truth is, he gave it to me a week or so before he was killed and asked me to send it back to a lawyer in his hometown for safekeeping. At first, he asked me to drive him to the post office, but I told him I'd just drop it off for him. He offered to pay the postage – asked how much it was. I wouldn't take his money, though."

Sarah waited while Poppy took a couple long sniffs of oxygen.

He adjusted his tubes and went on. "After your grandpa turned up dead, everyone clammed up. I tried to get the detective to look into that professor, but I couldn't come up with any real details. Just the fact they'd argued. My best guess was the professor might have been involved with the Huntingtons. They're the biggest shots around here, and I hear they are big collectors of Lincoln stuff."

Sarah's face turned pale. The pieces were coming together, and it was looking more and more like she was neck deep in some kind of huge conspiracy.

Poppy reached for Sarah's hand. "Say I didn't mean to upset you. I was just trying to tell you what a good man your grandfather was. You know, good character runs in a family, and you've got your grandpa's blood in you."

Sarah smiled in spite of what held like anchors hanging from the corners of her mouth. "Thank you, Poppy. No one has ever told me anything that beautiful before."

Poppy's words echoed in Sarah's head on her way back to the Vagabond after dinner. For the first time in her life, the notion of keeping her bloodline flowing had her attention. It gave her the same warm feeling that came over her as a little girl when Grandma tucked her in bed at night. The thought of Elliot entering her life at just the right time had the same effect – the opposite feeling from her lonely room back at the Vagabond. Maybe stopping at the Starbucks on Hill Avenue could help her sustain the afterglow of her evening with Poppy's family.

The postage stamp sized lot was full, but Sarah smiled at her luck. Two men were coming up the steps from the coffee shop and angling toward a row of parked cars. The older man was stocky and well dressed. The younger one wore a hooded sweatshirt. He was tall with an athletic build.

At first, Sarah was too lost in her thoughts to take more than casual notice of the two men. But when she recognized the well dressed one, her eyes bulged and her heart seized up for a moment. When blood started flowing to her brain again, her heart started pounding like an arrhythmic bass drummer who'd run amok. It was Jackson Andrews, Jr. – she was sure of it. The tall one could be Henri Rothschild.

Sarah glanced away, hoping to become invisible by avoiding eye contact. Of course, that wouldn't do any good. So she looked back at the two men, scrutinizing their faces for the slightest tics.

As they crossed in front of her car, Andrews glanced in her direction and offered a polite smile. Sarah looked away again. It was dark. Parking lot lights reflected off her windshield's tinted glass. Maybe he didn't see her. But out of the corner of her eye, she thought the two men picked up their pace as they approached their parked car. And Andrews's polite smile had faded from his face.

Not wanting to wait for them to make the next move, Sarah pulled forward and turned her car into another lane of parked cars, edging away from Andrews's spot while keeping a keen eye on her rearview mirror. The breath trapped in her lungs filtered up out of her nose as the realization struck her – they hadn't turned back to follow her on foot, but that didn't mean she was safe.

Sarah continued to cycle through the remaining rows of parked cars as if searching for an empty space. Her shoulders knotted tighter with each turn of the steering wheel, and by the time she cycled back to Andrews's black Mercedes, her knuckles were aching and ash white. His engine was idling, and the car's backup lights told her he'd already shifted into reverse. His brake lights were glaring like beacons.

She hesitated, pretending to wait for him to back out of his spot. But it occurred to her that he might back up and block her path so he and Rothschild could jump out and charge her car. Not wasting another second, Sarah surged forward, bolting past Andrews's parking space. At the street, she launched her car into the sparse traffic heading south on Hill Avenue. A few moments later at Colorado Boulevard, she took a free right, but didn't stop when she got to the Vagabond. He might be tailing her.

After an hour of circling through the streets of Pasadena and neighboring communities, Sarah pulled into the Vagabond parking lot, convinced that Andrews wasn't following her.

Chapter Twenty Three

Sarah's morning shower cascaded down her face and washed over her body for an extra fifteen minutes while she plotted how to coax Juan into cooperating. He could be the first step in linking Moran's murder to Grandpa Lake's. And if she pulled that off, Hetherington would have to start taking her seriously. Not that being a murder suspect wasn't serious enough.

She continued fine-tuning her pitch while crossing Colorado Boulevard and walking another block to Andy's Coffee Shop. Along the way she checked the time display on her cell phone before stuffing it into her bag. – ten minutes until nine o'clock.

Twenty minutes later, Juan came through the door. He wasn't smiling. His face was pale, and he kept glancing over his shoulder as he approached her. A plain white business-size envelope dangled loosely at his side, pinched between the index finger and thumb of his right hand.

As Juan sat down across from her, he dropped the envelope on the table and pushed it toward her. His eyes were dilated as if he'd just come in from in the dark – except the morning was bright and crystal-clear.

"A man gave this to me out on the street," Juan said as he shifted his eyes back and forth from the envelope to the glass storefront. "He showed me a picture of you on his cell phone and told me to give it to you."

"What did he look like?" Sarah fumbled with the envelope as she started opening it.

"He was Caucasian, wearing a hooded sweatshirt and big sunglasses. He pushed the cell phone up to my face before he started talking, so I didn't get a good look at him."

Sarah started to unfold the single sheet of white paper. "Was he tall, short, young, old?"

"I didn't see him well enough to know how old he was." Juan studied the back of the paper Sarah was scanning. "Everybody looks tall to me."

Sarah covered her mouth as she gasped.

"Is it something bad?" he asked.

She dropped the paper onto the table and looked at the window, jerking her eyes back and forth to see if the man was still lurking out on the sidewalk. Half the men out there fit the sketchy description Juan gave her, except none wore hooded sweatshirts.

Juan stood up next to the table, staring at the note. It was a collage of block letters cut from a newspaper and magazines. He knew that wasn't a good thing. He didn't have to read what it said.

Sarah grabbed his wrist. "Don't leave Juan."

"Sorry Ma'am, this is way too dangerous."

"Please," she begged him. "Did he have an accent – like French, European or anything like that?" Henri Rothschild came to mind. After all, he looked like someone who could kill and she'd just seen him in the area the night before.

Juan shook his head as he pulled away from her and bolted toward the door, mumbling something. It wasn't clear whether he was answering her question, or if he was just saying, "No more. Don't ask me to say anything more."

Sarah watched Juan as he pushed through the door. She couldn't make herself call after him. Her whole body, even her tongue, felt dead.

After a moment, she looked down at the note. "GRANT PARK – MIDNIGHT – THE BENCH

BEHIND   BASKETBALL   COURTS   –   BRING
JOURNAL – NO GAMES."

"I don't have the journal," Sarah muttered under
her breath as a thick fog rolled through her head. How
had they found her so soon?

The server cleared her throat before asking for
Sarah's order. Sarah jerked around and stared at her in
silence. Once more, Sarah looked down at the threatening
message. The server asked again for her order.

Sarah kept studying the note. "I'm sorry. I'm not
really hungry anymore."

The server fumbled with her order pad. Sarah felt
the weight of her eyes staring down at her.

After a moment, Sarah gathered up the note and
envelope and stuffed them into her bag. When she slid to
the end of the bench she stopped and fumbled for her
billfold.

The server stepped back to make room for her to
stand.

Sarah tried to smile as she stood and laid a five-
dollar bill on the table.

Out on the sidewalk, Sarah decided it was time to
check out of the Vagabond. Getting rid of her rental car
seemed like a good idea, too – just in case they were
tracking it somehow. She felt like one of those fake ducks
in a shooting gallery – sitting on a rotating perch while
some strapping guy takes a shot and knocks it over to win
his girl a big bright purple stuffed toy.

But as Sarah waited for the pedestrian signal to
change, an idea hit her. She reversed course and headed
to the City College bookstore. After that, to a nearby
convenience store. Her shopping list included a few
supplies for making a fake copy of Grandma Cassie's
journal. A leather bound portfolio, an old fashioned
fountain pen and a bottle of beer were the key

ingredients. Just one can of cheap pilsner would do, but the clerk at the convenience store insisted on selling her a six-pack. Sarah shook her head. It wasn't like she planned to drink something that looked the color of pee.

With one can stashed in her bag, she discarded the rest in the dumpster behind the Hill Avenue Library. A quiet corner inside the library was just the spot to work on re-creating Grandma Cassie's journal. Except, she'd soft-pedal the references to Lincoln's diary, and Grandma's worries about the diary's authenticity needed embellishment. Henri Rothschild, or whoever was after her, needed to believe Grandma's journal wasn't important because it didn't validate the diary.

At six o'clock when the library closed, Sarah still had six more hours to make the fake journal seem as genuine as possible. She moved up Hill Avenue to Starbucks to continue her work. It was a riskier venue as evidenced by her close call the previous night. Keeping an eye out for Andrews and his companion slowed her progress, so she made up the time by substituting a latté and pastries for dinner. After finishing her journal's entries it was time to transform it into a decades old artifact. An old trick she recalled from one of her contract FBI assignments would come in handy.

The case involved a Russian antiquities dealer who tried to sell some Tsarist era manuscripts. He said the documents were spirited out of Russia shortly after the demise of the communist regime. He was accused of trying to pass off fakes as authentic relics. At first, the dealer insisted everything was on the up and up. But the FBI agent Sarah was interpreting for described the process the suspect used to make the fakes. The FBI lab proved the documents had been treated with ingredients that go into making pilsner beer. The lab even identified the exact American brand, the production lot and a dozen local stores where the beer had been sold.

The agent explained that after the dealer soaked the leather bound documents in beer and rinsed off the excess suds, he had run them through a clothes-dryer, or possibly, a microwave oven. The dealer was speechless. He knew they had caught him red-handed.

The notion of confessing gave Sarah a shudder as she stopped in front of the St. Anthonys Church, not that she was Catholic – though she'd been told there was a priest perched on one of the branches of her family tree. Sarah was a private person. Thinking that God or anyone else might know what was on her mind, even the idea that angels were watching her, creeped her out. And besides, if any of that stuff was true, they weren't using their eavesdropping skills to help get her out of trouble – were they?

Instead of passing through the massive entry doors to the sanctuary, Sarah circled around behind the church, scanning the other campus buildings for signs of life. A knot at the base of her neck unwound a bit when a short, lean man wearing a clerical collar and black shirt came out of the back door to the church. That meant she might escape the gauntlet of rituals the initiated use to detect outsiders entering their sanctuary.

The short, lean man smiled at her and introduced himself in a high pitched voice as Father Jim, parish priest. Sarah scrutinized his large crooked nose and cinnamon complexion. She hadn't expected to find a foreign missionary who resembled Gandhi overseeing a Southern California parish.

When Sarah described her predicament, Father Jim shook his head and invited her to his office. He pointed to a boxy two story building across a wide concrete sidewalk from the sanctuary. The knot in her neck dissolved completely. She didn't imagine they enforced secret rules for kneeling, dipping and crossing oneself inside an ordinary looking office building.

But disappointing God by forgetting to dip her fingers in the holy water as she entered the sanctuary would have been a light burden compared to the guilt complex Father Jim dished out when he grilled her about why she wanted to go to Grant Park at midnight. And her answer, "I'd rather not say," didn't win any grace from the parish priest.

Determined, Sarah crossed her arms and legs and insisted, "Look, I need to meet someone there. Someone with information about a missing relative."

"It doesn't sound like a friendly place to meet."

"I can handle it. I've gotten through most of my life pretty well on my own."

"Truthfully, what kind of trouble are you in?"

Sarah stared at him, her arms still folded tight across her chest.

Father Jim continued pressing her for an answer, but after a couple of attempts, he relented, acknowledging that he understood the concept of free will. He also told her he knew about the trouble people got into when they made bad choices, and when they ignore Godly counsel.

Sarah leaned forward in her chair and laid her hands flat on his desk. "Do you have a laundry. I need to rinse out a few things – maybe even a drier, too?"

He stared back at her, chewing on his reply.

Sarah squirmed in her chair. "I packed pretty light and these clothes are starting to get a bit grody."

"Look, Sarah, we get a lot of people coming through here looking for Band-Aid help. We try to get them to look at curing root causes to their problems, not just treating symptoms."

Sarah nodded, stifling an impulse to smirk. She didn't have any root causes.

Father Jim reiterated that he thought she was foolish to wander into a city park at midnight. With budget cuts, there was no lighting after ten o'clock – only security lights at the apartments across the street and streetlights along Cordova, which was half a block away from the basketball courts.

Sarah leaned back in her chair and studied her slender fingers. "My grandfather was murdered about a block from here back in the 50s. The police won't help me because they think it's ancient history. They have this idea that I'm just grasping at straws, getting in the way of their investigation into a recent murder. I'm meeting someone who has a lead for me. He's paranoid and doesn't want to be seen talking to me in public. And I don't know what he's worried about, anyway. The killer he's supposedly protecting is probably dead by now. That's all there is to it."

Father Jim leaned forward and folded his hands on top of his desk, shaking his head. "Yes we have a laundry. I'll show you the way. And if you need a place to stay, we can put you up for the night – or a few nights, whatever."

"Thank you, Father. By the way, there's one more thing if you don't mind."

His smiled receded. "Yes?"

"I think your gardener knows something about my grandfather's murder."

Father Jim sat back in his chair and studied her eyes. "Do you mean Juan?"

"Yes."

"How would he know about that?"

"I think he saw it happen. Or at least he knows someone who did."

Father Jim leaned over his desk again, bowing his head. He muttered something she couldn't decipher.

Sarah stared at the top of his head. "I need his help."

Father Jim looked up and expelled nearly all his breath, saving just enough to mutter, "Juan is missing."

Sarah shook her head. "Are you sure?"

"He's always in his quarters at nine o'clock sharp every night. By six in the morning he's in the yard tending the plants. Sometimes he leaves for an hour or so, but he always tells someone where he's going and when he'll be back. It's usually to the library, next door." A faint smile broke out on Father Jim's face. "I think he feels guilty when he leaves us unattended."

Sarah rubbed her forehead. "Well maybe he just decided he needed some space."

"But no one has seen him since he went to meet a friend around nine o'clock this morning. Nothing like this has ever happened before."

"I may be the one he met this morning. I saw him at the library yesterday afternoon. That's when he told me about Grandpa Lake's murder and agreed to let me buy him breakfast."

Father Jim stood up. "He's never said anything about any kind of murder to me."

"He told me he couldn't talk about it because he was protecting a priest's vow of silence." Sarah focused on a crucifix hanging on the wall behind Father Jim.

"Did he say which priest?"

"No, only that he's dead." Sarah studied Father Jim's eyes. "Would he still have to honor the priest's vow if the priest who swore it was dead?"

"It's a matter of conscience for Juan," he said. "Laymen don't have a duty to maintain a privilege like we in the clergy do."

"I hope I didn't dredge up a bunch of bad memories that he's beating himself up over."

"Does your meeting tonight have anything to do with Juan?"

"No."

Father Jim picked up his office phone.

"What are you doing?"

Father Jim glared at her. "I'm reporting a missing person."

"Please, don't mention anything about me."

Father Jim put down the phone. "What are you hiding?"

"Nothing, I swear. He was fine when he left me. Just a little upset, that's all." She hoped he didn't notice that twitch in her eye.

Father Jim picked up the phone again. "Just to be safe, I'm filing a missing person's report, anyway."

"It would still be a good idea if you didn't mention me. The police aren't exactly taking me seriously right now. You don't want my baggage getting in the way of them finding Juan."

Father Jim lowered his head. "I can leave you out of it for now, but if someone gives me the smallest reason to involve you, all bets are off."

"Is there anything I can do to help you look for Juan?"

Father Jim shook his head. "No, I think you have enough on your plate tonight."

"I'm terribly sorry."

As Father Jim guided her to the laundry, he explained that Grant Park was just a couple of blocks away. She couldn't miss the tennis courts at the corner of Cordova and Chester Avenue. Going left down Chester, she'd pass the tennis courts and a narrow service road that led to the basketball courts.

But before he let her go, Father Jim insisted that he'd be waiting up until she was safely tucked in bed. If that didn't happen by one o'clock, he'd call the police. Confidentiality wouldn't be a consideration. He said she wasn't Catholic, so the rules didn't apply.

Sarah wasn't sure about his version of the rules, but she didn't argue.

Chapter Twenty Four

At a quarter till midnight, Sarah tucked the phony journal into her bag. It looked genuine enough. And most of the beer smell disappeared after a baking soda bath and a second round in the clothes dryer.

Keeping her eyes peeled, she crossed Holliston Avenue heading west on Cordova toward Grant Park. Being early wasn't part of the plan. It was an impulse, a tribute to Poppy's work ethic. Of course, the sooner her stalker was happy, the sooner he'd leave her alone. Maybe he'd be early, too. And there was another reason to get back to the church. What if Juan had run away because of her?

She took steady breaths of the stale night air along Cordova Avenue, a wide, lighted street lined with trees, bungalows, box houses and low-rise apartments. Interior lights filtered out of several windows, suggesting a few people might be struggling to sleep on what had turned out to be an unseasonably warm night. They'd be able to hear her screams if things got out of hand. Her pace slowed and her heart pumped faster as stories filtered through her head about people getting mugged in broad daylight, surrounded by diffident bystanders. So there was no guarantee anyone would help her. She scanned the shadows for anything that didn't belong.

At the Chester Avenue intersection, her heart went into overdrive. It was a narrow lane with no streetlights. The trees that bordered both sidewalks arched toward the middle of the street, creating the illusion of a vortex that led into another world. The perfect place for the black-cloaked Lincoln aficionados to pop out of the darkness and start chasing her.

A short distance past the tennis courts she craned

her neck and peeked between rows of shrubs that framed the opening of a path into the park. Her heart pounded inside her chest as she stepped back, calculating her approach. A second path appeared to veer off just a few yards further down the sidewalk. It was wide enough to be the service road Father Jim mentioned. She took slow, deep breaths and edged her way in its direction, clutching her bag close to her side.

From the sidewalk she saw a bench not more than five yards down the service road. It as in plain sight even in the darkness. Was her stalker close enough he could hear her heart thumping?

Sarah looked at her cell phone. It was ten minutes before midnight. A noise. She jerked around, stepped back from the opening and held her breath, trying to block out every distraction in case the sound returned. Her eyes scoured the darkness.

There it was again. It came from behind a low picket fence just to her right. She swallowed her breath. Maybe it was only a squirrel rummaging through the dumpster behind the fence.

Proceeding down the service road, Sarah inhaled a long draw of night air and let it out slowly. Her steps were short and light. In spite of that her foot kicked up some loose gravel. The pebbles rattled as they skidded away along the asphalt path. She crept past the bench, her eyes darting back and forth, scanning for the slightest movement around her. To her right were the outlines of two basketball half-courts painted on a concrete pad at the edge of the tennis courts. No mistake about it. This was the place. Sarah took another deep breath, exhaling it without hesitation.

Surveying as much of the park as she could make out from the edge of the basketball courts, nothing caught her attention. Her cell phone display read eight minutes before midnight.

Then came another noise. Maybe something or someone moved about twenty yards beyond the basketball courts near some kind of structure – a picnic shelter, or maybe restrooms.

Sarah froze. Only her eyes moved, trying to track whatever had snagged her attention.

A cell phone rang from somewhere behind her.

She spun around. Its tone was synchronized with a light that flashed from the park bench. Should she answer it? The ringing stopped, but just for a moment. When it started ringing again, she dashed over to the bench and stared down at the display. The word "Blocked" glared back at her. The cell phone continued to ring.

When Sarah answered, it was the same garbled voice she'd heard on the other occasions – the night Agents Salazar and Conrad intruded on her at dinner, the other afternoon in the Sheriff's parking lot, and the night she bolted from the Hilton. "You're early."

"I know."

"Do you have it?"

Sarah's spine quivered. The tiny hairs on the back of her neck stood up like quills rising through her flesh. This person was a killer and he was watching her. Did she dare lie to him?

"I asked if you have the journal."

She hesitated for a moment. "Yes."

"Take the phone and walk across the park. I'll call you when you get to the other side."

"No."

"What did you say?"

Her whole body trembled. "I'll leave the journal right here, next to the phone. You can come and get it when I'm gone."

"I'm in charge here. Do you understand?"

Sarah reached into her bag and fumbled for the phony journal. A whiff of beer vapors gave her pause. Or was it her guilt-ridden imagination? She flipped the phone shut and dropped it on the park bench along with the journal. After making a quick scan of the area, she bolted. If she could just make it back to Cordova Avenue without hearing the footsteps of some oversized goon closing in on her.

Sarah had only taken half a dozen steps out onto Chester when a figure streaked into the intersection at Cordova. He stopped short under the streetlight and squared around to look at her. She couldn't see his face. He wore a hooded sweatshirt.

Both stood frozen, silently sizing each other up. He was the hunter and she was his prey.

He drew his shoulders back and headed toward her, calculating his steps.

She stole a glance to each side, straining to see as much as possible without losing track of him. A quick peek over her shoulder down Chester told her she was toast if he wasn't alone. Her mind whirled, processing all of her options for escape. Trying to race him through the park wouldn't work. Besides, that's where he was trying to lead her. But turning and running away from him, deeper into the devil's tunnel, sent a new chill down her spine.

He picked up his pace as he closed in on her.

Sarah clutched her bag to her side and focused on his gait. There'd be a gait. Everyone has a gait. She knew about gaits from more than a hundred lacrosse matches and what seemed like two lifetimes worth of practices.

He started to trot halfway down the block.

She measured the cadence of his steps, the length of his gait.

He was a quarter block away.

She watched his lateral movement. Few people run straight up and down. Most sway side to side. There's a pattern to the lateral movement and a variance off of center. She had his measured.

He was ten feet away.

She centered herself and anchored her feet, just as if she was loading a spring.

He threw both arms out to his sides and tilted his torso forward, committing to a line of attack. A hint of light reflected off something in his right hand.

She dodged right as he made a sweeping arc with his right hand. Her pelvis caught his hip, throwing him off balance.

He reached back and across his body as he changed directions in mid-air.

Something stung her back..

They both tumbled to the ground.

In one continuous motion Sarah lifted herself off the pavement and tried to launch into a sprint.

He grabbed at her ankle, collecting the hem of her pant leg in his vise-like grip.

Chester Avenue was no lacrosse field and her opponent wasn't constrained by any rules. She kicked at him with all her strength as he jerked on her leg. He was relentless like a jackal gnawing its uncooperative prey into submission. The stinging on her back was swallowed up by a dull ache as he started crawling up her leg.

Sarah twisted onto her back so she could kick with more power.

He deflected her assault with his right forearm as he clung to her leg with his other hand. The shiny object still glistened in his right hand.

Voices broke out up at the intersection. Sarah could tell that one had an accent, a high pitched one like Father Jim's. She wasn't sure what they were saying.

The attacker froze and looked toward the voices.

Sarah launched her foot at his head, catching him square in the jaw.

His head snapped back and he lost his grip.

Even while scrambling to her feet she started sprinting toward the voices.

Father Jim and another priest ran toward her.

With her arms wrapped around Father Jim, she looked over her shoulder to see her attacker running into the park. The other priest followed him as far as the basketball courts.

Sarah's knees went wobbly as she pressed her forehead into his chest and gasped for breath. Her voice cracked. "I'm fine."

Father Jim stroked the back of her head.

"I thought you weren't going to follow me," she protested. Her words were muffled by his coat.

"Forgive me, Father, for I have sinned," he whispered in reply. "I lied."

Sarah shook her head. "He'll come back, you know."

"At least you're alive for them to come back to."

Sarah leaned back without breaking his hold, giving herself just enough freedom to wrap her arms around herself and rub off a chill that didn't belong to the stale night.

"Is 'thank you' in your vocabulary?" Father Jim stared at her.

"Thanks," Sarah said in a quiet voice.

Father Jim slid his hand down to the small of her back and nudged her close again.

Sarah flinched.

"Are you sure you're okay?" he asked.

She reached back to massage the soreness and flinched again. As she brought her hand forward, the source of her pain was obvious. Her hand was smeared with blood.

Father Jim's voice pitched higher. "You're hurt."

Sarah yanked around, trying to take a peek at the wound.

Father Jim leaned in for a closer look.

"We'd better get you back to the church and take care of that. You might need to see a doctor."

"No doctors." Sarah stared hard into his eyes.

Father Jim pulled off his clerical shirt, rolled it and pressed it into the wound. "We'll try to fix it. But I can't make any promises."

"Can we get the journal first?" She took hold of the shirt and continued applying pressure, freeing Father Jim's hand.

Father Jim gestured toward the service road and watched her take a few steps before he followed.

At the bench, Sarah hesitated, not sure whether to take the cell phone as well. She stared at it as if it might bite her hand when she picked it up. The slight chance the phone could yield some fingerprints or DNA played on her mind. At last there'd be evidence to corroborate her story for Detective Hetherington – that is if he gave her a chance to tell it. She looked at Father Jim. Her eyes begged for guidance.

He smiled and nodded. "Maybe you can convince the detective it's evidence."

After debating with herself a bit more, Sarah bent over and picked up the cell phone. If nothing else, it would keep the phony journal company in her bag.

As they walked back to St. Anthony's Church,

Sarah looped her spare hand around Father Jim's elbow. "Is it okay if I hold on to you?"

He smiled and nodded. "Are you sure you're all right?"

Sarah brought the bloody shirt around and inspected it. "The bleeding seems to be slowing."

Father Jim stopped to pull up her shirt so he could check out the damage. "It looks a little iffy. You might need some stitches. But that's not what I meant."

She rolled up her shirttails a few inches and cinched them around her stomach to hold the makeshift bandage in place. "Absolutely no hospital. A couple of butterfly bandages should do the trick. It can't be as bad as some of the slashes I've gotten from lacrosse."

Again he asked, "Sarah, are you all right?"

She looped both hands around his forearm and looked up at him. "Truthfully? I'm scared to death."

"Wouldn't you be safer in police custody?"

She pulled away without letting go of him. "What? Locked up in a tiny cell waiting for them to stick a needle in my arm. No thanks. Detective Hetherington is as much a danger to me as that stalker."

Father Jim cupped his hands over hers and squeezed. "That's going to require some explanation."

Sarah started to whimper.

Father Jim drew her against his chest and held her tight.

She kept her face pressed against his chest and convulsed with tears, intermittently gasping for breath.

Father Jim kept stroking her head. Now and then he tilted it back so he could wipe tears from her cheek.

When she was all cried out, Sarah leaned back and looked straight into his eyes. "I just want to go home. I don't belong here. What in Hell is happening to me?"

Father Jim drew her close again. "Those who endure the hardest preparation are called on to finish the greatest tasks. I don't know what you've been called to, but rest assured, you won't have to go through it alone."

Sarah buried her head in his coat and muttered, "Did you find Juan?"

Chapter Twenty Five

When Juan shuffled into the kitchen the next morning, Sarah and Father Jim kept their conversation on track without the slightest pause. Juan slid into the chair nearest the door, keeping his head down. He didn't even peek at them.

Sarah had spent the last hour schooling the priest on the basics of lacrosse. She had come clean with him about all the details of her predicament while he was changing her bandage earlier. The issue of Juan's whereabouts and well-being would have occupied their attention, but each of them heard him shuffling back to his quarters just before daybreak. Father Jim was an early riser by habit, and Sarah's throbbing wound had kept her awake most of the night.

After several minutes of glancing furtively in Juan's direction, Father Jim got up and eased his way over to the old gardener. He squatted across the table as if trying to find a pathway into Juan's field of vision.

Juan kept his head down, avoiding eye contact with the priest.

Father Jim straightened up to look at Sarah. "So Sarah, what are your plans?"

Sarah nodded to the priest and turned to study Juan's slumped figure. "I have to prove to Detective Hetherington that the Andrewses have killed before. That'll make it easier for him to see they could have killed again."

Sarah joined Father Jim standing next to Juan and leaned over, trying to make eye contact with the old gardener. But she didn't fare any better than the priest had. She turned away and held up her hands in mock surrender. "And I have to convince whoever's chasing me that Grandma Cassie's journal isn't worth their effort."

Father Jim bent down again trying to catch Juan's eyes. "Now look son, I understand you made a vow, but it isn't necessary for you to keep it. It's not your job to protect the priesthood, especially when your silence helps a killer."

Juan still refused to make eye contact with him

Sarah chimed in. "And you're putting an innocent person in jeopardy."

Juan rubbed his hands. "You don't understand, neither of you do."

"What don't we understand?" Father Jim asked.

"She's not the only one in jeopardy. My life is worthless if I help her."

Father Jim palmed the back of his neck. "How?"

Juan's eyes were bloodshot and his face was drawn. "Yesterday, he came back and threatened me."

"Who came back?" Sarah asked.

"The one who gave me the note."

"Was it the man who killed my grandfather?"

Juan shook his head. "He was a young guy. He said he worked for powerful people who could kill me and get away with it."

Sarah walked in front of Juan and looked him straight in the eye. "Where were you last night?"

"I – I saw what the note said. I went to the park after dark and hid behind some bushes across the street. I wanted to protect you, but I got scared when I heard all the commotion. It was like I got paralyzed. I stayed there until everyone was gone."

"After that?" Father Jim pressed.

"I spent the night at a shelter. I was too ashamed to come back here. It was the second time I failed." Juan buried his head in his hands and moaned.

Father Jim draped his arm around Juan.

Sarah folded her arms across her chest and gritted her teeth. "You said it was the 'second time.' What was the first?"

Juan blurted through his sobs. "If I hadn't been such a coward I might have saved your grandfather."

"What do you mean?"

Juan began blubbering out his secret. "On the night he died, I had been hanging out around the library with a friend – a girl the priest had warned me to stay away from. We were making out in the garden on the other side of the library when we heard a man yell for help. He sounded like he'd been hurt bad. I peeked around the corner into the alley and saw two men running toward us. We hunched up against the library as low as we could so they wouldn't see us. They ran behind the library and out onto the sidewalk toward the church. I recognized one of them. He was the professor."

"And you didn't go help the poor guy who was hurt?" Sarah glared at him.

"My girlfriend ran home and called for help. But I told her not to get involved. I was afraid the priest would kick me out of the church if he found out I was still seeing her."

Sarah bit down hard on lower lip.

"I followed the two men to the church. I heard them talking to the priest. The professor wanted to call the police. His bully friend slapped him and told him he wasn't going to throw his life away over some sentimental fool who wouldn't follow through on a deal. The priest told them he was calling an ambulance. When he started to dial the phone, the bully told the professor they should get out of there. When they came out of the priest's office, they caught me listening outside the door. The bully shoved a closed-up switchblade into my hands. I looked at it. My thumb slid across the wet blood. It nearly fell out of my hands. The bully laughed and said I'd been stupid enough to touch a murder weapon. I had a dead guy's blood on my hands. He made me bury it in the garden and said if I ever snitched, he'd dig it up and give it to the police. They'd find my fingerprints on it and send me to the gas chamber. He said it was just as well. I should have never come across the river, anyway. This wasn't my country."

Sarah glowered at him as she asked. "Had you ever seen the bully before?"

"No. But the professor came to mass regularly, up until that night."

"Have you seen the bully since that night?" She held her cold, hard stare.

"Only once. He and his son threatened me one New Year's Eve before the Rose Parade a long time ago. A couple of police stepped in. But first, the bully told me that his son would make sure I kept quiet, even after he was roasting in Hell."

"Was it his son who gave you the note at Andy's?"

"No, that guy was a lot younger. But, he could have been a grandson. He was tall like the bully."

"You said he worked for powerful people. Did he say who?" Father Jim asked.

"Only that they had more money than I could imagine. He said they've bought politicians all over the world, and they owned railroads and banks. He said they're so powerful they even have streets named after them. So it would be nothing for them to turn me into dust."

"Why don't we go dig up the knife?" Sarah

started walking toward the door, expecting Juan to follow.

"He already made me dig it up and give it to him."

She turned around. Her opened wide. "Who made you?"

"The man who gave me the note. He said he was going to use the knife on you and after he did, he could help the police trace the knife back to me. So I'd better keep quiet."

"How did he know about the knife?"

"I don't know."

Sarah stomped back to where Juan was sitting. She leaned over and got in his face. Her voice strained like an over-wound violin string. "If you were so afraid to tell the truth all these years – so afraid that you let my grandfather die and so scared that you would have let that goon kill me too – why are you telling us all this now?"

"I stayed awake all last night, ashamed of who I am. I decided I don't want to die a coward. I realized that spending an eternity in heaven knowing that I'm nothing but a scared worm – that would be worse than burning in Hell."

Sarah looked down and shook her head.

The disposable telephone in her bag started ringing. It had to be the one from the park because her old phone was turned off. "Damn," she muttered. "I forgot to turn it off." When she reached into her bag and pulled it out, the display read the same as before, "Blocked."

Sarah flipped the cell phone open.

"Hello."

The voice on the other end was garbled, just like before. "That was very bad form."

"I tried to give you what you wanted. What was your problem?"

"I make the rules."

"Then go find someone else to play with."

"Cute. But you have something I want."

"It's not what you think it is."

"Really?"

"It doesn't say where the diary is, and it doesn't say what's in it. It just says my grandma's crazy ex-boyfriend bragged about having a diary that belonged to Abraham Lincoln."

"But your grandmother believed it was real."

"All of us Morgan women are crazy. Aren't I proof of that?"

The voice laughed. "You're ballsy."

"Sorry that's neither standard equipment nor an option on this model."

He laughed again, an icy laugh that sent a chill up and down Sarah's spine. "I always get what I want. Next time, no funny stuff."

Sarah flipped the phone shut. She looked at Father Jim and shrugged.

"Well?" Father Jim asked.

"Well, it was the guy from the park. He really wants Grandma Cassie's journal."

"Did he set up another rendezvous?"

"Not yet, but I need to get ready for him when he does."

Father Jim disagreed. "It's time we got the police involved."

"I told you that won't work. They think anything I tell them is just a decoy to throw off their investigation of Dr. Moran's murder."

Father Jim grinned. "Come on now, I'm a priest. Why wouldn't they listen to me?"

"Are you kidding, Father?" Sarah countered. "Don't you follow the news? I don't want to offend, but you guys don't have the best of reputations these days. And besides, they'll just say I've conned you."

Juan stood up and threw his shoulders back. "I'll do whatever you say."

Sarah's scrutinized the old gardener's face. After several moments of holding a grim expression on her face, she smiled. "I guess I can give you one more chance. As I recall St. Peter got three." She turned to Father Jim. "Do you have a credit card?"

"I have one for the church."

"If I pay you back in cash, would you mind going shopping with me?"

Panic registered all over his face. "Hey, I'm celibate. I don't have to go shopping with women."

Sarah couldn't stop herself from laughing out loud.

He winked. "I guess I can charge it to the Benevolence Fund."

"No worries. I'm good for it. And what I have in mind is probably beyond your budget, unless the Vatican has loosened up these days."

Father Jim winced.

After visiting a wireless store and the spy shop a few doors from Andy's Coffee Shop, Sarah and Father Jim were back at St. Anthony's. They'd bought a netbook computer with internet service, a cell phone just like the one Sarah had turned off when she went into hiding, and a 'buttoncam' – a hidden camera she could wear under her blouse. The wireless accounts were set up in Father Jim's name.

Sarah showed the priest how to track the new cell phone using an application on her old phone. Since she'd be leaving the old one with him they also covered how to access her Contacts. In the process, Sarah had to explain to Father Jim about the couple dozen voicemail messages from Angela on her old cell phone – which she insisted on ignoring. The priest bristled at her rudeness, but that didn't phase her.

One of the contacts she pointed to on her phone was Detective Hetherington. His phone number and email address would come in handy if Father Jim had to call in the cavalry to help Sarah out of a jam. Of course that assumed the detective would care about her health and welfare.

She told Father Jim he should only call Hetherington if he received a distress message from her, or if he saw something bad going down on the video feed she'd be broadcasting back to the church from her buttoncam over the internet. When he had a handle on all the details, they switched phones. Father Jim took her old one, Sarah took the new one with a copy of her Contacts.

With the phones configured, Sarah set up the buttoncam which included replacing the buttons on her blouse with ones that matched the lens on the camera. Fortunately, one of the buttonholes lined up pretty well with the V in her bra. Her small breasts never got in her way on the lacrosse field, but for this purpose, it seemed that a little more cleavage might have been helpful. Sarah buttoned up one notch above the camera, just in case her stalker was the kind of guy who liked to stare at exposed flesh.

Sarah explained that she'd only be able to broadcast the video feed if her computer was close enough for it to receive the wireless signal. About a hundred feet. But the internet connection shouldn't be a problem since the computer came equipped with a built in dial-up connection.

"You'll be able to monitor the webcam on my cell phone with this app." She pointed to an icon on her old phone's display.

"So." Father Jim's patience had worn thin. "If you want my help, you have to let me in on what you're planning – every detail. And if anything changes, you have to clue me in."

"Okay. I'm going back to Redlands to start narrowing down the field of suspects. I think I'll start by finding out everything I can about Dr. Burgess and his secret society. And, I need to bring Elliot into the loop. His phone may be tapped at this point, so I need to talk to him face-to-face."

"So I'm supposed to use all this technology to keep tabs on you."

"You've got it, Father."

"I can handle that."

"Oh, and one more thing."

Father Jim cocked his head.

"If you see Angela's name show up on the display, ignore it. No matter how many times she calls."

Father Jim grimaced. "Wouldn't a friend who's that concerned deserve a little more trust?"

"Look Father, please just ignore her. Hopefully, she's filled my voice mailbox with messages already, so anyone else who tries to get in touch will just hit a dead end – communication-wise that is."

Chapter Twenty Six

Sarah tasted the adrenaline rushing through her veins as she scurried out to the church parking lot. Grandpa Lake's killer, Dr. Moran's killer, the diary, the guy who was after Grandma Cassie's journal – they all had to be connected. But how? Or were they were in fact one and the same.

Father Jim insisted Sarah take his car. Whoever was stalking her wouldn't recognize it. And it was exactly what she expected for a priest – an inconspicuous, light blue, hybrid coupe. There were plenty of them on the road. Almost as many of them as there were light-colored sedans.

She opened the navigation app on the new cell phone and entered her destination. So much for the priest's rules, but how was he going to know about it? Anyway, if he did find out, it wouldn't be the first time someone ragged on her for adlibbing. The lacrosse girls whined about it regularly. Of course scoring a goal helped them get over it fast. That's another reason they always let her play first home position.

San Marino's stretch of Huntington Drive reminded her of women who wore distressed denims and Akoya pearls to their weekly pedicures. For them, money was more of a cachet than something they flaunted. The two-lane-wide median and it's understated landscaping served the same purpose. Why use two lanes of prime real estate when a yellow stripe would get the job done, unless you were trying to make a subtle point. The area's architecture was no different – a fusion of Spanish mission and new world capitalism. It was the perfect setting for Jackson Andrews' office.

Without much difficulty, Sarah found a diagonal

parking space right in front. The solid door just feet from the curb meant that Andrews wouldn't be tipped off before she walked in, unless he was in the habit of peeking through the bay window's drapes to check out the sound of every idling car. Even in that was the case, he'd be out of luck. Father Jim's hybrid coupe could run over someone and not be heard.

Sarah studied the office layout as she eased the door open. Andrews was in plain sight, conferring with his assistant about the day's schedule. He jerked back when he looked up and saw her walking through the doorway.

"Sorry to barge in unannounced." Sarah grinned.

Andrews forced a smile. "Not at all, Ms. Morgan. But, I only have a couple of minutes. What can I do for you?"

"Can we have a minute in private?"

"Certainly. This way." He ushered her down a narrow hallway into his inner sanctum and closed the door. "What's this about?"

"I want to talk about the diary."

He pointed to a cozy arrangement of leather stuffed chairs and a coffee table in the corner. "Have a seat."

"That's not necessary. I won't be long."

Andrews held out both hands inviting her to get to the point. "Well?"

"I came to tell you that it belongs to me and I want it back."

Andrews coughed back his surprise. "To start with I don't have it, and to end with you're not in any position to make demands." He walked to his desk and reached for his telephone.

"You know where it is, and you're not in any

position to do that." She pointed to his phone.

"Oh, really?" He picked up the receiver.

"I have a witness who will testify that your father killed a man some fifty years ago. The victim happened to be my grandfather."

Andrews froze. She watched his eyes grow big as his mouth tried to form a response.

"That's right, and I imagine you know exactly what I'm talking about."

Andrews put down the phone. "That's ridiculous."

"Why? Because you think you can keep scaring that poor gardener into keeping quiet."

"What, some illegal who's looking to trade his way out of deportation?"

"He was an eye witness."

"You're splitting hairs. The truth is there's no corroborating physical evidence."

Sarah figured he already knew all about the knife, including where it was at that very moment. "You've thought this thing through. I can see that. Which means you know your father's guilty. Now all you have to decide is how much of a risk you're willing to take – now that a witness is willing to talk. And I think they call your behavior for the last several decades something like 'conspiracy after the fact.'"

"You came here to blackmail me."

"All I want is Lincoln's diary. Your father stole my grandfather from me. The least you can do is give me back the only piece of him he left behind."

"What makes you think I have it?"

"I'm betting you and your father were behind Moran's murder. And it only makes sense that the killer has the diary."

"That's logical, but it's just a guess."

"It's more than a guess. Whoever's been

hounding me to get my grandmother's journal never bothers to ask for the diary. He knows I don't have it because he does."

"Now I'm not the one hounding you, and I didn't kill anyone. But let's say I can get my hands on the diary. Can we make a deal?"

"The only deal I'll make is that I'll ask Juan to keep his secret."

"I'll need some time."

"How long?"

"A couple of days."

Sarah planted her hands on her hips. "I've got your number. I'll be in touch. In the mean time just remember, I'm not as afraid of the cops as you should be. Detective Hetherington and his uncle have wanted to solve my grandfather's murder since before I was born. And the older they get, the more important that becomes. I'm sure it's more important to them than finding Moran's killer. Of course, one could make the case that when you've solved one murder, you've solved them both."

"What makes you say that?"

"Both murders had the same motive, Lincoln's diary."

"My father and I both have alibis."

Andrews's cold stare gave Sarah the chills, but she camouflaged her reaction with her own steely glare. "We'll just have to see how well they hold up."

"I'll see you out."

"Don't bother, I can find my own way."

When Sarah stepped out onto the sidewalk, she looked back and peeked at the window to see if anyone was peering though the drapes. She didn't expect anyone would be, since Andrews didn't follow her into the lobby, and his assistant was preoccupied with computer issues.

Without wasting a stride, Sarah jumped into Father Jim's car and pulled into traffic. At the first intersection, she made two quick rights and cruised the alley behind Andrews's office. About halfway down the alley, an inconspicuous parking spot was perfect for her purposes. Shutting off the ignition and slumping behind her steering wheel reminded her of one of those stakeout scenes from the old TV police shows Grandma Cassie used to watch.

But unlike the all night ordeals TV screenwriters depicted, Sarah's suspect was on the move almost immediately. Andrews came rushing out the backdoor of his office, headed for the same black Mercedes she saw him and the hooded stranger get into in the Starbucks parking lot. It seemed logical that if Andrews was going to talk with someone about the diary, or even about her extortion attempt, he'd do it in person, not over the phone. He wouldn't take the chance that the police had already tapped his phone. Nor would he presume her performance was just a way to bait him into incriminating himself.

When he started backing out of his parking space, she lowered the sun visor and ducked down into the passenger seat of her car just in case he headed out in her direction. Her luck was better than she hoped for. He went the other direction and made a left turn onto Huntington Drive. She let some traffic get between them before following him. Her knuckles turned white as her grip tightened on the wheel.

Seeing his left turn signal flashing as they approached San Marino Boulevard quickened her pulse. She recalled seeing signs to Huntington Library coming down San Marino to Andrews's office. But his U-Turn at the traffic light confused her, and the right turn onto another street that angled into Huntington Boulevard came up too quickly for her to get her bearings. Not until they cruised past the Oxford Road entry to The Huntington – the gates at that entrance were closed – did her heart seize up. She was into full palpitations by the time they reached the main entrance.

Andrews's left turn into The Huntington sent her mind into overdrive. Follow him in, or keep going? What if he recognized her? Instinct took over as she turned the opposite way, rolling to stop in a residential neighborhood. Her eyes were locked onto her rearview mirror tracking Andrews's progress through the gate.

After convincing herself Andrews hadn't spotted her and he'd gotten far enough ahead that he wouldn't get a close look at her, Sarah turned the car around and drove through the gate. Within a few yards the road curved toward a security kiosk and the word 'Stop' painted in thick white letters on the pavement grabbed her attention. When she pulled to a stop, the guard handed her an information packet and told her admission tickets could be purchased at the Entrance Pavilion. Her lungs relaxed, releasing their entire deposit of suspended breath as she proceeded to the parking lot. The entry fee would be a small price to pay if she could track down Andrews and snap a photo of his accomplice on her cell phone.

Parking spaces were plentiful, but the dense landscaping between rows made it hard to locate Andrews's car. As she circled through the passenger drop-off area – hoping to catch sight of him on foot – she got a glimpse of him hurrying into one of the nearby buildings. And even though it would have been easy for her to grab a parking space and follow him in, the risk he'd spot her was too great.

Instead, she found his black Mercedes and parked

nearby to wait for his return, hopefully with his co-conspirators at his side. Thanks to her cell phone's zoom lens and enhanced resolution, she'd be able to capture good enough pictures to make a solid identification.

Chapter Twenty Seven

Second guessing herself came from listening to others. On the lacrosse field, Sarah shut out everything except the ball, her stick and the goal. Nothing else existed. Not spectators or opponents. Especially not her jealous teammates. All their voices melded together into a muted, unintelligible hum. They were just background noise. But when she was alone, the critical voices that momentarily escaped her consciousness during the heat of battle flooded into her zone and echoed a clear message, "Stupid move."

After slinking down in the driver's seat of her car for ten minutes, parked a few spaces from Andrews's car, Sarah began wondering if she'd made the wrong choice. Any of her teammates would have blurted out, "Yes," if they had been sitting next to her. The only thing that ever silenced their criticism was scoring. But The Huntington parking lot didn't offer the same opportunities as the teal grass and loamy soil of a lacrosse field.

When Sarah stepped out of her car and started toward the concrete apron leading to the building that Andrews had disappeared into, she glanced up to the rooflines of the surrounding structures. Every muscle in her body tensed. The Entrance Pavilion's roof would be a good spot for a sniper to set up. Realistically though, it was far more likely she'd get caught by Andrews as he exited the building. And her life was on the line just the same. Nailing Andrews was about the only way she could stop Hetherington from railroading her.

As she stood at the top of the half dozen steps that spanned the width of the federal period style building it didn't take much to picture Andrews standing in front of her as the entry door flew open. They'd be face to face. He'd accuse her of stalking him. Her side of the story wouldn't count. He was the one with powerful friends. Realizing that made her wonder – had she been brave or just plain stupid to confront him in his office about a half-hour earlier? If it was bravery, where had her bravado gone? She winced as she stepped across the threshold.

Although Andrews was nowhere in sight, it didn't take long for Sarah to attract attention. In less than a minute a scowling security guard noticed her and approached.

"Ma'am, can I help you?"

Sarah stammered. "I – I'm looking for my, uh, boss. I dropped him off out front and found a place to park. He must have forgotten I've never been here with him before."

"Is he a reader?"

"Excuse me."

"Is he registered to do research at the library?"

"No. I mean, I don't know. He has a meeting with someone."

The security guard studied her face as if he was memorizing every feature.

Sarah looked down. "I suppose I don't sound like much of an assistant. Nothing like getting fired on my first day."

"Well, if it's Andrews you work for, he'd be doing you a favor."

Sarah looked up and smiled. "He seems a bit stiff."

"He's a pompous ass. But I'm not telling you anything you won't find out sooner or later."

"Did you see him come in?"

"Yeah, he met up with Ms. Coulter and headed over to the Tea Room. Let me show you." The guard led her through a labyrinth of corridors that wound through the restricted research area of the library. Along the way, he pointed out several high security areas where valuable artifacts were kept. When they arrived at a locked exit door, he handed her a Visitor's Guide that he'd opened to a map of the grounds. Using his finger he traced the route to the Tea Room, then he warned, "She's more of a bitch than he is an ass. People say if this place was a zoo, she'd be eating hyenas for lunch." He laughed from the pit of his stomach. "And gorillas for dinner. Just keep your mouth shut and don't give her any reason to grind you into hamburger."

Sarah's pained smile was the best thank you she could muster. Having a name for Andrews's accomplice should have made her day, but it sounded like Ms. Coulter could give Hannibal Lecter the shivers. Sarah's spine tingled as she walked toward the Tea Room, hoping not to come face-to-face with Andrews.

Glancing at the map in the Visitor's Guide, she noticed that both paths from the Tea Room converged at one end of the North Lawn which was not far away from her. It was a spot they'd have to pass to get back to Coulter's office. When Sarah got to where the paths joined, the woods bordering the lawn gave her perfect cover to lie in wait. Tucked between a rotund tree trunk and some dense bushes, she readied her cell phone's zoom photo app to snap a critical piece of evidence that could link Andrews to the conspiracy that killed Professor Moran.

Half an hour passed before Sarah decided it was time to stretch her cramping legs. That's when Andrews appeared on the path with a tall, thin blond woman. Sarah slid the zoom control as far to the right as it would go, enlarging both figures so the details of their faces were obvious. The woman's angular features made her appear gaunt. But just as Sarah tapped the shutter icon, a security guard charged her from several yards away. He was motioning with his left hand for her to emerge from her cover as he talked into a walkie-talkie strapped to his shoulder.

The guard's gestures caught the Coulter woman's attention, interrupting her conversation with Andrews. When Andrews caught sight of Sarah, he gripped Coulter's arm and launched into an animated explanation, no doubt about the deranged female stalker who had followed him onto the grounds. In short order, both Coulter and Andrews started toward her.

Sarah's heart sank, realizing she had handed the advantage to Andrews. He'd have no problem calling the police on her now. He had her red-handed. A law-breaker. A stalker. That's what they'd focus on. Her words wouldn't carry the least bit of weight. They'd call her story a diversion, or worse, a lame stab at excusing her misbehavior.

Her eyes darted back and forth between the security guard and the approaching co-conspirators. Rushing out into the open toward the Entrance Pavilion would give her a direct path to the parking lot, but that wasn't an option. Going deeper into the trees was her only hope. But she'd have to get creative to elude their pursuit. That guard could communicate with the entire security force, and all of them knew every possible hiding place on the grounds. She needed to lose them at least long enough to study the map and visualize a clear escape route.

Sarah bolted toward deeper cover. The security guard broke into a run, this time yelling into his walkie-talkie. Andrews and Coulter joined in the chase. It helped that Sarah was in top form for lacrosse. Her athleticism helped her pull away from their pursuit, zigzagging around trees and hurdling low lying shrubs. After a few dozen yards, she stopped short when the woods ended at a concrete path. To her right, the parking lot was visible through a gauntlet of tree trunks, but she'd be easy to spot. To the left were dense trees and shrubs lining the walkway. After scurrying to her left for about ten yards, Sarah ducked into some bushes and held her breath, waiting for the security guard to make his next move.

As she hoped, the security guard headed straight for the parking lot where half a dozen more uniformed guards had started to assemble.

Andrews and Coulter barreled out of the woods a minute later, gasping for breath. They never looked her way, not even while they collected themselves and reined their pulse rates down to a level that wouldn't threaten to trigger a stroke or a hear attack. When they headed to the parking lot to join the others, Andrews ambled with a slight hitch the way last place runners walk as they cool down after losing a race. Coulter drew back her shoulders and stomped forward in what came close to an abbreviated goosestep.

Five of the seven security guards, together with Andrews and Coulter, fanned out through the parking lot. The other two guards headed up the path that ran along the woods past where Sarah was hiding. She let out a long sigh about half a minute after they cleared her position and were out of earshot.

Sarah took what she knew would be a brief intermission in the hunt to study the map. Somehow, she had to make it off the grounds without being detected. After that, she'd figure out how to recover the priest's car before they locked the gates to the entrances. As she oriented the map, lining up her position with landmarks that were tall enough to see from points along her planned escape route, her head dropped and her shoulders slumped. Security cameras were mounted everywhere. On trees, lamp posts, more than likely on the roofs of buildings as well. It would only be a matter of time before they found her. And they'd be able to follow her every step, radioing her positions to the search patrol on the ground.

She panned a complete circle to pick her next cover and to be sure there were no guards close by before she crouched through the undergrowth that bordered the North Lawn. Her aim was to follow the perimeter of the North Lawn to an intersection of pathways behind the Art Museum building. From that point, it might be possible to sneak across about ten yards of open space before picking her way through the Rose Garden. Next, she'd lose herself in the Japanese Garden and navigate the dense undergrowth to the border of the grounds, which hopefully led to a residential street.

Except for the occasional snapping and cracking of twigs under her feet, Sarah got to the corner of the Museum without incident. But her timing was terrible. Two security guards were scanning an area near where the two paths came together. They were close enough she could hear the chatter on their walkie-talkies. From the sounds of it, Andrews had demanded local police join the search, including two K-9 units that were inbound from Pasadena. The guards shook their heads and laughed out loud when the voice at the other end of the radio described her as a deranged bitch who was stalking one of the foundation's board members.

Being called a 'deranged bitch' didn't bother Sarah. What sucked the wind out of her was getting confirmation that Andrews had taken full advantage of her blunder. He no longer feared the police would give any credence to her accusations about him or his father. And the idea of two German Shepherds punctuating the point by tackling her with their angry fangs made her ankles sting. Seconds later an excited voice from the squawk-box blurted, "We have her on visual right behind your position. Now don't let her get away, or you'll be on permanent night shift. Do you copy?"

The guards spun around and both focused on the base of a large shade tree about a yard from the shrubs behind which Sarah was crouched like a sprinter waiting for the starting gun. According to the map, her best cover was between the Art Museum and the Rose Garden. Only a short portion of the north end of the Tea Room was open space. For that short distance the guards would find it easy to track her with the security cameras. After that there'd be plenty of dense vegetation to cover her until she was off The Huntington's grounds.

As she lowered her head and took a deep breath, her hand rested a couple inches from an egg-shaped stone. As if she was imitating a slow-motion replay, she cradled the rock between her thumb and index finger and lofted it a couple yards beyond the base of the nearby tree. Both guards broke toward the sound of the stone skittering through the underbrush. When they stopped short at the edge of the shrubbery, Sarah broke for daylight, angling across the back side of the Art Museum toward the Rose Garden. The guards turned, stumbling off balance, and gave chase.

Another reason her teammates let her play first home position was that she was fast. Faster than any other player in league. She outran the guards, making it safely to cover.

A little more than a half an hour after her brush with the security guards at the North Lawn, Sarah had worked her way past the Japanese Garden to the public restrooms near a service entrance off Euston Road. According to the map, Euston intersected Oxford not far from the entrance to the parking lot. The underbrush near the restroom provided a good place for her to stay out of sight and scout out some prospects to retrieve Father Jim's car. Her stomach knotted up when she considered that she knew very few trustworthy people. Maybe none or one or two or four, not counting Grandma Cassie, of course. But Grandma was dead and the others were Elliot, Poppy, Father Jim and possibly Juan, who weren't accessible at that moment.

Sarah watched a young couple push a baby stroller up the path to the restrooms. He went into the men's room. She guided the stroller to the women's side. Sarah figured they'd be safe, but that's also why they wouldn't want to take the risk. After all, what was her story? Please put your baby in harms way to help me escape from the security guards and cops who want me for stalking a Huntington board member.

Two girls in their early twenties sporting lacrosse jerseys approached the restrooms from the direction of the Desert Garden. They wouldn't be turned off by the risk, but her teammates back home never hesitated to turn on her when they were off the field and the chips were down. Sarah passed on the two jocks as well.

A tanned hunk of a guy showed up right behind the two girls, also from the Desert Garden. As Sarah studied his face, he gave the impression he was shadowing them. Even if she could get his attention, his price would probably be too high. And if she didn't oblige, he'd try to force it out of her. To be precise, he'd likely try to force it *into* her.

After the first meager wave of prospects cleared the restrooms, three nuns appeared from the vicinity of the Lily Ponds. If she had been a young man and they were priests, Sarah would have passed. But how could three Sisters be any different from thee angels? She stood up and followed them into the restroom, hoping The Huntington was sensitive enough not to install cameras inside.

She stood at the sinks, waiting for the nuns to finish their business before starting her pitch. As the first of them began to wash her hands, Sarah interrupted. "Excuse me. I think I've gotten myself into some trouble and could really use your help."

"What can I do for you, Child?" the nun asked.

"You see, I'm having trouble with a guy who has been stalking me today." Her throat turned as dry as sandpaper.

"Have you reported him to security?"

"Uh, no." Sarah ran her hand though her hair. "That's kind of the problem. He is a security guard."

Another nun joined their conversation. "That makes it complicated."

"Right. And I'm afraid if he follows me back to my car, he'll be able to trace my plates and find out where I live."

"That wouldn't be good," the third nun chimed in.

"Well, I was hoping I could find someone to take my keys and bring my car down to the service entrance here on Euston." Sarah pointed toward the restroom wall that paralleled The Huntington's boundary.

"I don't think that would be too hard to do. Sister Elizabeth can follow Sister Justine and me down here in your car." The first nun said. "We were just about ready to head out anyway."

"Yes, I think we're done here," Sister Elizabeth agreed.

Sarah smiled for the first time since leaving the church parking lot in Father Jim's car.

"I can't thank you enough," Sarah offered.

"Say nothing about it, dear. God put us on this earth to help each other in times of need."

Sarah's smile faded. "By the way, we'd better not go out together. This place is covered with security cameras. I don't want to get you in trouble."

After Sarah gave the nuns directions to her car and handed Sister Elizabeth the keys, the three of them headed out of the restroom where they ran into two security guards. The guards smiled at each other when Sister Justine told them in a voice loud enough to be heard inside the restroom that she and her friends had seen the woman they described wandering on one of the paths in the Desert Garden. They'd be glad to lead them to the very spot.

Sarah loitered a few more minutes, seated in one of the bathroom stalls, giving the Sisters time to lead the security guards out of sight. When the time was right, she stole her way into the underbrush and headed straight for the boundary wall. The wall was short enough for her to clear with little effort, and the curbside landscaping on the street side provided plenty of cover. While she waited there for the nuns, she spotted six police cars as they sped up Oxford through the Euston intersection.

Chapter Twenty Eight

Once Sarah got Father Jim's car back, she wasted no time hurrying toward Redlands. Barreling down the eastbound lanes of I-210, she picked up the cell phone from the park and dialed the number on Dr. Burgess's business card. There was no sense taking the chance of him passing along the new cell phone number to Hetherington.

Dr. Burgess didn't answer with the cordial I-can-be-nice-to-someone-who-wants-to-give-me-valuable-artifacts-tone. "Yes, I remember you. You're the one the police think killed Dr. Moran."

She latched onto the first response that entered her mind. "'Think' is the key word."

"Yes, as in you think I killed him – or I'm apparently one of a half-dozen dead-ends you've been feeding Detective Hetherington."

"So you two have been talking behind my back."

"Just enough for me to give him my alibi, and for him to tell me how close he is to bringing you in."

"If he had any evidence he'd already have me locked up."

"I believe his exact words were, 'Anything that walks like a duck and quacks like a duck is a duck.'"

"Well, I've never heard of a duck killing anybody."

"And he said he doubts you have any intention of making a donation to the Shrine."

"He's clueless about a lot of things."

"Yeah? Well we're not interested in anything you have."

"Is that because you already took it from Dr.

Moran?"

"We have an excellent memorial here. It doesn't need to be associated with murderers."

"Then get ready to give back anything that connects you to half the folks in your little secret society."

He choked. "Come again."

She was fishing and he knew it.

"I'm thinking you and half your little secret society were behind Moran's murder. You killed him to get your hands on Lincoln's diary. And now, you want my grandma's journal, too."

"You're insane!"

"All of us Morgan women –"

The call dropped or he'd hung up.

It was time to go to the next phase of her plan. She pulled off the Interstate and turned into a gas station. While she filled up, she used the cell phone from Grant Park to dial Father Jim's landline.

"Hi Father, I need you to ask Juan to do something for me."

"He left just after you did, and he's not back yet."

"Okay, then can you do something for me?"

"Sure, what do you need?"

"Activate the voice distortion app we downloaded on my phone and call Detective Hetherington."

"Sure, I think I can handle that."

"Tell the Detective that Dr. Burgess's alibi is bogus and the people who corroborated it are part of the conspiracy that killed Moran. Tell him you have specific information to back up the claim. Call me on this line to tell me how he reacts."

"Gotcha."

"Oh, and one more thing. Tell Hetherington not to bother tracking the call. Make him believe you'll be gone by the time they figure out the location you're calling from."

"Good idea. But Sarah, I don't think you're going to like this. You got a text message from Angela."

"And –"

"Arrive @LAX tomorrow 4:20 p.m."

"No. I can't deal with her right now. I just have to hope she won't know how to find me."

"You can only hope."

Sarah finished fueling up and got back on the eastbound Interstate, grinding her teeth and swearing under her breath. How was Angela going to figure out exactly where she was? Was it some app she'd installed on their cell phones? Was that how Angela always kept tabs on her back home, knowing when to 'drop by' to join her for coffee or where to 'run into her' for lunch? Certainly Angela didn't plan to step off an airplane in one of L.A.'s half dozen airports and start examining twenty million sets of eyeballs until she found Sarah's.

While Sarah was rehearsing the tongue-lashing Angela would get the next time they saw each other, the cell phone from the park rang. Father Jim wouldn't be calling back so soon. The display read, "Blocked."

"Hello."

Just as she feared, there was a garbled voice on the other end of the line. "Let's try this again. This time we'll do it right."

"Pardon me. You must have the wrong number."

"Nice try. I know it's you."

"What do you want?"

"I told you what I want."

"Yeah, the journal. But that won't be the end of it – will it?"

"I just want to make sure the journal is authentic

before I'm done with you."

There was a beep on the line. It had to be Father Jim calling back. "Oh, the low battery alarm is beeping. I'll have to buy a recharger." She clicked the Power Off switch and flipped the phone shut.

The words "done with you" echoed in her head. After she took a couple of deep breaths, she grabbed Father Jim's cell phone and scrolled for the priest's office number.

"Sorry about that, Father. I had to turn off the other phone. Did you talk to the Detective?"

"Yes, but I think I struck out."

"What did Hetherington say?"

"Well, he was sure it was you who was calling. He said if Dr. Burgess's alibi was made-up, it took a big conspiracy. He interviewed six different people – even some visitors at the Shrine whose names were in the guest book – and all of them backed up his story. He never left the library campus."

"So he didn't take me seriously." Sarah sighed. She squinted and rubbed her forehead with the back of her phone hand. After a couple of seconds, she put the phone back to her ear. "Say, the bad guy called me again. I think I'm just going to have to do a face-to-face so I can find out for sure who I'm dealing with. So, standby like we talked about and wait for me to broadcast a video stream. It may take a few hours before that happens."

"Sarah, Detective Hetherington wants you to come in."

"You know I can't do that. I'll just get railroaded all the way to death row."

"Juan can tell them about Andrews and the knife."

"Yeah, but there's nothing to corroborate his story. We don't have the knife. It'll just sound like another smoke-screen."

"We can give it a try. The truth is on our side."

"I'd rather have the knife or the diary on my side."

"Just be careful."

Sarah laughed. "I'm not sure I can fit that into the plan."

"God be with you, Sarah."

"Thanks, Father. By the way, does He let you pray for non-Catholics?"

"He listens to everyone, Sarah. Some people are just more in tune with what's on His heart, so it looks like He listens better to them. But he cares about everyone the same."

"Well just in case he plays favorites, pray for me. Will you?"

"I'm way ahead of you on that."

"Thanks, Father."

She hung up and powered on the other cell phone for the rest of her drive back to Redlands. Making the bad guys angrier by not answering wouldn't improve her chances of survival. After all, they had a knack for finding her.

A couple minutes later, she grabbed Father Jim's phone and scrolled the contacts for Elliot's number.

No answer. She frowned and hung up.

After making the transition from the Orange Freeway onto I-10, Sarah tried calling Elliot again.

This time he answered, and the sound of his voice made her smile all over. "Elliot, it's me, Sarah."

"Sarah, are you all right?"

"I'm okay. How are classes?"

He laughed. "Classes are fine, but that's not why you called."

"I do care about your classes."

"I'm glad you care. But look, you have more trouble than you need already, and I should be helping you."

"Well, I hate to ask, but I do need a favor."

"I'll do my best."

"Can we meet somewhere?"

"Where are you now?"

"I'm on I-10 headed into Redlands. I'm just coming up on the Ontario Airport."

"Yes, take the Milliken Exit North and go to the Ontario Mills Mall. Make sure you go to the main mall entrance. Do you still have your GPS?"

"Yeah, I can plug in the name of the mall."

"Okay, wait for me at the Starbucks inside. It's on the back side of the mall. The concourse wraps all the way around the inside, so if you just keep walking either direction you'll eventually come to it."

"Thanks Elliot. You're a lifesaver."

"Say, I have some bad news."

"What's that?"

"Both Andrewses have iron clad alibis. They were closing a deal on some rare documents and spent the whole morning of the murder with clients and lawyers."

"Sure, and one of the lawyers was probably John Easley. I bet the clients were other members of the conspiracy."

"What makes you say that?"

"Easley was Moran's lawyer, and the other night he was chumming it up with the Andrewses and some French banker at a secret society meeting the Shrine's curator drug me to."

Elliot laughed. "You didn't tell me about any secret society. What's that about?"

"I'll spare you the details. Anyway, since that meeting, I've gotten a strong feeling the French banker whose name is Henri Rothschild – if you can believe it – was their triggerman. I'm almost sure he's who I saw driving away from Moran's house the morning of the murder. And I think he's the one who's stalking me for Grandma Cassie's journal. But all the others are up to something, too. Dr. Burgess, the Andrewses, Easley. Huntington Library is involved in it as well."

"What makes you think it was Rothschild you saw driving away from Moran's?"

"I don't know. And he was about the same size as the creep at Grant Park." Sarah bit he lower lip.

"Wait. What creep at Grant Park?"

"I'll fill you in when I see you. But there is something that doesn't fit, unless Henri Rothschild is working with someone else."

"What's that?"

"At dinner the other night, Andrews pointed the finger at someone connected to Stanford. That's the name he whispered to me."

"Well, it could be that Andrews was trying to throw you off his trail. But I'm not so sure you should stay so focused on the Andrewses. They're not the violent types."

"That's so not true."

"What do you mean?"

"I found proof in Pasadena that old man Andrews killed my grandfather."

"You what?"

"I met an old gardener who saw him do it. But he's been afraid to talk, until now."

"Why would he come forward all of a sudden?"

"I guess because he felt guilty about the fallout from Grandpa Lake's murder, and the only way it can ever be over is to bring old man Andrews to justice."

"Sorry, Sarah. I want to be there for you."

"That means a lot to me, Elliot. I want this all to be over so I can sh– I mean, I want you to know your friendship means a lot to me."

"I can be patient."

"You won't have to be for much longer. I promise."

Chapter Twenty Nine

Sitting inside Starbucks at Ontario Mills Mall, Sarah touched Elliot's wrist just like the last time they were together, but this time she didn't pull it back. She rolled her hand to one side, cupping her slender fingers, waiting for him to slip his hand into hers.

Elliot's hand didn't move, though he used his other hand to take a sip of his mocha.

Sarah pulled her hand away from his wrist and played with her cup.

"Yeah, it's frustrating," he said. "Without their alibis the Andrewses would be the perfect suspects to get you off the hook."

"Those alibis don't mean they weren't involved in a conspiracy. I didn't get a chance to tell you on the phone, but I went to see Andrews, Jr. I told him I'd go to the cops about his father killing my grandpa if he didn't turn over Lincoln's diary. And no sooner than he thought I'd left, he ran out to his car and tore off to Huntington Library. I followed him. And I snapped a picture of him meeting with a woman named Coulter who's one of the execs at the Research Library."

"Way to go girl. You're turning into a major league sleuth."

Sarah blushed. She touched his wrist again, this time closer to his hand. Again, her hand lingered there waiting for him to make a move. "Yeah, I'm sure." She looked down at the table.

"I'm serious."

"Well, I need to find something tangible to connect Henri Rothschild to the Andrewses and that Coulter woman at the Huntington Library."

"There is something that links the Andrewses to both the Rothschild Bank and Huntington Library. Old man Andrews has worked with both of them for decades. Supposedly, Andrews helped General Patton get some contraband Nuremberg documents out of Germany after World War II. It's likely the Rothschild's helped. The documents eventually wound up at the Huntington Library."

Sarah grinned. "Now we're getting someplace. The Andrewses want Lincoln's diary because it's worth a ton of money. The Huntington will help them cash in on it, but only if they get clear of Moran's murder. The guy who calls himself Rothschild probably worked for them and killed Moran in the process of stealing the diary. So they try to frame me. If they're successful that puts Rothschild and The Huntington in the clear, and it comes with a bonus. Without anyone to challenge them, they can produce a phony will and claim that Moran left the diary to the Huntington Research Library. They pretend to sell it for an undisclosed price and give the Andrewses a huge commission. Grandma Cassie's journal undermines Moran's claim of ownership of the diary and his right to bequeath it. The journal proves it belonged to my family and there's no record we got paid a fair price for it. On top of that, Grandma's journal might also connect old man Andrews to Grandpa Lake's death."

Elliot nodded. "And the younger Andrews is pointing the finger at someone from Stanford as a decoy to throw you off. It also makes you come across looking more than a bit loony. If Andrews is in tight with The Huntington folks, picking on Stanford makes sense. The bad blood between those institutions goes all the way back to the days of Collis Huntington and Leland Stanford. And with today's tough economic times, competition between those two charities for major donors has gotten pretty intense."

"Intense enough to kill?"

Elliot shrugged. "I don't think Moran's murder was part of their plan."

Sarah looked out the door. Her focus wandered into the concourse. "I think the knife is critical. DNA would prove that old man Andrews used it to kill for the Lincoln dairy once before. And if Henri Rothschild was the guy who made Juan dig it up, that connects him directly to the Andrewses."

Elliot shook his head. "Okay, but playing devil's advocate – before we give both Andrewses the gas chamber, there might be another angle we've missed. Let's say Henri Rothschild does have the knife. Does he have any other connection to the Andrewses?"

"You said there was the thing about General Patton."

"I mean something that relates to either the diary or the murders?"

"If Henri Rothschild isn't involved with the Andrewses, how would he know about the knife?"

"Maybe the Andrewses don't know Rothschild has the knife. Maybe he found out about it from someone else and took it to get leverage on them." Elliot sat straight up in his chair.

Sarah caught a glint in his eyes.

Elliot continued, "Maybe Henri Rothschild heard that Moran bought Lincoln's diary and killed him when he refused to sell it. Somehow, he heard about the knife. Someone could have known that Andrews killed your grandfather – maybe the gardener talked before, or maybe that professor at USC confessed before he died – so Rothschild figured the Andrewses were perfect scapegoats to cover his crime. A DNA test would prove the old man was guilty of one murder. If he killed once, he could kill again, right? Now Rothschild could be pretending to be some goon chasing after your grandma's journal. Eventually, he's planning to convince the police that it's the Andrewses who are stalking you, trying to tie up loose ends, trying to be sure the journal doesn't link them to your grandpa's murder." Elliot leaned back in his chair and folded his hands behind his head.

"And why would he need Grandma's journal?"

"For the same reason you said the Andrewses want it. It might prove the Andrewses killed your grandfather, so he could use it as leverage for blackmail."

Sarah leaned forward, resting both forearms on the table. "Somehow we have to get the Andrewses and Rothschild together to see who blinks first."

"Good idea, but how?"

Sarah touched Elliot's hand. This time he laid his hand on top of hers. Her heart stopped. She couldn't hold back her smile.

Elliot smiled back.

Sarah gasped and pulled away. She bent over and pretended to look at something on the floor. "Don't look, but there's a cop just outside the door. He's talking into the radio thing on his shoulder."

"You need to get out of here. I'll try to distract him while you duck out the back."

"I'll call you."

Elliot got up and moved toward the store's entrance. He stopped at the condiment bar before he sidled past the policeman and pulled something out of his wallet. The officer had to turn his back to the storefront to see whatever it was Elliot wanted to show him.

Sarah darted for a door at the back of the store. The sign read, "Employees Only." She bumped into a barista who was taking a cart of garbage bags outside to a dumpster. Sarah held her index finger to her lips, staring the young woman down. "Shhh," she said.

When the barista nodded, Sarah bolted down a long narrow hallway and crashed through a set of double doors into the mall's rear parking lot. The bright sun stunned her eyes. After a few seconds, she scanned her surroundings to get her bearings and to be sure there were no police in the area. Father Jim's car was on the opposite side of the mall from where she had come out. She took her time making her way back to her parking spot, not wanting to draw undue attention. Her heart didn't stop thumping against her chest until she was back on the freeway driving toward Redlands.

A half hour later when Sarah called Elliot, he explained that the officer was looking for a lost kid. It was a false alarm.

"Too bad." Sarah sighed. "I was enjoying spending time with you."

"Me too."

Sarah's next words got stuck in her throat.

Elliot rescued the conversation. "Are you going to call Hetherington?"

"No, I don't think so. He won't take me seriously until I have the knife or the diary. Do you have any other ideas?"

"I could call the Andrewses and tell them you've hired me to get a good price for your grandmother's journal. You can set up a meeting with your stalker when he calls back. We'll try to get him and the Andrewses to show up at a rendezvous spot at the same time. If they both show, we can stand back and watch the fireworks."

"Isn't that awful risky?" she asked. "I mean what if they talk to each other and figure things out? After all, we're dealing with killers."

"At least we'll know they're in on it together. I can record the whole thing on my cell phone. That and the testimony from your friends at St. Anthony will be enough evidence to get Hetherington to change his focus."

"I like that better than me doing it all alone. At least Hetherington won't just assume that I made a bogus recording."

"Say, what are you doing for dinner tonight?" he asked.

"Uh, do we have time to eat?"

"We aren't in control of the timeline here."

"I guess you're right."

"Why don't you come to my place? We can strategize there and I can cook for you."

"Hmm. Ramen for dinner? That's what college guys live on, right?" Sarah chuckled.

"Seriously, I'm a pretty good cook."

"Is that what all the girls say?"

"Enough. Is it a date?"

"Yes. I'd like a date." She beamed, wishing Angela was around to witness the moment – but only that specific moment.

"My place isn't far from the University. I'll text you the address."

"What time?"

"If you come over now, you can help me cook."

"You're on."

Sarah pulled her car over to the shoulder and waited for his text message. When it arrived, she copied it to the navigation app on Father Jim's phone and was on her way. Her heart was too well anchored in reality to soar. She wished that her first date with a nice guy like Elliot could have come under better circumstances.

Elliot's quaint little box house, a rental, sat in the

shadow of Alumni House, a gracious old mansion up on a hill. One of Redlands's decorative orange groves stretched down from the mansion to the base of the hill, stopping abruptly across the street from Elliot's house. During the 1920s, the mansion had been the University President's residence.

Elliot greeted her with a broad smile and a kiss on her cheek.

Sarah closed her eyes, letting the warmth from his lips tingle on her flushed face. After a moment, she looked toward the kitchen and said, "What's for dinner? I'm starved."

"You'll have to wait a bit –" he picked a package of Ramen off the counter. "– unless we hear from the Andrewses and your stalker. In that case we'll only have time for this." He waved the Ramen under her nose and winked. "Good things take time."

She smiled at him.

"It's a Sicilian dish. I call it Penne con tonno, pasta with tuna."

"Mmm – sounds yummy."

"While I'm getting things ready, go ahead and pour yourself a glass of Grillo and try some antipasto."

Sarah picked up the bottle and looked at its label. "I thought you said Grigio as in Pinot Grigio."

"No it's an entirely different thing. It's white, but more full-bodied and earthy. Only a hint of sweet. The grapes that go into this one are grown at sea level."

She sipped the wine and studied Elliot's culinary handiwork. The wine was almost as delicious as she was imagining he could be.

Dinner passed without a word from the stalker or a return call from the Andrewses. And that suited Sarah just fine. The gleam in Elliot's eyes made her hope hers sparkled as bright as they felt. But their flirting wasn't restricted to the way they looked at each other. Even though Sarah's friends complained about the dearth of men in her life, she knew all it would take was for the right one to come along. He'd be something like what she pictured her father and grandfather had been like. Elliot was the walking, talking, sweet smelling personification of that vision. Sarah got more reckless with each sip of wine and with every delicious bite of dinner. And Elliot gave no sign he minded in the least.

When Elliot reached across the table and cradled her hand in his, she put her other hand up to her chest. That's when the buttoncam grabbed her attention, and her nerves short circuited. No. The camera. He'd think it was meant for recording him, that he was somehow under suspicion. Of what? After all he was helping her.

Sarah wanted to sop up every second of his attention, but she had to get rid of that damned camera. Her smile weakened. "I'm sorry. I need a bathroom to freshen up."

He scratched his head then pointed down the hall. Her soft kiss on his cheek, the way her lips lingered intentionally, hopefully he got the message his patience would be rewarded.

As Sarah grabbed at her bag, it slipped out of her hand and dropped to the floor next. Several things spilled out, including Father Jim's phone and the cell phone from the park. She scooped up her bag and darted down the hall while Elliot collected her phones and billfold.

Inside the bathroom, Sarah freshened up and disconnected the buttoncam. As she dropped it into her bag the missing button caught her eye, the button that had been replaced by the camouflaged camera lens. Not only was the button missing, but there a small slit where the camera lens poked through the inside flap of her blouse.

The next button down was lower than where she normally felt comfortable buttoning up. A broad grin broke across her face. She shook her head and laughed to herself. So what if her intentions were as obvious as a billboard?

When Sarah walked back to the table, Elliot wasn't smiling. The sparkle had disappear from his eyes.

She felt her eyes go dull as well.

Elliot handed her the cell phone from the park. "I think the enemy called while you were freshening up. It said 'Blocked.'"

"Did you answer it?"

"I figured I'd better not."

"Good thinking." Sarah fidgeted with the hole her missing button left behind.

"We need to set a time and place for our rendezvous, just in case we aren't together when they call again."

"I have a solution for that."

"You know the area. You pick."

Elliot smiled as he grabbed a pen and tablet. He scribbled some directions and drew a map. "Here's how to get to the rendezvous point. The first one who confirms the meeting can text the other with the time."

"Sounds good."

Elliot leaned toward her and fingered the hole where the missing button belonged. "Pop a button?"

Sarah wobbled as she leaned toward to him. "I guess I just couldn't hold something in."

He tugged on her blouse, drawing her onto his lap. Her chest nearly pressed against his. The only thing that held them apart was his hard fist knuckling into her exposed skin. Her face went flush. Her heart raced. A rare heat washed over her. She felt defenseless. Her layers of aloofness were too compromised to hold back the emotions that were welling up inside her.

Sarah opened her mouth just a bit. Elliot edged his lower lip between hers. Its softness made her limp. The tip of her tongue traced the edges of his lips. He slipped his tongue into her waiting mouth. She cradled the back of his head in both hands.

Elliot's cell phone rang.

"Don't answer," she whispered.

He pulled away from her and reached for his phone.

Sarah stood up and straightened her blouse.

"Hello."

From the moment he greeted her at the front door, Sarah had doubted she was going to be lucky enough that night to fall asleep in Elliot's arms. But a girl can dream, can't she?

After a few moments of him saying nothing – he only listened – his face turned sallow and his eyes narrowed as if by closing them he could regulate his intake of pain.

Sarah stood back, covering her mouth with one hand.

When Elliot pressed the End button, he looked up at her. His eyes were empty, like a lost child. "Aunt Agnes is in ICU. She's had a stroke."

Sarah sat back down on his lap, pulling his head against her chest. "You'd better get to the hospital right now."

He pulled back and looked up at her. "But we have work to do."

Sarah stood up, straddling his lap as she smoothed the contours of his shoulders with her hands. "You should be with her. I'll call you if I hear from them. Or I'll text you like you said."

Elliot gripped her wrists. "Say, why don't you crash here for the night?"

Sarah slid one leg over his knees and stepped back. "Look, I'll just be in the way. I can find a motel."

"You sure?"

Sarah was all too familiar with the pangs she imagined were stinging his heart at that very moment. In fact, her heart had started aching again, as well. "Positive. Now get going."

Chapter Thirty

Sarah's expectation of a restful night's sleep at the Comfort Suites was unrealistic. She dozed on and off during the night, waking up at one point and pouring through a local telephone book for hospital listings. Calling one of the areas hospitals only resulted in awakening her to the reality she didn't know Elliot's last name, much less his aunt's.

An hour later, still wide-eyed and staring at the digital clock display, she picked up the house phone and dialed the front desk. The clerk made it clear that there were dozens of hospitals within a hundred miles of Redlands that handled stroke victims. Without knowing which of the seemingly hundreds of suburbs Aunt Agnes called home, finding Elliot would be a daunting task even with a last name.

Sarah hung up the phone and crossed over to a small computer desk just a few feet from the bed. She slumped into the chair and opened the new netbook, part of her haul from the shopping spree with Father Jim. Her other computer was still back at the Hilton and it probably would stay there. The cops could locate her through its IP address if they wanted to, so it was more of a liability than an asset. And who knew – the Hilton staff would probably call Hetherington if she showed up to collect her belongings.

After setting up the netbook and testing the buttoncam, she flopped back on the bed, finally falling into a hard sleep just before dawn. But it didn't last. A couple of hours later she was jolted out of bed by the alarm clock. Whoever rented the room previously had left the alarm set to 'On.' Half of her wanted to burrow under the blanket and ignore everything. That half would have won except for the rational half's insistence that she had to be alert when Henri Rothschild – or whoever her stalker was – called.

Sarah sat up in bed and stared into the bathroom. She was clueless about what to do next. Maybe a hot shower would put her mind in motion. Her best inspirations always came to her in the shower.

Just thinking about the shower cascading down her face and the smell of clean hair gave her a spark. She started digging through the local phone book. Attorneys – Criminal attorneys. Pictures stared up at her and bold red letters jumped off the pages. Mostly DUI. There were lots of ads for DUI, but what about murder?

One ad showed a headshot of a tanned, chiseled chin, no-nonsense looking guy, probably in his forties. The caption read, "Twelve year veteran – FBI." Those three letters and the calm in his face were enough for Sarah. She picked up Father Jim's cell phone and dialed the Law Office of Attorney Ed Fulton.

A fist pump and mouthing "Thank you" were her reactions to the receptionist's news that Fulton had an open slot in an hour. That wouldn't give her time to hand wash and dry the clothes she wore the day before. But, hey, it wasn't a date, and he probably saw a lot worse every day.

What caught her off guard was discovering that Fulton's office was across the street from the San Bernardino County Court House. Bambi would have felt safer crossing an open meadow during hunting season. The couple of blocks between the public parking lot and Fulton's office put her in full view of a horde of law enforcement personnel. Stepping through the doorway into Fulton's office, gave her a small shiver of relief.

Sarah's sense of relief would have given way to

something akin to a caffeine surge if the priest's cell phone log had shown at least one call from Elliot when she checked it while waiting for her appointment. It would have been nice to know how Aunt Agnes was doing. Grasping for straws, she scanned the call log on the cell phone from the park, but thumped her forehead with the heel of her hand remembering she hadn't given Elliot either number. She clung to the desperate hope he might check his recent calls and get curious about who had called.

A few minutes later, Sarah's body tensed as the receptionist led her to the conference room. And from the second Ed Fulton entered the room, she barraged him with disjointed details about the mess she was in, laced with emotional outbursts about the injustice of it all.

After indulging her predictable anxiety, Fulton took charge of the conversation. "Ms. Morgan, I'm acquainted with Detective Hetherington, and he's an excellent investigator, as well as a fair and decent man."

Sarah folded her arms across her chest and sank back in her chair. "Aren't you supposed to be on my side?"

Fulton smiled. "I am on your side. I just don't want you to think this is going to be a cake walk. Hetherington isn't some lazy bureaucrat who's just taking up desk space until he retires."

Sarah leaned forward. "Well, what do you plan to do?"

"First, I'm going to take your case. But I don't want you playing any more cat and mouse games with whoever it is that's trying to get your grandmother's journal."

"Speaking of the journal, are you going to get it back for me?"

"Yes. Eventually they have to share whatever

evidence they have."

"He wants me to turn myself in."

"I'll talk with him about that. It doesn't appear as if he's been trying very hard to bring you in. You said your friend, Elliot – he was the one who told you Hetherington wants you to come in, right? But the detective hasn't talked with you directly."

"Actually both Elliot and Father Jim, the priest in Pasadena, mentioned it, but I haven't exactly been in contact with Detective Hetherington. I've sort of gone underground."

"Has Elliot called the phone you left with the priest in Pasadena?"

"I haven't talked to the Father since yesterday afternoon, so I'm not sure if Elliot's tried to get in touch on that number."

"Why don't you call the priest from my landline?"

"What should I say?"

"Just tell him you're calling from an attorney's office. That should relieve him a little. Then tell him you're okay and ask him if anyone has tried to contact you."

Sarah dialed Father Jim's direct line while Fulton made some notes in her file. When she hung up, she told Fulton what she learned.

"He said the only calls that have come in are from my friend Angela. But Hetherington came by the church with a detective from the Pasadena Police Department. He said they were able to track me there from the GPS signal on my old cell phone that I left at the church."

"Did they take your phone?"

"The priest told them that he didn't know where I was and that he didn't have my phone."

"I'm surprised he lied."

"Oh, he didn't. He gave the phone to the church secretary when she told him the police were there looking for me."

"Sly move."

"But Hetherington did ask a lot of questions about my grandfather's murder. He asked if Moran ever came to the church asking questions about Lake Matthews or Martin Deery."

"And he hadn't, right?"

"Not that Father Jim knew about."

"Did Hetherington interview Juan?"

"No, he was still out."

"Well, if the elder Andrews killed your grandfather and Moran knew about it, the professor was probably blackmailing the old man. So, Hetherington's questions could make sense. But you said both the Andrewses had iron clad alibis."

"That's what Elliot said. But that doesn't mean they weren't part of a conspiracy."

Fulton smiled at her suggestion of a conspiracy. "I think you said that Moran knew Deery."

"Deery was Moran's advisor."

"So it's possible he knew both the Andrewses and your grandfather. And old man Andrews was funding Moran's pet research project, even though he despised what it was about."

"That's what I was thinking."

"And the Rothschild angle came from Andrews."

"No, that was my idea. Andrews told me to focus on someone from Stanford."

"So what we have is a lot of finger pointing. Hetherington says you killed Moran. You say it was Andrews or Rothschild, and Andrews says it was someone connected to Stanford."

"I guess so."

"Well, the Rothschilds and the Vatican are everyone's favorite targets when it comes to conspiracy theories. So I'm not surprised to hear at least one of them dragged into the mix. But the Rothschilds don't sound like promising suspects to me. I mean, why would they kill someone to get the diary when all they have to do is pay for it?"

Sarah bristled. "Are you trying to point the finger back at me?"

"Actually, I'm starting to believe that the Andrewses are behind Moran's death. They just didn't pull the trigger. And maybe Henri's real name isn't Rothschild."

"Well, I'm pretty sure it's the guy who calls himself Henri Rothschild who wants Grandma's journal."

"We don't know for sure who's behind that. You can't identify the voice. You don't have a phone number to trace. The closest you have to a visual was someone under a street light a block away in the middle of the night."

"So how do you explain Andrews feeding me that stuff about Stanford?"

"Maybe he hoped you'd sell it to Hetherington. There's nothing more distracting in a murder investigation than conspiracy theories that involve rich and powerful people. Accusing someone from the Stanford charities might be far fetched, but at least it's not trite."

"But there's the secret society meeting in the basement of the Lincoln Shrine. And what about Andrews tearing off to the Huntington Library right after I –"

Fulton broke in. "After you tried to extort him?"

"Okay, how do we prove it was them?"

"Certainly not by stalking anyone. Anyway, it's not my job to prove who did it. I just have to get a jury to believe that there's reason to doubt that you did it. Hopefully it'll be a reason the other side didn't take seriously enough to fortify with bullet-proof evidence."

"But that sounds pretty risky. We'd be relying on twelve people to be reasonable. Most of the time it's not good odds to get one person to be reasonable."

Fulton shook his head. "Well, I need to see what kind of evidence Hetherington is working with. In the meantime, stay under his radar and don't pull any more foolish stunts."

Sarah forced a smile. "I'll do my best."

Chapter Thirty One

By the time she got back to Father Jim's car Sarah's stomach felt like it was straining to digest a rock. Putting things in Fulton's hands was supposed to take away some of the pressure. But, it wasn't working that way. Instead, it reminded her of the time Angela talked her into riding the Ferris Wheel at the Wicomico County Fair. They got stuck at the top when the motor seized up, and Angela kept wondering if the operator was back in his trailer half stoned.

Talking to Elliot would make her feel better, but she had to get away from the courthouse and all those cops. She kept her eyes peeled all the way back to her car, on the look out for anyone in uniform who might be paying her undue attention. It was like picking a path through a swarm of Mako sharks in an inflatable runabout. Sarah didn't breathe right until she scooted past the Hilton and jumped onto Eastbound I-10, headed for Redlands.

Desperate for a latté and moral support, she parked outside the Starbucks on Orange Street and dialed Elliot's cell phone. No answer. It went straight to voice mail. She left a message. "Hi, Elliot, it's Sarah. Gee, I hope everything's okay. I mean, how's your Aunt Agnes? Are you hanging in there okay? I wish I could be there for you. By the way, I think I forgot to give you this cell phone number. You should be able to find it in your recent calls log. I left my old phone in Pasadena with the priest."

After hanging up, Sarah went inside and ordered a latté. The first sip released the morning's accumulated tension. But the cell phone from the park started ringing and that knotted her up again. Before she pressed Answer, the storm clouds of depression started closing in around her.

She couldn't bring herself to say 'Hello.'

"Sarah, guess who?"

She put her hand on her forehead and mumbled, "Satan?"

The garbled voice laughed a sinister laugh. "Not quite, but we can make your life seem like Hell."

"It already does."

"We can make it worse. We can hurt people, people that matter to you."

"You wouldn't."

"Can you pull up YouTube on your phone?"

"Maybe."

"You should check something out. Do a search for 'big bang bingo.' It's a sample of our work – almost live from the parking lot at the Vagabond Inn, the one across from Andy's Coffee Shop. I hope you carried rental car insurance."

The phone went dead.

Sarah scrambled for Father Jim's phone.

The video was only about 20 seconds long. It panned around the Vagabond parking lot, and then zoomed in on her subcompact rental car. Without warning, the car burst apart, throwing a blast of orange flames and smoke straight up in the air. Next, it focused on a woman. It was her. She was walking past the spy shop across the street from the Vagabond, stuffing her cell phone into her bag.

She couldn't' believe her eyes. These guys, whoever they were, meant business. Sarah replayed the video, just to be sure her mind wasn't playing tricks.

A few minutes later, she was still numb, frozen to her seat. Her latté was cold, and so was she, shivering in spite of the summer-like temperatures outside. The cell phone from the park rang again.

"Have you seen our little production yet?"

Sarah couldn't make her mouth move.

"Just to be sure Hetherington connects the dots, we dumped your amateur bomb making diagram and some of your leftover supplies in a trash can down the hall from your room. Nice touch – using the cell phone activated detonator. But you shouldn't be so sloppy if you want to make it look like you're being chased by real powerful people."

The caller was gone.

Sarah jumped up from her seat, stuffed the phones into her bag and raced back to the Comfort Suites. He made his point. They could hurt, maybe even kill. She couldn't let them do that – to anyone. They knew about Juan. But did they know about Elliot and Poppy as well? Maybe they even knew about Father Jim. They'd been watching every move she made. Now, everybody she cared about was in jeopardy. God, did they know about Angela, too?

Chapter Thirty Two

On the nightstand, a text message alert sounded on Father Jim's phone. Sarah reached for it. "Let it be Elliot," she whispered.

The message came from her old cell number. It was Father Jim. "Call Urgent."

Sarah's thumb punched Call Back.

Just as she placed her call to the priest, the disposable phone rang. Sarah's heart jumped. She recognize Elliot's number. She picked up the phone with her free hand and answered it.

"Hey Sarah, sorry I haven't called. Things are still touch and go. I know you've been trying to keep a low profile, so I wasn't going to call until there was a significant change."

"It's okay to call me, really. I was worried."

"How are things with you?"

She heard Father Jim faintly on the other line. "Hello, are you there?"

"Look Elliot, can you hold on? Father Jim's on the other phone and it sounds important. I want to know how you're doing."

"We're as well as can be expected. You go, I'll catch you later."

"Okay, please call me soon." Sarah juggled the two phones, trying to catch Father Jim before he was gone.

"Damn, he hung up."

She redialed.

"Hello."

"Father Jim?"

"Sarah, Is that you?"

"Yes. What's going on?"

"I know you've got your hands full out there, but I figured you'd want to know. It's Juan."

"Is everything okay?"

"He's – pretty bad off. Someone beat him up. He's in the hospital, ICU, barely hanging on."

"What happened? How?"

"He's been unconscious since they found him. We're not sure how it happened."

"Is he going to be okay?"

"No telling at this point. I would have called earlier, but the police have been hanging around. I thought it best to wait till they left."

"I'm coming back. I have to be there for him."

"I don't think there's much point in that until he wakes up."

"I want to be there when he does. I have to know who did this."

"The police will be coming back."

"I'll just have to be scarce when they do."

"Are you sure?"

She dumped the disposable phone in her bag. "I'm already on my way."

Sarah breathed a deep sigh as she pulled onto Westbound I-10. It was past lunchtime and traffic was lighter than it might be later in the afternoon. And he concierge's tip was a big help. Almost as soon as she merged onto the freeway, there was an exit to Highway 210 towards Pasadena. He had said it was a much faster route. And this time she didn't have any trouble stretching the speed limit. All she had to do was go a little slower than the fastest car on the road and hope her GPS could keep up with her. It was set for Glendale Memorial.

At eighty miles an hour, it took Sarah fifty-four

minutes to make it to the hospital. Her knees wobbled when her feet hit the pavement of the parking lot. Her throat felt like she'd eaten sand and her nerves were short-circuiting like a power plant imploding under a terrorist attack. Moments later, she found Father Jim in the lobby waiting to escort her to ICU.

Juan was still unconscious, though he had made enough progress to breathe on his own. An RT was wheeling back the ventilator as Sarah and the priest walked up to the viewing window outside Juan's room.

"He looks more peaceful with those tubes out," Father Jim said.

"Who could have done something like this?" Sarah pressed the heel of her hand to her forehead and rubbed the corner of her eyebrow.

"The world is full of evil. It lurks in every corner. Who's to say how or why it chooses its victims."

"Yes, and I'm the one who provoked the evil."

"Sarah, it's not your fault."

"But it had to be whoever's stalking me. I told Andrews that I'd talked to Juan."

"At this point we can't be sure of anything. It could have been a mob of ignorant punks who wanted to make an example out of him. It's not immigration they're angry about. They're just afraid of losing their jobs, or of having to work harder or of having to face the responsibility of taking care of other people in need. We don't know who did this or why. What we do know is that Juan's in the Father's hands."

Sarah forced a smile. She wanted to contort in anger, beat her head with her fists demanding revenge. But that would take too much energy, too much resolve. If the bad guys wanted her to give up, turn herself in to be their scapegoat, they'd found her weak spot. Maybe she should let them have their way.

Sarah clamped her hand over her mouth as she surveyed Juan's broken frame from his swollen, bruised face to the IVs in his arm. His right hand – it twitched. It could have been a momentary, barely perceptible quiver, but to her it was a convulsion.

She grabbed Father Jim's arm. "My God, did you see that?"

Father Jim moved closer to the viewing window. He kept his eyes peeled, ready to detect the slightest sign of consciousness.

Sarah yelped. "Look. His eyes."

Juan's eyelids fluttered.

Father Jim grabbed her wrist. "Come with me."

"Will they let us?"

"I'm a priest, for God's sake." Father Jim lurched toward the door, dragging Sarah into Juan's ICU bay.

Sarah leaned over the bed, gazing into Juan's eyes. "Juan, this is Sarah. Can you hear me?"

Juan blinked. He strained to focus on her face.

Sarah clutched his hand. "I'm so sorry about this."

Juan's mouth quivered.

Father Jim made a sign of the cross with a small vial and touched two fingers to Juan's forehead. "Take it easy, my son."

"Who did this to you?" Sarah fought back tears.

Father Jim called out, "Nurse."

No sooner than he'd called out, a swarm of hospital scrubs flooded into the room.

One of the nurses barked, "I'm sorry, she'll have to leave. No family."

Father Jim retorted, "She's with me."

"A Sister?" asked the nurse.

"Yes." Sarah replied. She wouldn't let a priest lie for her.

Juan squeezed Sarah's hand. He sputtered in short bursts, his voice barely audible. Sarah turned her ear close to his lips, straining to hear him. "De – termination – is more – more im – portant – than anything. Don't – give – up."

Sarah turned her head again so she could lock onto his eyes. Trying to talk was useless. Her tongue curled up when she opened her mouth.

He begged her with his eyes to persevere.

A nurse nudged Sarah out of the way and started barking instructions. "He needs to save his strength. The detectives are on their way up to talk with him."

Father Jim caught Sarah's eye and nodded toward the door. As they started to back out of the room, he offered the nurse his own instructions. "We'll get out of your way for a bit, but be sure to let me know if he needs me."

The nurse nodded as her eyes zeroed in on Juan and a new battery of instruments that she'd just hooked up.

Sarah was only a couple of steps from the doorway when she turned and found herself staring into the chest of a plainclothes detective. A quick glance out into the hallway showed he wasn't alone. A uniformed cop trailed right behind him. "Excuse me," she said, stepping aside to let them pass.

The detective studied her for a moment.

Sarah looked down, avoiding eye contact, hoping she'd be invisible if he didn't see her eyes.

The detective glanced at Father Jim. "Family?"

"No. She's with me."

The detective turned back to Sarah. "Did you know the victim, here?"

Sarah shifted her eyes from side to side, avoiding direct contact with the detective's stare. "We only just met. Haven't had much chance to get acquainted. I just came to support Father Jim."

"Do you have any idea who might have done this?"

She kept her eyes down. "I'm afraid I can't be much help."

"Well if you think of anything, let the Father know. He knows how to contact us."

"Sure."

Sarah eased past the detective and out into the hallway.

Father Jim lingered in the room for a few moments to talk with the detective.

Sarah fidgeted, resorting to tracing the seams between floor tiles with the toe of her shoe. When Father Jim joined her, she'd been counting ceiling tiles. Without saying a word to each other, they made their way to the lobby where they found a private place to talk.

"Did he say anything at all about who attacked him?" She studied Father Jim's face, hoping to glean the truth whether or not he had a clue what it was.

"I'm sorry Sarah. He slipped into a coma as soon as you left the bay."

"Where did they find him? Who reported it? Someone must have seen something."

"I called a detective friend of mine when Juan didn't show up at the church. He left right after you did and never came back."

"You mean he's been gone all this time?"

"Yes, so I had the detective check the ER's, morgues, lock ups, everywhere. He called me when Juan turned up here."

"Did your friend talk to the EMTs who brought him in?"

"All he got from them was the pick up location, Finkbine Park. A couple was on an early morning walk and saw him struggling to pull himself onto a bench. By the time the aid car got there he was unresponsive."

"Let's go then."

"Where?" he asked.

"To the park where they found him. Maybe we'll get lucky and find someone who saw something."

"Sarah, I can't leave him." Father Jim dropped his head and fingered the rosary he carried looped around the palm of his left hand. "He may need me."

"You're right, Father. You stay here. I'm going to snoop around the park to see what I can turn up."

"I understand," he said. "Keep in touch."

Both stood up and left the lobby in opposite directions.

Chapter Thirty Three

Sarah sat on the park bench where the EMTs found Juan. She stared at the ground and took a deep breath, letting it out slowly. Her eyes misted over as she fought back tears that didn't care what passersby might think. She was spent. There wasn't enough energy left to worry about the Andrewses, Rothschild, The Huntington, the mysterious man from Stanford, not even Detective Hetherington.

No one had seen anything, at least nothing they were willing to talk about to a stranger. As far as the neighborhood would attest, the attacker was invisible, or maybe it was Juan they didn't see. But coming up empty on leads was only part of what seemed to pull into a deep void.

Her nerves were raw from waiting for word about the old gardener, whether he had pulled through. And her wits were almost at an end from worrying about Elliot. But maybe it was selfish of her. What did she have to offer him, anyway? Wasn't the whole Elliot thing just about using him to fill some emptiness deep inside her? What gave her the right to be rescued by a knight in shining armor, anyway? She should be standing on her own two feet. Besides, white knights were just myths. Weren't they?

When the disposable cell phone rang her heart almost jumped into her throat at the thought it could be Elliot. But the word "Blocked" on he display knocked her heart right through the pit of her stomach – to the lip of that black hole.

The garbled voice didn't waste any time with small talk. "I have someone who wants to talk to you."

Sarah could hear the voice-distortion being turned off. "Sarah?"

It was Elliot. Her jaw dropped.

"Sarah, it's Elliot."

The reality that Elliot might be in danger didn't register with her right away. She blurted out, "How's Aunt Agnes?"

"They want to trade me for the journal."

"Oh my God! Are you okay?"

"They haven't hurt me, yet."

The distortion was back.

"You two love-birds can catch up after I have what I want. I'll call you with the drop site and rendezvous time. And leave the cops out of this. Come alone or there won't be enough left of your boyfriend to cuddle up to."

The line went dead.

A voice inside her head screamed, "My God! They've kidnapped Elliot."

Now, two people were in harm's way because of her, and one of them might die any minute, assuming he was even still alive. Juan was fighting for his life because he stepped up to help her. And Elliot, the man her heart was always meant to love – someone snatched him away and was threatening to kill him too. She was a jinx, a curse, a death sentence for anyone who got close.

Sarah's head spun like a computer caught in an endless loop of bad code. How was she going to save the person who was supposed to save her? Both her hands rummaged through her bag for Fulton's business card. Staring at his picture calmed her just as it had when it first caught her eye in the telephone book. She dialed, but got no answer. It went directly to voice mail. Sarah hesitated. She heard the beep and hesitated again, then tapped End Call.

Chapter Thirty Four

It took Sarah an hour-and-a-half to get back to her motel in Redlands from Glendale. Trying to see the road through broken-hearted eyes was like driving without wipers through pelting rain in pitch dark. Rush hour traffic didn't help matters. And during the entire drive, not a single useful idea came to her.

After getting up to her room, she sat on the bed and buried her face in her hands, crying harder than she knew was possible. In time, either she had cried herself out, or had made up her mind that hiding wasn't a viable answer. Pacing around the room, treading the same path over and over didn't work, either. It lasted until she decided her pointless motion wouldn't get her anywhere. This time when she called Fulton and got his voicemail, she left a message.

While waiting for her attorney's return call, Sarah sat at her netbook computer and double-checked, triple-checked, the video feed. On every test, she locked the computer screen, pressed the buttoncam against her chest and reminded Father Jim it was just a test. When she finished each transmission, she unlocked the screen and watched the recorded video. Occasionally, she rubbed her hands together. The room felt like winter.

An hour later, Fulton called back. He'd been out to dinner with his wife. Even though he usually forwarded his office line to a cell phone after hours, he always turned it off when they were having a date night.

After Sarah told Fulton about Elliot and the ransom drop, he told her to meet him at his office right away. He'd help her figure out what to do.

As soon as she tapped End Call, the cell phone

from the park rang.

The garbled voice sounded more menacing than ever. "In exactly half an hour, be at the Redlands Bowl. Come alone. Your friend will be sitting in the first row, middle section. Walk down the center aisle from the back row. When you get to the front, turn and walk past him. Don't stop or speak or sit down. Toss the journal onto the stage, then go directly to your car and drive to the library entrance across the street. If I'm satisfied with the journal, your friend will meet you in front of the library in less than five minutes. If I'm not, you can kiss his ass goodbye, and yours will be next. Don't think you'll be able to hide. I'll find you."

Half an hour wouldn't be enough time for her to go to Fulton's office and get back to the Redlands Bowl. On top of that, she was afraid he'd try to convince her to play it safe, rather than do what her heart was telling her had to be done. Leaving Elliot out to hang just wasn't an option. When Elliot was safe, maybe then Hetherington would take her seriously. Elliot could convince him to believe her.

Right on time, Sarah stepped out of her car and surveyed Redlands Bowl. It was as surreal as the videos of astronauts standing on the moon looking down on Earth. What if she never made it back? Glancing over at the Shrine, she closed the car door. The place looked lonelier and scarier than it had the night Dr. Burgess led her into its eerie underbelly.

A chill trickled down her neck. Facing the garble-voiced monster all by herself put a frosty edge on the warm desert night.

Father Jim's cell phone rang. Her old phone number glared up at her from its display. She stopped and turned back toward the car.

"Father Jim?"

"Hi Sarah. I'm afraid I have bad news."

Sarah's body went rigid. An ache pierced her throat and rolled like a hurricane through her whole body. Tears welled up in her eyes, blurring her vision. She tried to yell out at the top of her lungs, cursing against the evil that took her innocent friend's life, an evil that fed on raw greed and the lust for power. The words she wanted to scream were stuck in her ravaged throat.

Father Jim continued, "He didn't make it. Juan fell into his Father's loving arms just a few minutes ago."

Sarah opened the car door and slumped into the driver's seat. No words, only moaning poured out of her.

"Sarah, are you okay?"

"I – I'm –"

"Do you want me to come out there? My secretary called – Angela's at the church. Hetherington sent her there to talk you into coming in. I can bring her if you want."

Sarah's chest heaved and her entire frame started to convulse. Through her tears, she tried to mutter, "I can't do this anymore."

"Sarah, are you there?"

The message alarm rang on the other cell phone.

Sarah looked down and blinked away her tears so she could read the text message. Her eyes focused long enough for the words to glare up at her. "Now or he dies!"

"Father I have to go." She tapped End Call.

Wiping her eyes dry, Sarah slid out of the car again and planted her feet on the pavement, not sure she could take the next step without collapsing. One hand pressed down on the roof of the car, holding her steady. In her other hand she clutched the phony journal and the cell phone from the park. The phone's message alarm blared, and the display flashed, "NOW."

She straightened up and took a bead on her target. Damn Lincoln's diary. Instead, she visualized wrapping herself in Elliot's arms, just the two of them in some remote place, untouched by the world's ugliness. That vision gave her the courage to arc her way along the back row of the Redlands Bowl.

Picking her way down the dark center aisle, she imagined herself driving for a lacrosse goal, weaving through a gauntlet of alpha women who hacked at her stick under the delusion they could force her succumb to their pressure. She was standing tall in a strange place, facing the greatest challenge of her life under the worst circumstances imaginable.

A smile flashed across her face when she caught a glimpse of the back of Elliot's head. He was slumped, but only slightly. Her foot pressed down on something hard and smooth. It was pebble sized, and it was stuck to the rough concrete walkway, so it couldn't be a loose rock. Her parched throat felt like coarse sandpaper as she edged forward.

Elliot turned his head slightly to the side. Maybe he saw her out of the corner of his eye or heard her footsteps. Maybe he sensed her presence as lovers sometimes can. She smiled again – for an instant.

Sarah raised her eyes and scanned the wings on each side of the stage, trying to detect the slightest movement. Something from her left side caught her ear. It could have come from behind the stage. She kept moving – not wanting to upset whoever 'they' were – but at a slower pace. As she got closer to the stage, a porch light pulled her eyes off track. It was more than a block away, across the street from the Bowl. She almost hesitated.

Just a few steps from Elliot, she inhaled a deep

breath of stale night air. Were the kidnappers going to text her again as she closed in on the stage? Maybe they'd throw in a change of plans at the last minute just to catch her off guard or to flush out anyone she'd brought along to help. After all, they were experienced killers. They hadn't just killed Moran. They'd probably killed Grandpa Lake and now Juan, too. For sure, they would cut down anyone else she cared about. She and Elliot could be next. Yes, they promised to let him go. But murders don't keep promises.

Sarah rubbed the phony journal's leather binding. It felt weathered enough. The church's clothes dryer and microwave had added years to its short life, and the beer smell was too faint to detect. She slipped one thumb inside its leaves and probed the inside front cover. Its pages could pass for decades old paper, at least long enough to get Elliot out of harm's way.

She wondered how closely they'd scrutinize it. And assuming they let her and Elliot go, would they take the bait? Would they even see her note at the end of the journal telling them to meet her to negotiate a deal for the real journal? Her throat refused to swallow.

They'd only given themselves five minutes, and the best light around was in the parking lot behind the stage. Was that it? They didn't need five minutes. Had they simply lured her into a trap? Were they going to grab her, kill Elliot to punish her, and then kill her after they tortured her into telling them the truth?

Sarah didn't have a choice. Elliot was in danger and that was her fault. She had to do whatever it took, make any sacrifice they demanded.

At the end of the aisle, she turned to her right, looking down at Elliot as she stepped past him. He appeared to be all right. She took as much time studying him as she thought they'd allow. His belt was wrapped tight around his ankles. His hands tied behind his back. So grabbing his hand and bolting out of there would be impossible, for sure. The kidnappers would be on top of them both before he could get loose from his bindings.

Elliot looked up at her and forced a brave smile. She read the warning in his eyes. He knew how dangerous his kidnappers were. She dared not utter a word. That was his kidnapper's instruction. Her eyes said she'd do anything for him.

In the next instant, Sarah turned, kissed the journal as if saying a gentle good-bye to Grandma Cassie herself, and lofted it onto the stage. On hearing it slap the concrete and seeing it skid to an abrupt stop, she gave Elliot a final glance and hurried back to her car. As instructed, she drove to the library entrance and parked facing the Bowl. She'd be able to see him right away if her bluff succeeded.

Sarah kept one eye on the dashboard clock, counting down the five minutes. With her other eye she stared, unblinking, through the windshield, desperate for a glimpse of Elliot's silhouette emerging from the darkness of Redlands Bowl.

After four minutes, Sarah saw a shadowy image moving toward her from across the street. She scrambled for Father Jim's cell phone. Her fingers trembled as she scrolled through the contacts for her own number, tapping the display to dial it.

"Father Jim."

"Sarah."

"Father, go back to the church. I need you there. I'll explain later. Just get back there as soon as you can. I think –"

She strained her eyes, filtering through the darkness to make out the image of the person who was walking toward her.

"Sarah, are you there?"

"Just get back to the church as soon as you can and get ready to monitor the video feed." She tapped End Call.

As the figure stepped into the light of the library parking lot, Sarah was certain it was a man, a tall man with a strong, athletic body. Her heart jumped at the possibility it could be Elliot.

With her motor still running, Sarah shifted into drive. She kept her left foot on the brake, and her right one was poised over the accelerator. She strained to recognize enough features of the person moving toward her to be sure it was him. She was ready to unlock the door when she was sure.

As he got closer, the glow from her headlights brought his body into sharper focus. But his face was still covered in darkness. Sarah's heart rate accelerated with each step he took in her direction. His hands appeared to be empty.

When he was about ten feet away, his pace quickened to a trot. Sarah kept her eyes trained on his face. Her pulse spiked and any remaining moisture evaporated from her throat. Her right foot was now applying a touch of pressure to the accelerator, though her left one was still holding the brake pedal firmly to the floor. She had the car in launch mode.

At the instant he touched the front passenger fender, she recognized his face. It was Elliot. Her left hand hit the unlock button. The click of the door locks resounded like the soaring scores from a Tchaikovsky ballet.

In a matter of seconds, Elliot was sitting next to her. She had an impulse to throw her arms around him and whisper "Thank God!" But her survival instinct kicked in. She jammed her right foot hard to the floor as her left one flew off the brake. The car screeched as she made a hard right out of the parking lot. It wasn't until she was cruising up Orange Street, racing through a gauntlet of traffic lights, that she looked at Elliot. "Are you okay?"

He sighed as he looked out the passenger window. "Yeah, fine. Man, did they have me scared."

Sarah leaned across in front of him to get a better view of his face. She had missed him more than anyone at any time in her life. "Hey." She reached over to touch his face. "They hurt you."

Elliot jerked his head away from her. "Not all that bad."

"No, it looks terrible." She cupped his chin in her free hand and tried to turn his head toward her. His left eye was swollen. His cheek was bruised. "I have to take you to a hospital."

"No, I'm serious. I'll be okay. We just need to get some stuff to put on it."

"I'm so sorry. I can't believe I dragged you into this."

"No, you don't have to apologize. I wanted to help." Elliot let out a nervous laugh. "I just didn't plan on it being so intense."

"I can't believe it. First Moran, then Juan and now you." Tears trickled down her cheek.

Elliot stared straight out the windshield. "There's a Wal-Mart not far away. They're probably still open." He directed her to the west end of town.

Neither said anything for a couple of minutes. The silence gave Sarah a hollow feeling. Sure, Elliot was safe. But had she lost him anyway?

"Who were they?" she asked.

"I couldn't tell for sure. I tried to get a rise out of them by using names like Stanford or Huntington and Andrews. I got no response. I even tried to play the Rothschild card. And for the record, I didn't hear any French accents." Elliot laughed the way people do when they're too nervous to do anything else. "I wouldn't want to play poker with them, that's for sure."

Sarah chuckled, too. Hers was a nervous laugh that didn't fit her sadness. "Want to go home so I can take care of that?"

"No." Elliot's voice cracked. "After we get something for it, let's go to your motel. It'll be safer. You did get a room, right?"

"Yes I got a room, but not much sleep."

Both of them went quiet again for a couple of minutes. Sarah stole glances at Elliot. He kept staring straight ahead.

This time Elliot broke the silence. "You said something about Juan. What happened?"

Sarah wiped a tear from the top of her cheek. "He's dead. They must have gotten to him."

"Who?"

"I'm not sure. They beat him and left him for dead."

"Was he able to tell anyone what happened?"

"No."

"That makes one more reason we have to nail Moran's killer."

As she pulled into a parking place at the Wal-Mart, Elliot reached for the door handle. "I'll just be a minute. Why don't you hang here and give Detective Hetherington a call to fill him in on the kidnapping."

"Be sure you get some antiseptic."

Elliot smiled and shook his head as he slid out of

the car.

When he returned, Sarah reported she'd only gotten Hetherington's voice mail. She left a message, but was sure he'd just think she was flaking out again.

Elliot tried to reassure her.

Sarah's face turned somber. "Yeah, but I don't think I care about finding Moran's killer or the diary, anymore. You can go with me to see Hetherington in the morning. Maybe after what happened to you and Juan, he'll let me off the hook and start being a real detective."

Chapter Thirty Five

On their way up to the motel room, Elliot hovered close to Sarah as if he was shielding her. She kept glancing around, scanning for any sign of a trap, even though she hadn't been foolish enough to tell them where she was staying. But there was no guarantee they hadn't already tracked her down. After all, they had resources.

In the hallway, Sarah fumbled for her room key, pretending to lose her balance for a second. It was an excuse to lean closer to him and breathe in his scent. Even perspiration can smell sweet on someone you love. She smiled at him like a nervous bride and unlocked the door, nudging it open so they could go in. His eyes said he was nervous, too.

Sarah had made up her mind that nothing, not even a phone call from the kidnapper would keep Elliot and her from picking up where they left off the other night. Before they pulled out of Wal-Mart's parking lot, Elliot had filled her in on Aunt Agnes. She was recovering well. Out of the woods. At least they could relax about that. And curling up in the safety of his arms, just being held, would make the rest of the insanity dissolve away. Perhaps if they practiced that position enough, it could become a habit. That's what had been missing from her life all these years.

As he pressed his chest against her back, she felt their hearts beating with one rhythm. The ebb and flow of their breathing was like an ocean kissing the sands of an unspoiled beach. Elliot's love could take the sting out of Juan's death. His love could save her from the black hole that was always trying to pull her into its emptiness.

Elliot put his hands on her shoulders, guiding her

into the room. Once across the threshold, she turned to stare into his ocean blue eyes and hint at how delicious she remembered his kisses were.

But just as the door clunked shut, he clutched her mouth with one hand, not letting her breathe except through her nose. With his other arm, Elliot threw a chokehold around her neck. She strained to break free.

He jerked her tight against his chest.

"Now listen carefully," he said. "I'm going to take my hand off your mouth, but if you so much as peep I'll snap your neck in two. Do you understand?"

Sarah bobbed her head up and down as best she could.

He pushed her farther into the room, stopping just short of the bed. Easing his hand off her mouth, he turned her around and leered at her.

Sarah started to mouth "Why?"

He put his hand up to her mouth.

She begged him with her eyes to explain that he was just putting on a show to trick the goons who had kidnapped him. They must be watching somehow. Closed circuit TV. Maybe he was wearing a camera, too.

Elliot reached into his pocket and pulled something out. Sarah glanced down quickly at his hand, but didn't get a clear view at what he was holding. She didn't want to take her focus away from his eyes for more than an instant, hoping to read some hint that his sudden turn wasn't for real.

He raised his right hand up to the side of her face. She heard a click next to her ear and caught a glimpse of something shiny out of the corner of her eye. He pressed its coldness against her cheek. It was thin and made of metal with a razor sharp edge. That's all she could tell for sure.

"I'll use this if you don't cooperate." His voice

was like ice as he drew the dull side of the blade along her face to her throat. He turned its sharp edge into her flesh with almost enough pressure to make an incision.

She didn't dare nod. He could cut her with no effort. Even her slightest move would be enough to slice the blade's edge deep enough to draw blood. He wasn't putting on a show. He was serious, and she had to kick into survival mode, find that zone she always slipped into when a lacrosse match was on the line. This was sudden death in the truest sense of the word.

"Let's go over to the night stand, nice and easy."

Sarah brought her hand to her chest as they moved in sync, almost as fluidly as ballroom dancers, until they stood next to the nightstand that held the motel telephone.

Still holding the blade tight against her throat, Elliot nodded toward a notepad and pen. "Now pick those up."

Sarah leaned forward and stooped a bit as he yielded the knife just enough to let her reach the pad and pen. If he'd given her just a smidge more slack, she might have bolted for the door. But that would have been more stupid than brave.

"You're going to write a little note. I'll dictate."

Sarah cradled the pad in her left hand and poised the pen to write down what he instructed.

"I've done something terrible."

Sarah scribbled it, hardly registering the words. Her brain was reeling through myriad possibilities like a computer scanning an enormous database for one discrete record, a failsafe escape route.

"I'm tired of running."

Nothing about this made sense.

"I can't live with what I've –"

An alarm went off in her brain. Sarah protested, "I can't do this."

"Keep writing." Elliot knuckled his thumb into her neck, a reminder of the fatal consequences of disobeying.

Sarah stiffened. She would have to make time her ally.

"I said keep writing." He pressed the blade tighter against her flesh.

She recalled her mantra from lacrosse. "Keep the ball in play."

Sarah asked him to repeat his ugly words "I can't live with what I've done" before she finished writing them.

"I killed Dr. Moran in a fit of rage when he wouldn't give the diary back. He said he offered to give her a fair price, but she just wanted to see it put to good use."

Sarah's face grew hotter with every word she scribbled on the pad.

"Now we're going to set your little good-bye note over there on the desk next to your computer."

They edged toward the corner of the room where she had set up her netbook to broadcast its live video feed to Father Jim. The computer was open with its screen saver shooting stars into a black void. A tiny blue light flashed near the top of the keyboard, telling her the processor was active behind the locked screen.

As Elliot turned her and shoved her toward the bathroom, Sarah dropped the pad and pen on the desk. Her head reminded her heart why she never trusted people. But her brain refused to process the thought that Father Jim might let her down as well. He was her last chance for salvation.

"You're going to get undressed and take a little

bath."

Sarah balked. "What do you think you're going to do?"

"Move." He shoved her forward.

After they crossed the room, Elliot pushed her into the bathroom and waved the switchblade in front of her. "Do you like my little heirloom?"

Sarah's eyes grew wider.

"I got it from a mutual friend. You remember Juan don't you?"

"What did –?"

He cut her off. "Shh. I'm the one who gave Juan the note at Andy's Coffee Shop. I made him dig up the knife. It was me who cut you while we wrestled on the street next to Grant Park. And after you told me Juan was going to spill his guts to the cops about old man Andrews, I went back to make sure he kept his mouth shut."

Sarah choked back the urge to vomit.

"You see, I killed Dr. Moran. I already knew he was blackmailing Andrews over some poor schlup he killed more than fifty years ago. Then I overheard the good professor on the phone arguing with the son. He said something about the murder weapon, a knife that had been buried by a poor Mexican gardener at a church in Pasadena. A couple weekends of field research was all it took for me to find the sorry little wetback."

Sarah started to object, but he shushed her.

He went on, "I was just looking for the right opportunity to take over his little gravy train. When I found out about Lincoln's diary, I decided it was a bonus, just what I needed to make my mark on academia. Then you came along. It didn't take a genius to figure out what you were after. That made you the perfect patsy to take the rap." He laughed a cackling kind of laugh. "You just fell into my lap." He laughed even harder.

Sarah shook her head.

"So I rushed over to Moran's house to kill him before your appointment. But I wanted him to cough up the diary first, especially after you showed me that poem. Of course, he claimed he didn't have it. He said your mother wouldn't sell it to him. I knew he was playing me. He kept insisting he didn't know where it was, so I bashed him over the head with a marble bookend of Lincoln's bust. It was just sitting there on his desk, begging me to use it on him."

"How could you?" Sarah found her voice.

Elliot gave her an icy stare. "And you – you made it so easy."

"But the cops won't buy a suicide."

"What, with all the crazy, neurotic notions you've thrown at them, 'some rich and powerful conspiracy is out to get me.'" Elliot laughed again. "Yeah, they've got you pegged as a paranoid bitch, off your rocker. They'll buy suicide all right, especially when I deny the whole kidnapping story and tell them you made it all up to con the priest into helping you. They'll be convinced you killed Moran in a hysterical fit. You couldn't stand the guilt, so you killed yourself. Case closed. I get off scot-free."

Sarah glowered at him. "Yeah, what about Grant Park? Father Jim saw you there."

"He saw some guy you hired off the street. The two of you wrestled a little bit. He gave you a little flesh wound and ran away."

"Juan told Father Jim everything. Hetherington will believe a priest."

"Only hearsay from some old wetback you bribed to corroborate your fantasy. You just didn't count on a bunch of racist vigilantes beating him to death. Now start the water and get undressed. I promise it'll only hurt for a little while. Besides, think of it as a family reunion. Your blood and your grandpa's on the same blade."

Sarah's olive face turned deep purple.

Elliot chortled, "That's right, how sweet. Your blood mingling with his."

Her stomach roiled and she ground her teeth. She wanted to lunge at him, grab the knife, twist it back into his gut and slice him open. But he'd probably overpower her and she'd be finished. Playing along would buy enough time for the cavalry to show up – at least she hoped they'd show up in time – it was her only real hope. "You're sick!"

"Yeah, sick enough to kill, and not just once. Now turn the water on and don't make me raise my voice."

Sarah looked down at the bath. "Hot or cold?"

"It's your bath. Why should I care?"

She reached over and turned on the water to the hottest setting. When she tested it, she jerked back and shook her hand, keeping her eyes on him. "Too hot."

Elliot grimaced.

Sarah reached over and turned the water all the way to cold. She tested the water again. "Too cold."

"Stop stalling."

Sarah held up both hands in mock surrender.

Elliot motioned toward the bath with the switchblade.

Like a safecracker dialing in on the last notch of a combination lock, she rotated the water temperature control to just left of center. After she tested the water once more, she locked onto his eyes as if taking aim at her opponent's net. "Just right."

He stared back. "Now get undressed."

"Aren't you forgetting something?" she teased.

"No. I've got everything under control."

"What about the diary? I can't tell you where it is if I'm dead."

"As if you know where it is."

"Who says I haven't been bluffing all this time?"

"If you knew where it was, you wouldn't have come all the way out here for a showdown with Moran. You see, that poem you showed me gave me a pretty good clue to where it is."

Sarah's shoulders slumped a bit and her stare softened. "I don't get it."

"You don't have to. Now just get undressed like I told you."

Sarah dropped her hands to her waist and made a production of unbuttoning her jeans before she wriggled them off her hips. She took her time, knowing he wouldn't rush her as long as he was being entertained. She kept her eyes focused on his and mimicked a shy grin.

"I like it when a girl goes right for her pants. That shows that she wants to get right down to business." He winked at her and laughed.

She tossed her head to one side and puckered her lips, continuing to stare into his eyes. "In your dreams."

"Whatever."

Sarah reached for the bottom button on her blouse. She found a scosh more bravado and teased him by tracing her upper lip with the tip of her tongue. She toyed a bit with the bottom button before she undid it.

Elliot swallowed his breath.

Sarah cocked her head. "At least I get to see the regret on your face while you stare at what you'll never have a chance to enjoy."

Elliot waved the blade in her face again. "Don't

press your luck. I can have anything I want. And right now, I want this to be over with."

Sarah undid another button, slow and careful so she didn't expose the camera. "Do you mind if I make this a bubble bath?"

"That's a bit much to expect from a place like this. Don't you think?"

"I can improvise." She nodded toward the stash of toiletries next to the sink.

"Just hurry up." He waved the blade toward the vanity.

Sarah reached over and picked up the shampoo as she held her blouse together so the camera stayed hidden. When she eased back over to the tub, she undid another button, giving him an unobstructed view of her flat, bare tummy. Her survival instinct had tapped a previously underutilized talent. It was the kind of thing she played out in her mind when she fantasized about keeping the right man happy if he ever came along.

She pulsed small spurts of shampoo into the bath water, emptying the entire bottle. Bubbles fluffed through the tub.

Elliot's eyes showed his impatience.

Sarah sat down on the toilet to watch the tub fill. She bent over and caressed her bare legs and feet. Only the two top buttons of her blouse remained fastened. "I would have shaved my legs this morning, if I'd known."

"You're pushing it," Elliot warned.

Sarah stood up and toyed with the waistband of her panties, curling her lips into a pout. "Sorry it's not a thong." How long would this striptease keep him engaged?

Elliot leered at her. "Enough."

Sarah rolled the waistband of her panties down

about an inch. "I wish you deserved this."

"Enough I said." He stepped toward her, waving the blade.

Sarah threw up her hands "Sorry, it just came out. No one ever told me how to act when I'm being killed." She kept an eye on his face as she reached down to finish unbuttoning her blouse.

"What the hell is that?" Elliot blurted.

Sarah clutched the spy camera against her chest.

"It's not what you think. I wrote a message in Grandma's journal. I told the kidnappers I gave them a fake. For them to contact me to negotiate for the real one. The camera was so I could tape them when they showed up – get their confession. Honest. I wasn't taping you. I forgot I had it on – all of the excitement of getting away."

"Let me see that thing," he bellowed as he lunged at her and grabbed for the camera.

Sarah ducked around him like she'd done so many times eluding over-zealous defenders.

Elliot reached at her, trying to tackle her with his left arm.

Sarah dodged his grasp and dove at his ankles. As Elliot tumbled over her hip, she pivoted away and scrambled out the bathroom door. The splash behind her came seconds before his pained yelp. "Oh shit!" She turned to see him flailing in the tub, rubbing his eyes. The switchblade was no longer in his hand. She scanned the bathroom floor, but didn't see it anywhere.

Sarah scurried to her feet and raced toward the motel room door, stopping in her tracks at what sounded like an explosion in front of her. The door jolted loose from its hinges as if someone had slammed it with a wrecking ball. Behind the door, men were yelling. "Police! Get down! Get down!" One of them was on top of her before she could even think of dropping to her knees. She heard boots thumping past her, flooding into the room.

"He came through," she whispered as tears of relief spilled from her eyes.

Chapter Thirty Six

Sarah glared at Elliot as two SWAT Team members jerked him through the doorway into the hall. Her heart turned to granite as she stared at his back. In an instant, the man she imagined she loved was as good as dead to her. The turn in her emotions took less time than it had for her to slip back into her jeans.

She stood motionless for a long minute, guarding her room's threshold the way gargoyles cling to their perches warding off evil spirits. Her eyes stayed fixed on the empty doorway even after the sound of the elevator's descent faded away.

When the echoes of Elliot's footsteps no longer reverberated in her head, Sarah shrugged. She walked over to the computer desk and yanked the thumb drive out of her netbook's USB port so she could hand it over to Fulton. He in turn passed it to a detective.

"We thought you were getting a kick out of playing Undercover Sarah." Fulton's words were the first anyone had ventured to speak loud enough for her to hear since the SWAT Team secured the room. "By the way, your friend Hetherington is on his way. I can't wait to see him eat humble pie."

Sarah grimaced. "Yeah, I'm surprised he didn't come along with the SWAT Team."

"He called me right after he dispatched them. He told me to stay back until they cleared the room. I thought he'd be right on their heels. Maybe he's too embarrassed to face you." Fulton winked. "Having an amateur catch his bad guy has to sting."

Sarah smiled. "Hey, believe me. It wasn't planned. Elliot wasn't supposed to be the bad guy."

Her grin dissolved. The word Elliot left a bitter

taste on her tongue. And labeling him the bad guy didn't make it go down any better.

"Look, if you're not attracting the right kind of guys you need to try something different."

She glared at him. "Shut up."

"Look at it this way. You got your man, just a little differently than the way you wanted to. In fact, you got two of them. Elliot confessed to killing two people on live video and he fingered Andrews for your grandfather's murder. I'm sure a couple of search warrants will turn up the evidence the police need to put both Andrewses away."

Her eyes brightened a bit. "I was lucky. I didn't set up this spy cam to catch him. And if Father Jim hadn't done his part, I'd be dead."

Detective Hetherington's voice grabbed her attention from out in the hall. "I understand someone's been trying to relieve me of some of my caseload."

"That would be me." Sarah glared at Hetherington.

Detective Hetherington looked at her. "I guess I owe you an apology – and my thanks."

"Well, I can't imagine what gave you the idea I could have killed anyone in the first place."

"I'm sorry. Somehow, I got it in my head you came out here to even a score. I have to confess. I was probably trying too hard to avoid the same trap my uncle fell into." Hetherington glanced away. "Even the best make mistakes, you know."

"Yeah, I know."

"Say, I brought you a peace offering. It was in my desk. I finished reading it this afternoon." He cleared his throat as he handed her Grandma Cassie's journal. "You should finish it."

"Believe me, I will."

"Can we step out in the hallway. I've got something I want to tell you, privately." Hetherington looked directly at Fulton, hoping he wouldn't object to a one-on-one with Sarah.

Fulton nodded. "Hey guys, let's give these two the room, okay?"

"Thanks." Hetherington tapped Fulton on the shoulder as he passed by on his way into the hall.

When the room was theirs, Hetherington cleared his throat again. "His name was Tyrone Wallace. We served together in Nam."

"Whose name?" Sarah held her breath. Her throat grew tight and pressure built up behind her eyes as she studied Hetherington's face.

"That's your father's name."

Sarah's eyes bulged. "You knew him?"

"Yes. He was a war hero. He saved our platoon from an ambush while we were picking our way though rice paddies. I was one of those he saved."

"Why didn't you tell me?"

"You'd dropped out of sight before I made the connection. Before that, I'd been distracted by the notion you were out here getting revenge for your grandfather's murder. You see, I figured out the victim in my uncle's cold case was probably your grandfather. And at first, I thought your mother and grandmother having the same names as your father's fiancé and mother-in-law-to-be was just a weird coincidence. By the way, you did a good job of losing yourself. We couldn't trace you by either your cell phone or your laptop's IP address."

"Yeah," Sarah swallowed hard, choking back tears. "I ditched them for some new ones."

"It was only after I talked with your friend back in Maryland –"

Sarah interrupted him. "What happened to him?"

"Your father?"

She nodded.

"When he got back home he planned to marry your mother, but some folks had other ideas. That sort of thing didn't set well with a lot of people back then." He paused. "Are you sure you want to know all the gory details?"

"Why would anyone care about them getting married?"

"Uh, your father was – he was mulatto."

Sarah stared at her hands, turning them over so she could examine both sides. She caressed her forearms. Her olive-brown complexion always made her wonder about her ancestry, but being part Black wasn't something she'd ever considered. After a moment, she walked to the bathroom door, peered in at the mirror and looked herself over, twisting her dark curly hair around her slender fingers. She turned back to Detective Hetherington, smiling.

He returned her smile.

Sarah threw back her shoulders and stood at least an inch taller than her physical height. Her smile dissolved. "How bad?"

"It was real ugly. It sent your mother over the edge. They kept her institutionalized while she was pregnant and for nearly a year after that. Your grandmother took care of you from the day you were born."

Sarah bit her lip. "Did you know Grandma Cassie or my Mom?"

"I met your grandma when I went back to stick my nose into the investigation before you were born. She was pretty overwhelmed. Of course, I ran into a brick wall with the local authorities. I kept in touch with her by phone for a few months after I left town, long enough to know she was going to be okay."

Sarah dropped her head and lowered her voice to a near whisper. "What was he like?"

"There's an expression, 'Still waters run deep.' That was your dad. Some guys talk a lot and talk big, but do very little. He was quiet. He was a deep thinker, but he acted big."

"Wow. I finally find someone who knew him, and we meet like this."

"Yeah." Hetherington looked away, avoiding her bloodshot emerald eyes.

Sarah edged forward and folded her arms around him. She started to cry.

He hugged her tight. His coat muffled her sobbing as he swallowed his own tears.

When Sarah was all cried out, at least for the time being, she looked up at him through bleary, aching eyes. "Did they ever catch the people who murdered him?"

"We pretty much figured out who did it. But the local cops weren't interested in pursuing it. It wasn't exactly something anyone was ashamed of."

"Where did you bury him?"

"Segregation was still pretty much alive and well, especially in those rural areas. He's in what they used to call a 'colored' cemetery. I kept the little funeral program. It's in my desk at home. I'll get it to you before you fly back."

Sarah thumbed the edge of Grandma Cassie's journal, the real one. "Does it say what happened to the diary?"

"That depends on whether your mother followed your grandma's instructions."

"What do you mean?"

"Near the end of the journal she told your mother what she should do with the diary."

"How did Grandma know she'd read her journal? That's just not like —"

"Maybe you didn't know your mother as well as you thought you did. You know, the younger generation never does."

"Well, what did it say?"

Hetherington winked, "Who says I read it? There's nothing about it in my report."

Sarah missed the glint in Hetherington's eye as she caught sight of Father Jim and Angela walking into the motel room. By reflex she threw herself into the priest's arms, barely waiting for him to cross the threshold. Hetherington excused himself, assuring Sarah he'd be in touch. He patted her on the shoulder as he stepped through the doorway.

Angela had made Father Jim drive her to Redlands as soon as they saw the video feed of the SWAT Team crashing through the door into Sarah's room. It wasn't as if she had to insist, though. Father Jim was just as eager to see Sarah as she was. After all, that was why he was a priest, to help save desperate people.

Fresh tears seeped out of Sarah's eyes as she buried her face in Father Jim's shoulder. "Thank you, Father," she murmured. "I would have been dead without your help. Why couldn't I have been there to save poor Juan?"

Father Jim brushed back the damp curls from Sarah's eyes and wiped tears from her cheeks. "Like many people, Juan spent most of his life under the tyranny of fear. But now he knows the voice of perfect love. And love casts out all fear."

Sarah smiled at him. "I've been hiding in a prison

of fear, too. I was afraid of the truth. I could have pressed Grandma Cassie for the truth, but I didn't. I think it's time I decided to be free."

Father Jim smiled back. "I think Juan would agree."

Angela edged toward them, clearing her throat.

Sarah turned to her. "I was fine, really."

"Yeah. A homicide detective calls me all the way from California with a bunch of questions about you and you call that fine."

"Well –"

"And the second time he called he asked if I'd fly out here. He said they were looking for you near Pasadena."

"What did he expect you to do?"

"He said they traced your phone to a church in Pasadena. He wasn't getting much cooperation from the priest or his staff, so maybe if I showed up there they might agree to talk you into meeting with me."

"So you were going to help him set a trap?"

"It was for your own good. But after my plane landed, he called again. He was worried about you. He said he knew your family, and he had uncovered some new evidence that could clear you of the professor's murder. He thought you were running scared from someone who could hurt you badly and he hoped I could convince you to accept protective custody."

Sarah sighed. "Apparently Father Jim tried to tell me that the last time he called, but I hung up on him before he got a chance."

Angela stretched out her arms. "Do I get a welcome hug?"

Sarah walked into her open arms. When the two women embraced, Sarah whispered in Angela's ear, "I was so pissed at you for butting in. But I'm glad you came."

"I'm your friend. I belong here for you."

"Yeah, I guess I'm hard to get through to. But you can be such a self-absorbed little drama queen. Know what I mean?"

Angela stepped back. "Well, all the drama is just my lame way of trying to get your attention."

"Okay. I'll work at paying attention."

Father Jim excused himself saying he didn't want to rain on their reunion. He was convinced they needed some one-on-one time and promised to call Sarah when he had details about Juan's Funeral Mass. Sarah assured him she'd be there. He deserved at least that much from her.

After Father Jim left, Sarah invited Angela to stay the night with her. They'd get some sleep and drive to Pasadena in the morning. But as Angela slept, Sarah couldn't escape the lure of Grandma Cassie's journal, especially her instructions about Lincoln's diary. When she'd read that passage, she sat straight up in bed and shook Angela's shoulders. "That's it. That's what the poem was all about. That damned Elliot had it figured out."

Shaking the sleep from her head, Angela protested, "What are you talking about?"

"The diary – I know what Mom did with the diary."

Angela sat up and focused on Sarah's eyes. "Where is it?"

Sarah leaned in close to Angela and whispered. "It's safe, as safe as it can be right now."

"Well tell me."

"Just be patient. I'll show you as soon as I can. But Pasadena comes first."

Chapter Thirty Seven

Agents Salazar and Conrad dogged Sarah's every step starting the morning after Elliot's arrest. The first time she caught a glimpse of them was when they parked outside Poppy's house. It was the first place Sarah and Angela stopped on their trip to Pasadena for Juan's funeral. They'd just agreed to return for New Years Day and the Rose Parade when Sarah glanced out the window and recognized Agent Conrad sitting in the driver's seat of a parked late model SUV. Angela picked up on Sarah's distraction and leaned over to poke her just as Poppy declared it would be just like old times, and they'd get to experience what Grandpa Lake had missed out on.

A couple days later, Sarah noticed the agents again. They were loitering about forty yards away from Juan's grave during his interment. They walked off just after she caught sight of them while she was laying a solitary long-stem red rose on top of the casket. She didn't know how else to honor a martyr.

She spoke to the agents for the first time as they got in line behind her and Angela to board the flight back home.

"Agent Salazar, are you and Agent Conrad headed back home on this flight, too?" Sarah asked.

Salazar smiled. "We go where our work takes us, and right now you're our work."

Angela whispered to Sarah, "What's going on?"

Sarah looked at Salazar. "I thought we were done."

Salazar smirked. "There's this diary thing. Have you forgotten? Government property."

"Did you talk to Detective Hetherington? Maybe

he found it when he arrested Dr. Moran's killer?" Sarah ignored Angela's raised eyebrow, hoping neither Salazar nor Conrad would notice the perplexed expression on her friend's face.

"We thought you could tell us what he found." Salazar cocked her head.

Sarah shrugged her shoulders. "My lawyer's going to check into that after we get home."

"Well be sure to keep us in the loop." Salazar smiled.

"I'll be sure to mention it to him." Sarah glanced at Angela.

"You do that." Salazar scowled.

As they navigated their way down the jetway, Angela tugged at Sarah. "Something tells me you're still not out of trouble."

"Shh – we can talk about it when we have some privacy."

When they took their seats, Sarah asked Angela in a half whisper, "How tight are you with your uncle, the judge?"

"I'm his favorite niece, why?" Angela knotted her brow.

"We might need his help. And based on what's in Grandma Cassie's journal, I expect we might need your dad's help as well."

Angela nodded and smirked as she pulled some reading material out of her carry-on. "I'm ready any time you feel like sharing."

Sarah smiled. "Hey, give me a break. I'm still getting used to this teamwork thing."

"The girls on our lacrosse team will be glad to hear that." Angela grinned as she looked down at her magazine.

Sarah slapped Angela's wrist. They both laughed.

For the remainder of the flight, the two friends talked very little. Angela read, and Sarah played Sudoku when she wasn't staring half a dozen rows ahead at Agents Salazar and Conrad. Her nerves continued to fray throughout the flight, and by the time everyone stood in the aisle to deplane, Agent's Salazar's smirk almost unwound Sarah altogether.

When Sarah and Angela emerged from the gate, Agents Salazar and Conrad were arguing with two dark suited men. The men kept their poise, but looked like they could incite fear in a pair of All Pro linemen. When one of them caught sight of Sarah, he waved off Salazar and Conrad and made a b-line in her direction. His counterpart had some final words with the two Federal Agents before he followed his partner.

"Ms. Morgan –" The grim faced suit held out his badge. "My name is Special Agent Edwards, FBI Civil Rights Unit. We're here to escort you and your friend."

"I don't understand," Sarah sputtered.

Angela grabbed Sarah's arm. "What the –"

"This is Special Agent Johnson. We'll explain en route. This way, please." Agent Edwards pointed toward the ramp Sarah and Angela had just used to deplane.

"What about our luggage?" Angela asked.

"Don't we get to make a phone call?" Sarah added.

"Please, ladies. This is a precaution to protect you from possible threats. When we get to the car, you can talk to Detective Hetherington on the phone. He'll explain everything."

Sarah and Angela looked at each other, speechless.

Special Agent Edwards set a quick pace. His partner Johnson hurried them along from behind. They headed back down the ramp and exited the terminal using a set of stairs that emptied onto the tarmac where a late model black SUV was waiting for them. When they'd buckled themselves in, Edwards pulled out a cell phone and dialed. After a moment, he handed it to Sarah.

"Hello." Sarah said.

On the other end of the line, Detective Hetherington explained that they were being taken into protective custody to assure their safety. Only an hour earlier, Hetherington had convinced the U.S. Attorney General's office to launch an investigation into her father's murder. The targets of the investigation were a retired minister in Wicomico County and several active and retired public officials, including present and former members of the judiciary and law enforcement. All of them had allegedly been involved in Klan activities, some dating back to the early 1950s. And as Hetherington pointed out, Grandma Cassie's journal was the smoking gun investigators had been looking for. It named names, cited sources and was a virtual encyclopedia of Wicomico County hate crimes that took place during the 1970s.

Sarah hugged her bag tight to her side. "Will I have to give up the journal again?"

Hetherington told her the Attorney General's office had arranged for a federal judge to seal it throughout the investigation and any trials. It would only be opened under the judge's supervision if the court needed to verify that copies entered into evidence were authentic. "Don't worry," he said. "No one will be allowed to see the particular part you want to keep secret."

When Sarah repeated what Hetherington told her, Angela hung her head and laughed.

"What's so funny?" Sarah asked.

"You're a surprise a minute. I used to think you were the most boring person I knew. I guess that's what my daddy means by, 'Still waters run deep, and deep is where the big ones hang out.'"

Sarah turned to Special Agent Edwards and asked, "Where are we going?"

"FBI Headquarters."

At FBI Headquarters Sarah sat through two hours of interviews. Some of the questions got personal about Mom and Grandma Cassie. Were there other family members? Did she remember any stories people told about her father as she was growing up? Sadly, she said, there were none. No one asked her about Lincoln's diary. Maybe Agents Salazar and Conrad would be in touch later. Solving her father's murder appeared to have priority now.

After the interrogations, she and Angela were driven to a judge's chamber at the federal courthouse. The judge darted into the room, introduced himself and thumbed through the journal. When he finished, he handed it to a bailiff and said, "Seal it." He gave Sarah a quick smile and thanked her.

Sarah looked at Special Agent Edwards and asked, "What's next?"

Chapter Thirty Eight

Sarah studied the elderly mocha-skinned woman sitting across from her. Grandma Wallace pretended to be indifferent to the TV talking heads whose grainy pictures clamored out the news.

"Ain't nuttin' gonna come of it." The old woman shook her head.

News of the FBI Civil Rights Unit's investigation into several prominent Wicomico County citizens had set the area abuzz. The first arrest was a retired white minister who allegedly incited the mob that tortured and murdered Vietnam War Hero Tyrone Wallace nearly forty years earlier.

"Maybe so," Sarah replied. A big part of her was grateful for the media attention. People had started talking as soon as a local journalist began poking around, trying to flush out stories with his whispers about a pending FBI's investigation. The reporter also led Sarah to her paternal grandmother.

"Never does. People don' care 'bout our kind." Grandma Wallace rocked in her chair.

"I really want to know what he was like."

The old woman rocked a bit harder. "Smart boy. Too smart, some said."

"How was he smart?"

"Numbers was his thin. Loved to work them numbers."

"Was he athletic?"

"Maybe cudda been. He was fas and strong. But it didn't interes' him. Said it was jes 'nother way the Man 'sploited us – sports and senin' our boys to war so their uns didn' have to get shot up 'n the like."

"So he didn't play football or anything?'

"Naw – was too busy stirrin' up trouble o'er Civil Right stuff. You know, King, Malcolm and the likes of them."

"Why did he go into the Army?"

"Draft board was rigged. The ol' judge tole him, either 'Nam or jail."

"Why would he have gone to jail?"

"White folk didn't need a reason back then. But spose it had somethin' to do with your mama, her bein' white an all. They was foolin' 'round an folk didn' like it. When he came home from 'Nam a hero, he thought thins would change. They didn'. Instead they got worse."

"What do you remember most about him?"

Grandma Wallace sighed. Her lips quivered. "I loved the way he laughed."

Sarah winced. She stood up and walked over to her elderly grandmother, folding her arms around her and hugging her tight. "I'll come back tomorrow, okay?"

Grandma Wallace nodded as she dug into her pocket for a handkerchief.

The following morning, Sarah and Angela overheard chatter in the local grocery about another arrest, a retired judge who spent his career protecting Klan members from prosecution. His charges included numerous counts of suppressing evidence and intimidating witnesses. In addition, several people came forward with eyewitness accounts that tied the judge directly to Tyrone Wallace's murder.

Sarah seethed. "The whole justice system in this county is corrupt."

Angela bristled. "One bad egg doesn't make the whole barrel rotten."

"You're supposed to be on my side here." Sarah complained.

"What gives you the right to judge people you don't even know?"

"Look, others had to know what that crooked judge was doing. And they kept protecting him, even after he retired."

"Are you accusing my uncle?"

"What makes you so sure he hasn't been covering for the old coot? How could he not know what his predecessor had been doing?"

Angela thumped her forehead with the heel of her hand. "And you accused me of being self absorbed. You're just another celebrity turned bitch. I liked you better when you were a brooding geek."

"Fine. I'm better off not having to constantly watch my back. I knew it would only be a matter of time before you stuck a knife in it."

Angela turned on her heels and stormed out of the store.

A week later, Sarah learned that the retired judge's plea bargain had led to several other arrests. One of the suspects had built a substantial local business that he recently turned over to his three sons. Their business dried up overnight. Things went downhill for the sons just as quick as they might have for the old man some forty years ago if he had stood up to defend a young war hero named Tyrone Wallace.

A month later, Sarah tuned to a cable news broadcast to catch a press conference with the head of the FBI Civil Rights Unit. She announced the arrest of a high-ranking Wicomico County law enforcement officer, accused of obstructing previous attempts by the Bureau to crack a cold case involving the brutal murder of decorated Vietnam Veteran, Tyrone Wallace. Sarah's throat almost seized up when the FBI spokesperson commended Angela's uncle, Wicomico County's presiding judge, for helping break the case.

When Sarah's pulse settled to a normal rhythm, she picked up her cell phone and dialed Angela. "Please pick up," she whispered.

On the third ring, Angela answered and Sarah blurted, "Humble pie doesn't taste very good. I'm sorry I made a lousy judgment without having all the facts."

"It happens." Angela's tone was tentative.

"But mostly, I was insensitive, stupid and selfish. I didn't even think about how any of this was affecting you. I'm sorry."

Angela snickered. "Look, I love you. I don't know why, but I do. I want to be your friend, and I can forgive you. God knows I've made my own share of mistakes."

"Would it be rude for me to ask for your help again?"

"Of course not. What's up?"

"I need you to go with me to meet with your uncle and your father."

"Hey, what are friends for? I'll drive over in the morning."

"Thanks, Angela. I don't deserve you."

"Look girl, it's not about deserving. If it was, none of us would have real friends."

Sarah hung up and placed a call to her confessor, her rock, Father Jim. He was used to her late night calls by now. He had been helping Sarah from long distance as she navigated the rough spots on her new journey, including counseling her on how to patch things up with Angela. Sarah knew he'd want to know they'd made amends. But he had a bonus for her. He broke the news that Detective Hetherington had been loaned to the FBI to consult on the Civil Rights investigation.

As the two women arrived at Salisbury-Wicomico County Airport the next morning, Sarah jabbered non-stop and bounced around like a kindergartener. It was a side of her Angela couldn't remember ever seeing. When they met Detective Hetherington at Baggage Claim and he agreed to help them sell the judge on granting Sarah's motion, she got weepy. Angela teased that she must have been drinking already.

On their way to the courthouse, Hetherington handled another piece of business by phone, convincing the Bureau to reign in Agent Salazar and her partner. They'd started snooping around again, trying to dig up leads on Lincoln's diary. Their presence revived the circus atmosphere that had started to die down after news of the arrests went stale. Most of the buzz in the area had begun to focus on Lincoln's missing diary and speculation about what it said.

In the judge's chambers, Hetherington convinced Angela's uncle that Sarah had the right, as Administrator of her mother's estate and as Grandma Cassie's only living heir, to consent to the plan on their behalf. That left two loose ends to be handled. Hetherington had to investigate Lake Matthew's family to determine whether Sarah could legally speak for his estate, and Sarah had to get Grandma Wallace's approval for moving Tyrone's body.

Hetherington turned up birth and death records proving that Lake Matthews had been an only child, and both his parents passed away years earlier. The DNA test results that Hetherington ordered could corroborate Grandma Cassie's claim that Sarah was Lake Matthews's only direct descendent.

It took some weeks for the FBI Crime Lab to complete its testing once the Pasadena Police Department sent them various pieces of evidence. When the DNA tests came back positive, Sarah was three-fourths of the way to her goal. At that point, it was all up to her elderly grandmother.

But when Sarah broached the subject, the old woman sobbed. "Of course I won' allow it. It – it's unchristian."

"But Grandma, it's just putting things right for a change. Making things the way they should have always been all along. Doing what they would want if they were here to speak for themselves."

"No, I say. He's wiz his own people. Thaz where he belongs."

"He loved my Mom. She was his people."

"But it's so unnatural."

"It's what's right," Sarah pleaded.

"Why can' you leave thins in peace? You're jes' like he was. Always stirrin' thins up."

Sarah planted her hands on her hips. "I'm right, then. He would have wanted to do this."

Grandma Wallace stared up at her with lips trembling, and her eyes couldn't hold back the flood of tears. Sarah leaned over and wrapped Grandma Wallace in a tender embrace, and after clinging to each other and crying together for several minutes, the old woman consented.

Sarah laid the paper out on the dinged up old wooden coffee table. "Can I find your glasses for you?"

"I don' need no glasses." Grandma Wallace stared at the neatly typed document. She took Sarah's pen and scrawled her name near the bottom. "There. God forgive me."

"God will. Thank you."

"Jes don't say anythin' more 'bout this to me, ya hear?"

"Thank you, Grandma. I'll see you again tomorrow, okay."

Grandma rocked in her chair, refusing to look at Sarah.

Later the next day, after calling on the judge, Sarah and Detective Hetherington connected with Angela who took them to meet with her mortician father.

Chapter Thirty Nine

Standing on the tarmac at Salisbury-Wicomico County Airport, Sarah clung to Angela's arm while Hetherington supervised loading the sleek black coffin into the back of the hearse. It had taken an eternity for Grandpa Lake to come home. An eternity and tons of support from friends, not to mention a mountain of bureaucratic paperwork.

At least the delays had given Sarah time to nurse Grandma Wallace's emotions and bring her to the point where she was at peace with having given her consent to the plan that was about to unfold.

After the coffin was loaded, Sarah, Angela and Hetherington piled into a waiting limo to follow the hearse as it made its journey to the cemetery and mortuary that Angela's father owned.

Hetherington studied Sarah's face. "Are you sure you're up to this?"

"I can handle it."

"Look, I can do this for you. I've seen some pretty gruesome stuff in my life."

"I don't have to look inside. I just want to be close by when he opens it."

"The smell could be brutal."

"I'll wear one of those surgeon's masks or something."

"You're determined aren't you?"

Sarah stared out the limousine window as Wicomico County's familiar landscape rolled by. Cozy pastures and slumbering farmlands extended from the road to creek beds lined with dormant deciduous trees of various types. All the brown and gray would turn luscious shades of green come springtime.

Some fifteen minutes later, the limo pulled off the highway onto the asphalt drive that ribboned through a broad manicured lawn. Trim evergreen shrubs edged the roadway, and neat rows of grave markers spread out over the emerald-hued grass. In the distance, a grayish-blue pond reflected the overcast sky. Its graceful fountain sprayed crystal-like streams in perfect arcs. Sarah absorbed the cemetery's solemnness, but as the limo approached the mortuary building, her heart raced again. The whole universe didn't contain enough serenity to calm her excitement.

The mortuary's post-mortem area reminded Sarah of the morgue scenes she'd seen on TV crime shows. Except it was less institutional, more like the atmosphere she'd expect to find in the basement of a cathedral. Reverent, even if it was chilly and functional. Sarah and Hetherington watched from a few yards away as Grandpa Lake's casket was rolled into place in line with the other three. Four brand new matching, empty caskets flanked the original ones.

Once Grandpa Lake's coffin was in place, the most elaborate of the original caskets was pushed over to a stainless table where Angela's father was waiting. He wore a protective mask and gown, as well as goggles and gloves to minimize the risk of exposure to transmittable diseases. His gauze mask was treated with chemicals to block out any particulate matter that might get released into the air. He'd insisted that Sarah and Hetherington wear the same kind of mask.

When he inspected the labeling on the casket and flashed Sarah a thumbs-up, she nodded back. Angela's father had told Sarah that Grandma Cassie's casket made an impression on him more than ten years earlier. It was top of the line. He remembered her original internment vividly. Sarah's mom had instructed him to prepare the body with sufficient embalming chemicals to stall decomposition for several decades. It wasn't routine, but he'd been able to accommodate that request, as well as her other one.

Angela's father worked on Grandma Cassie's casket with diligence and reverence for most of an hour before he opened its lid fully. Sarah held her breath. Her pulse quickened and continued to beat at what felt like an anaerobic pace while the mortician probed inside the casket.

Sarah's heart leapt when the mortician grinned and pulled something out of the coffin. She caught herself bouncing on her toes as he walked toward her. He kept his head down, staring at the delicate parcel he cradled in his hands. Hetherington pumped his fist as if his team had scored a touchdown.

When Angela's father stopped in front of Sarah, he looked up and his eyes gleamed through his goggles. "Is this what you were expecting?" He was as giddy as a new daddy.

Sarah couldn't make a sound. Her eyes misted over and her swollen throat went dry.

Hetherington put his arm around her. "I can't believe it," he said.

Sarah found her voice at last. "I can't believe it either."

Angela's father weighed in. "It's in remarkable condition for having been buried in the ground for more than a decade. But, I think it's clean enough you can take it home."

All three stared at the leather binding for some time before anyone spoke again. Then Sarah looked at Hetherington. Her smile had dissolved. "Do you think Agents Salazar and Conrad are lying in wait for us out there?"

"Not likely," Hetherington replied. "I talked with my friends at the Bureau as I landed. I made an appointment for us to meet with them tomorrow afternoon in D.C., and I invited the judge to come along."

"Do they suspect anything?"

"No. So far, everyone is buying the story that this is just a garden variety re-interment of family members."

"Okay then – if you don't mind, I'd like to spend some alone time with Mr. Lincoln's thoughts before we have that meeting."

"I think that's a good plan," Hetherington said. "I'll drive you to my hotel where you can spend the night. It'll be more secure than your apartment."

"I hope you don't plan to sleep out in the hall like Colonel Lamon used to do when he was guarding President Lincoln."

Hetherington shook his head. "I'll be next door. If you need me, just knock on the wall."

Sarah, Hetherington and Angela's father exchanged smiles and headed to the mortuary's lobby where Angela was waiting for them.

Chapter Forty

The first winter snow began about mid-afternoon on December 15 that year in Wicomico County, Maryland. Just flurries, but snow nonetheless. Nothing is as peaceful as the echoes of snowflakes floating effortlessly onto a frozen lawn, unless it's the reality of peace itself.

A subtle wind whistled around them and through the gnarly branches of massive oaks and elms that stood guard along the cemetery's perimeter. Sarah was with family, newly discovered family. Detective Hetherington was there too, standing next to her. Father Jim had just finished reading the Twenty-Third Psalm in a gentle, soothing cadence.

Sarah felt Juan's warm smile, radiating down on her from heaven. His funeral, more than a year before, had also made her swell up with pride. Sarah was satisfied, full and complete, just like the expression on her face. And there was Angela, standing where cherished friends are supposed to stand, on her left.

Sarah and Angela had become inseparable, and Sarah didn't mind it at all. She understood Angela's need for drama. It was much like Lincoln's need to immerse himself in meaningful work. Both were effective tools for combating depression.

During the months after Sarah's narrow escape from Elliot's sinister plot, Angela rose to the occasion and kept her friend safe from the black hole that wanted to suck her in. Whenever Sarah got discouraged over being bound up in red tape, Angela pushed her to continue the process they were bringing to a close on that frosty afternoon. Of course, there were some disagreements along the way, but friends persevere in spite of setbacks.

Sarah was getting her head around the truth that she didn't lose Elliot. She lost an illusion. He wasn't the real object of her love. Her love belonged to a dream. And Elliot didn't kill that dream. He was just unworthy of it. Sarah had resolved to see people truthfully. Not to disguise them in images of what she wanted them to become. Celebrating the truth about people meant knowing them at their core. She liked to call it 'touching their souls.'

She began taking emotional risks, investing herself in others. As the number of her friends increased, so did her appetite for connecting with them. Becoming a recluse wasn't the best way to protect her emotions.

The others standing near her hadn't known she existed, and visa versa, before her return from the ordeal in California. On her visits to town during the years when she was growing up in Grandma Cassie's home, Sarah had no idea they were family. But they were cousins, grandchildren of one of Grandma Wallace's sisters. There was room for them, now, in her new life.

Overhead a formation of swans flew past honking their last respects, their gentle whiteness set off against a canopy of solemn gray.

The ensemble of family members and friends stood with their heads slightly bowed, half-celebrating and half-grieving, holding four roses each. Four coffins were ready to be interred in pairs in two double graves.

One common grave was marked with a headstone:

Lake Matthews and Cassie Morgan – separated by mortality – side by side in eternity.

The other grave's headstone read:

Tyrone Wallace and Jennifer Morgan –
finally together – no longer broken, but
whole.

Grandma Wallace held the bright new American flag that had draped her son's coffin. Her chest swelled with pride. The flag was Sarah's gift to her, a reminder that her family had a rightful place among the ranks of American patriots. Tears trickled down her cheeks as the military chaplain – he officiated along with Father Jim – read Tyrone Wallace's commendations and talked about his bravery and dedication to country.

Thanks to Sarah's determination, the entire Wallace family was now clinging to the hope that they would see justice served, at last. DNA samples from Tyrone's remains were being compared to pieces of trace evidence from his decades old murder. Old guard families from miles around waited anxiously, hoping the trials that would soon start in Wicomico County wouldn't turn their lives upside down as the world righted itself.

To Sarah's ears the sound of the bugler's Taps and the thunder of the honor guard's salute were sweeter than any symphony by Mozart, Bach or Beethoven.

As the bugle sounded and the guns thundered, Sarah sighed, but not with regret. It was a sigh of contentment laced with pride. She had caught the bad guy, brought together her fractured family and uncovered the deepest secrets of Lincoln's diary. And she was determined to let some grand purpose consume her life so depression wouldn't swallow her up again.

Sarah held a marble slab. It was small, only about five inches by eight. It bore an inscription, Grandma Cassie's wishes for Lincoln's diary that she'd written in her journal.

*Let it be my pillow throughout eternity. It's
all I have left of him.*

She'd thought about using Lincoln's poem,

*I'll weep upon unhallowed ground
In rain or snow or dust
Until the sacramental crown
Has sealed its sacred trust.*

It was the poem, after all, and the promise of
unearthing Lincoln's diary that convinced the judge to
sign the exhumation orders.   Without the court's
permission, this day would not have been possible.
Nonetheless, Grandma's words were more precious to
Sarah than Lincoln's verse.

As Sarah laid the slab upside down on her
grandparents' grave at the base of its headstone, she
whispered, "Not any longer Grandma – not any longer.
You have all of him now."

Epilogue

On the morning she presented Lincoln's diary to the Abraham Lincoln Presidential Library and Museum, Sarah sat on the platform next to Dr. Burgess from the Lincoln Shrine of Redlands, California. Agents Salazar and Conrad were in the crowd.

Sarah explained her decision to release the diary to the public. It was a choice that sprang from her own tragic experience with secrets. She said, "Secrets make it possible for oppression to quiet the voices of hope and perpetuate the abuse of innocent people." Her selection of Dr. Burgess to read from the diary was her way of making amends for the unfair way she accused him of killing Dr. Moran.

Before Dr. Burgess began to read, he spoke about Lincoln's impact on history. "Among other endeavors, he ended slavery, preserved the Union, fought to vest both political and economic power in the hands of common people, championed universal suffrage and workers' rights, promoted technological advances in both agriculture and transportation, and advanced education by establishing land grant colleges across the country. No secrets that Lincoln might have kept due to a personal sense of shame can diminish the magnitude of his accomplishments. And for us today, knowing a deeper truth only engenders more respect."

Dr. Burgess read several excerpts from Lincoln's diary. All entries were made during the winter of 1864-65.

When Joshua Speed and I were young men we kept one another warm on dreary winter nights and attended each other's dark periods of melancholy. He was the one who rescued me when I sank to such depths that I was convinced I could not survive. I steadied him when his wits seemed to have abandoned him and in the times when he agonized over torturous decisions. Sadly though, Providence, family and ideals have separated us. We are no longer close, which in my present condition leaves me feeling that I am utterly alone.

Nonetheless, I shall call on my old friend one more time. On this occasion, instead of coaxing me gently back to living, his task will be to introduce this 'Hamlet' to the instrument of his fate.

A. Lincoln

If there is a God and Heaven, as my Bible assures me there is, then my dear Willie is amongst the angels. I miss him greatly and am eager to be with him again. It is a relief to know this weary frame will not hold out much longer.

A. Lincoln

Though I have preserved the Union, the task of keeping my house united has proved impossible. Two of my children have passed on, as well as my dear mother and sister, and, my father was someone whom I could not abide. Even my wife has threatened to leave me. It matters not that I have loved her and provided for her and our children, as a man should. How different life would have been had my dear Ann not left me so soon. Would that I could join her even now.

A. Lincoln

I hear that even my friends are my enemies now. Their alliances for justice and equality were merely masks they hid behind so others would not notice their reach for power. However, those two great principles dictate that I should press on to guard our Nation from the vagaries of victory, that the Almighty may not have snatched us from the jaws of defeat in vain.

A. Lincoln

When I was a young man, they deprived me of my knife and rifle. Even now that I command vast armies, yet I still have no means to end my misery. Truthfully, I lack the will to do so as well. It seems that there will always be some grand cause to consume me.

A. Lincoln

Not even my father was privy to what I placed into Mother's coffin. He hated my poems; she loved them. It would have been all the more tragic had she not taken my poetry book with her. So I made a pillow of it for her eternal sleep.

A. Lincoln

Recently, Hill has been angry with me, so much so that again he offered to resign. As oddly as it seems to his critics, I could not endure Washington without him. So I placated him and said that I would take my security more seriously, though I am not at all disturbed by the prospect of death. To the contrary, I find my heart quieted when I consider it might be like greeting an old friend after a long separation. I wonder if <u>this</u> shall be my fatal Jan'y.

A. Lincoln

Finally, news from the front brings a constant parade of encouragement to our hearts; nonetheless, mine appears to be all the more exhausted. One would think the flurry of victories should make it easier for me to extricate myself from these dark hollows, but that is not the case. Now that the great job is done, what more is there to work for?

I cannot tell how long I shall endure this present episode. It seems far more intense than the others which I survived, and the phantoms that torment me are now indifferent to the spell of the little blue masses.

A. Lincoln

I owe Speed a debt of gratitude for his assistance in arranging the recent meeting. The person in question proved to be a most competent resource. I am certain our collaboration will cause quite the stir in due course.

A. Lincoln

I have learned through fiery trials that the melancholy is something for which there is no cure. One must choose either to survive it or become its victim. Those are the only paths which have been given by the Almighty to those of us who have been predestined to bear the affliction. To survive one must be constantly restless with the status quo; for the companion of complacency is an unending pit which swallows up melancholy's victims.

Several evenings past, I dreamt that I had died. I would have thought that I would feel great relief seeing the burden of this life lifted from my shoulders. Oddly though, I was horrified. The sight of my own coffin and the shrouded face inside it startled me. I only hope that I can muster the resolve to press on with the great work that still lies ahead.

I must dispatch Hill to Richmond forthrightly to assure that an egregious error does not occur.

A. Lincoln

About the Author

DL Fowler trained as a military linguist after receiving a BA in English from USC. His skills as a communicator have contributed to his success over the years. As a novelist, he likes to get inside people's heads and write about what he finds there – keeping readers on the edge of their seats while he touches the depths of their souls. He lives with his wife near their three grandchildren in the Pacific Northwest.

8037620R0

Made in the USA
Charleston, SC
02 May 2011